W9-BXD-403

SONS OF THE 613

SONS OF THE 613

BY MICHAEL RUBENS

Clarion Books
Houghton Mifflin Harcourt
Boston   New York   2012

Clarion Books

215 Park Avenue South

New York, New York 10003

Copyright © 2012 by Michael Rubens

All rights reserved. For information about permission to reproduce selections from
this book, write to Permissions, Houghton Mifflin Harcourt Publishing Company,
215 Park Avenue South, New York, New York 10003.

Clarion Books is an imprint of Houghton Mifflin Harcourt Publishing Company.

www.hmhbooks.com

The text was set in Adobe Garamond Pro.

Library of Congress Cataloging-in-Publication Data
Rubens, Mike.
Sons of the 613 / Mike Rubens.
p. cm.
Summary: Isaac is struggling to prepare for his Bar Mitzvah when his older brother
Josh, a self-proclaimed "Super Jew" and undefeated wrestler, forces him into a quest to
become a man by shooting a gun, riding a motorcycle, falling in love, and more.
ISBN 978-0-547-61216-4 (hardcover)
[1. Coming of age—Fiction. 2. Brothers—Fiction. 3. Jews—Minnesota—Fiction. 4.
Bar mitzvah—Fiction. 5. Junior high schools—Fiction. 6. Schools—Fiction. 7. Family
life—Minnesota—Fiction. 8. Minnesota—Fiction.] I. Title. II. Title: Sons of the six
one three.
PZ7.R8295Son 2012
[Fic]—dc23
2011044352

Manufactured in the United States of America
DOC 10 9 8 7 6 5 4 3 2 1
4500373030

RO426844565

For My Parents

PROLOGUE

THE TRAGIC EVENTS AT TEMPLE ISRAEL SET THE STAGE FOR MY OWN INEVITABLE DOOM

"Today, I am a man."

Right then I knew that something was seriously wrong—I mean *seriously* wrong—with Eric Weinberg. Everyone in the audience knew. You couldn't miss it.

It wasn't just the anxious, weebly quaver of his voice, the nasal soprano of which didn't do much to support Eric's assertion of manhood. His skinny face, which was pale and pasty even in midsummer, had suddenly gone several notches whiter—beyond white, really, achieving a sort of ghostly translucence, and all the way from the seventh row of Temple Israel I could see the greasy sheen of sweat on his beaky nose and the trembling of his birdlike hands.

Even Rabbi Abramovitz—a man who must have witnessed the very worst of tragic bar and bat mitzvah flameouts—looked concerned. This was more than a standard attack of the jitters.

The rabbi had a famously rebellious left eyeball that tended to move and blink independently of the right one, which explains how an otherwise nice man can end up with a nickname like the Lizard. Now, though, his rebel eye was taking a break from its standard

Pong-like wanderings to cooperate with its rival. Both pupils were riveted on Eric, who had started to sway gently behind the podium.

"Oh, shit!" muttered my older brother, Josh, next to me. Then he grunted, probably from an elbow in the ribs from our mom.

I glanced at Josh. His muscly jaw was clenched, lips pressed together. He was trying not to *laugh*. This was *funny* to him. My friend Eric—well, maybe not *friend*, but at the least, ally of convenience in a hostile universe—was going to pieces up there, and Josh was staring at the back of the pew in front of us, eyes bugging out as he tried to maintain his composure.

On the stage, Eric was doing his best to continue, his reedy little voice coming from what seemed like very far away. I couldn't even look at him. He was giving off palpable waves of intensely contagious Panic, and my Panic immune system is extremely weak. My own skin was clammy. I pinched my thigh, hard, to distract myself from the terror bubbling and churning inside me.

I leaned forward to see past Josh's bulk, vainly hoping for some reassuring guidance from my parents. My mom didn't notice me. Her attention was focused on the disaster unfolding on the stage. She was employing one of her superpowers, the Smile: a fixed expression as placid and pleasant and unperturbed as a mirrored pond, capable of hiding even the most monstrous emotions.

Next to her was my nine-old-sister, Lisa. She had yet to master the mysteries of the Smile and was staring at the stage with undisguised eyes-wide, mouth-open horror.

Just past her, our dad was shaking his head subtly. He sighed—something I saw rather than heard, because by now my ears were filled with a dull roar. I'd seen our dad make the same gesture of weary resignation once before: when we'd all gone out to his favorite fancy restaurant for his birthday, and a fat businessman collapsed at a nearby table and my dad the doctor knew he had to abandon his perfect steak to go treat him.

I didn't want to look, but some irresistible force drew my eyes back to the stage. Rabbi Abramovitz had somehow managed to shepherd Eric to the Torah-reading portion of the ceremony and was holding the pointer for him, indicating lines on the scroll.

But Eric wasn't reading. He wasn't even looking at the Torah. He was standing there silently, his sunken zombie eyes fixed on something visible only to him, located somewhere behind and above all our heads.

"*Baruch* . . ." suggested the rabbi, gently prompting him.

Nothing. It was a horrible silent moment—sheer endless vacuum. No one even breathed. I wanted to scream or run or stab myself or do anything to end the pain, and I was furious at Eric for making me feel this way. Next to me, Josh was shaking with trapped mirth.

"*Baruch ata* . . ." Rabbi Abramovitz prompted again.

Eric's mouth stayed shut. From somewhere deep inside him came a sound like a sped-up foghorn played in reverse.

Josh was bent double, both hands clapped over his mouth.

"*Baruch ata adonai,*" said the rabbi.

"*Blaarrrgh!*" Eric responded, and spouted a thick stream of vomit in a bold arc over the podium.

The following then happened in rapid-fire 1-2-3 order: the dull, soupy *schplat* of Eric's breakfast hitting the carpeted steps; the unmistakable wet sound of an earlier meal exiting from his other end into his tighty-whities and cheap suit pants; and a two-part *thud-thud* as the bar mitzvah boy hit the deck, out cold.

Chaos. People leaping to their feet, screaming. The rabbi throwing himself over the Torah like a Secret Service agent protecting the president. My dad was already pushing past me to go render aid. My mom was covering my sister's eyes. Josh was standing, repeating "Hoooh, shit! Hooooh, *shit!*" in joyful disbelief.

It all swirled around me, people jostling me left and right, but I sat there, numb, expressionless, already in shock, my impending and inevitable doom now clear to me.

And then Josh, as if reading my mind, clapped a thick hand on my shoulder and said with a huge grin, "Guess what, Isaac—in three weeks, that's going to be you up there."

CHAPTER ONE

IN WHICH MY GUILT AND FEAR TORMENT ME AND VERY UNWELCOME NEWS IS DELIVERED

Guilt and fear are gnawing at the very core of my being. I'm in terrible, terrible trouble, and it's my fault, and the news my mother has just given me makes everything far, far worse.

"Josh will take care of us?!"

She must be kidding.

"Yes," says my mother. "Don't look at me that way! Your father and I have spoken with him. It will be fine."

I continue to stare at my mother in disbelief for several seconds. She's not kidding.

"Josh?" I finally manage.

"Yes."

"Will take care of us?"

"Yes!"

"Josh?!"

"Yes!"

"You think that will be 'fine'?"

"*Yes!*"

It's a Power Yes, delivered with a backward-leaning wind-up and emphatic forward thrust of the head, as if she's catapulting the conversation-ending-response at me. She holds the position, eyes wide, gaze boring into mine, searching for signs of unwise resistance. I zag.

"Dad!"

"Isaac, your father and I have already—"

"Dad!"

My father, his profile to me, holds up a distracted finger from across the room. I hear him saying something about blood gases into the phone.

"Isaac," says my mother, "I told you, we've discussed it already. Here, wash this." She shoves a potato into my hands.

"But—"

"Wash!"

I wash, gnawing on my lips, barely noticing what I'm doing. It's early evening, Thursday, not quite a week after the tragic events at Temple Israel. We're all in the kitchen. My mother is at the center island, chopping vegetables for soup. My father is ten feet away, wandering in a random pattern by the dining table as he nods into the phone, on a call now for thirty minutes discussing a patient. From the old radio on the counter come the opening bars of *All Things Considered,* blending with the comforting sounds of the neighborhood—a lawn mower humming on a distant lawn, birds singing, Lisa and her friends playing in the backyard, similar sounds repeated from lawn after lawn after lawn in a safe cocoon that extends for miles in every direction, everyone inside and outside that cocoon unaware that my parents have gone insane.

My father is going to Italy in two days for a conference. He'll be there for two full weeks. And now, my mother casually informs me, she will be joining him, because the organizers have suddenly thrown in a free ticket for her and what a fabulous opportunity and how could she miss it? But it will be fine, you see, because Josh will take care of us. It's insane. They're insane.

"Insane!" I mutter.

"What?"

"Nothing."

Boom. The house shudders. It's from the basement. Josh.

I still haven't recovered from Eric's bar mitzvah. When I'm awake I want to be asleep, just to escape the angst that eats away at my guts all day, but when I do manage to sleep—not an easy thing for me in general—I dream that it's me up there onstage, except I'm naked but for my semi-Jewfro and I can't remember anything and I'm totally unprepared. Which isn't that far from the truth. Hence the fear and guilt. What I need now is support and comfort and stability, not to hear that both my parents will be gone for two weeks at this critical juncture and that Josh will take care of us and it will be fine.

I scrub the potato, sweating, formulating strategies.

BOOM. Boom boom BOOM.

"What about renal failure?" my dad is saying into the receiver. "You know, maybe I should stick around."

A ray of light. "Yeah, maybe Dad should stick around," I second hopefully.

"He is *not* sticking around. It's been planned for a year, and he's speaking, and they're paying him, and he's not backing out now," she says, raising her voice to direct the last part of the sentence at him. He flaps a hand at her in exasperation.

"Well, why do you have to go?"

"Isaac . . ."

"Why-eee?"

3

Even I can hear the drawn-out, two-toned, childish whininess in my voice, but I don't care.

"Because I want my trip to I-ta-ly!" she says, jabbing the knife in my direction with each syllable. The knife point drops to target the potato I'm holding. "I think that's clean enough."

I look at the potato, which now has a bowl-shaped divot in it.

"Here. Peel," says my mom. The potato is swapped for a carrot. Peeler is supplied. I peel. *BOOM.* A small metal mixing bowl, resting unstably on a scrap of vegetable matter, rocks subtly and settles into a slightly different position. I glance over at my father. He's now leaning with his back against the long counter near the table, brow furrowed, drumming his fingers on his bald spot, the other hand pressing the phone against his ear. They have to know. I have to tell them. Now. I have to. Deep breath.

Mom, Dad . . .

Boooom.

I can't.

"Mom, I don't think you should go."

"I've got to get my hair done. You know, this is when I really miss New York, where I could find a competent stylist who—"

"Mom, my fart mitzvah is coming up in three weeks!"

"We'll both be back in plenty of time for—Did you just call it your fart mitzvah?"

"What if I'm not ready?"

"I don't want you calling it your fart mitzvah, Isaac. You're going to slip up and say it in front of the rabbi."

"What if I'm not ready?"

"'Fart mitzvah.' Honest to God. Herb, did you hear this? Did you hear what he's calling his bar mitzvah?"

More hand flapping from my dad.

Boom boom BOOOM.

"Mom, what if I'm not ready?"

"So what are we paying that tutor for?"

TO NOT SHOW UP!!!! I nearly scream. That secret is the specific source of much of my fear and all my guilt. Because that's what Yoel, the tutor, has been doing: not showing up. He's some sleepy-eyed Israeli guy with a shaved head and sunglasses who wears too much cologne. He came to the first two sessions, and then he basically . . . stopped. Each week he calls my cell about ten minutes after we're supposed to have started: "Hallo. Yitzhak? Theez eez Yoel." Then he explains that he can't make it this time but zee nest time for sure.

I can't say I've minded. Who wants to sit there with a bored, patronizing sabra practicing my Hebrew when I can be blowing s*** up on the Xbox? Except, it just kept happening. Each time. And soon the weeks were flying by.

"He seems like a very nice man," my mom is saying, scraping a mound of vegetables into the giant soup pot.

"Who?"

"Yoel. Your tutor."

"Um . . . yyyes."

You've probably gathered that I haven't done a very good job of communicating my situation to my parents. How was the session today? my mom asks each time, when she gets home in the evening. Fine, I always say. Except there are no sessions. And the longer I've waited to tell them, the harder it's gotten, and I've been feeling guiltier and guiltier, and now there's no time left and I'm not ready and I'm realizing that the person I've been lying to the most is me.

Booom.

My mother glances over at me. "Are you all right? You look ill."

"I'm fine."

"Isaac, you feeling okay?" My dad, from across the room, his radar instantly locking on to any hint of infirmity.

"I'm *fine.*"

"Judy, maybe I should stay," he says, covering the mouthpiece. "I'm concerned—"

"'Concerned about this patient,'" she says, finishing his favorite line for him. "I swear to God, Herb," she says, shaking the knife at him this time, "if you don't go, I'm divorcing you. Here." She tosses another carrot to me.

I don't know if you're Jewish or know how a bar mitzvah works. You have to memorize a lot of things that you'll be chanting. A *lot* of things. In Hebrew. I'm going to brag for just a moment now and say that I'm a very good student. I'm in AP English, AP history, and pre-calc. School comes easy to me. I was assuming that the Hebrew would come easy as well. It hasn't. It hasn't come at all, and there are only three weeks left, and I'm going to end up like Eric Weinberg, but worse.

True, his spectacular collapse was ultimately traced back to bad whitefish salad, something that eventually caught up with several other members of the bar mitzvah party. But I don't need food poisoning to make me throw up and faint onstage. I just need my own brain, undermining me like it always does. I've told you about my nonfunctioning Panic immune system. Give me an even semistressful situation and it's like someone has cast a spell on me, filling me with stupid. I start to sweat and shake and can barely get my

6

mind to work, and the few words that make it from my brain to my mouth tend to come out in the wrong order if they come out at all.

A flurry: *boom boom boomboomboom BOOOM.* The bowl resettles.

"How is poor Eric Weinberg doing?" asks my mom. "I hope the other kids aren't being mean to him."

I glance over at her. Sometimes I'm not sure if she's from this planet, or this universe. She might as well say, *I sure hope that gravity isn't in effect right now.*

I should give you some background: I live in Edina, Minnesota. There are 597 kids in my seventh grade class. *Four* of us are Jews. Everyone else has a name like Peterson or Jensen or Swanson or Schultz, and they look like the perfect blond Aryan youth in the old Hitler posters. I feel like a troll at an elf party.

So just the fact that you're Jewish and have to have a bar mitzvah is embarrassing enough. Being the kid who threw up, pooped in his pants, and passed out at his bar mitzvah is a total nightmare. Being that kid and having it all somehow end up on YouTube is a nightmare deep-fried in apocalypse sauce. It's still a mystery who put it online. All I know is that it was all over school in about a millisecond, and last I checked, the video had over twenty thousand hits. Twenty thousand! In two days!!

Do you know that painting *The Scream*? If you don't, you should check it out, because that's what Eric has been looking like at school—the character from *The Scream,* if that character had finally stopped screaming from sheer exhaustion. That, or Gollum from *The Lord of the Rings,* except a Gollum who's gone a few rounds with a Harry Potter dementor. In the hallway, I caught sight of Eric, shrunken and haggard, hugging the walls as he stumbled from class to class. I avoided him like the plague.

I'm not proud of it, but there it is. Obviously, being seen with him would mean instant social death. I may not be that high up on the social ladder, but there's no way I'm going to plummet back down to Eric's current level, a dank, sunless dungeon populated by creatures like Tim Simonson, who still snacks on stuff he digs out of his nose. That, plus I don't want to risk catching Eric's bad luck.

In some ways I should thank him. What happened to him shocked me out of my complacency, stripping bare the lie I've been living for the past six weeks. I need to change course now, to find a way to get ready.

The first thing I had decided to do: reveal everything to my parents, spill my guts. Maybe they'd postpone the bar mitzvah or let me convert to some other religion. Anything. I had been, in fact, working myself up to tell my mom, until the very moment that she told me she'd be going with Dad on his trip. But now it's all spinning out of control, all going nuts.

Boom boom BOOM. BOOOOM! Something final and decisive about the last one.

"Are you sure you're all right?" my mother says.

"You all right?" seconds my dad.

"I'm fine."

"Do you need to go sit on the toilet or something?" asks my mom.

"Mom, I'm—"

"Go sit on the toilet if you have to," says my dad.

"I don't need to sit on the toilet!"

"Well, what's wrong with you?"

"Mom, I really—I don't know, I just don't think I'm ready, and—"

"Give me that carrot."

"Are you sure you have to leave? I mean, what if there's a problem?"

"How could there be a problem? You're a grownup. Josh is here. He's a very different person from what he once was," says my mom.

"But my fa—my bar mitzvah! I still might need help!"

"Look," my mother says to me. "If you need more practice, Josh will help you—he loves that stuff."

Oh, God.

"Right, Josh?" my mom says to my brother, who has strolled into the kitchen on cue, absently tossing a heavy medicine ball up and down like it weighs nothing. He's sweating and breathing hard from hitting the heavy bag, which is what was vibrating the bones of the house.

"You're big on the Jew stuff," says my mom. "You can help Isaac, right?"

Josh grins that big predatory grin of his.

"Of course!" he says. "Stick with me, little bro. I'll take care of you." And he dots the end of the sentence by chucking the medicine ball at me.

"Great," I rasp from the floor, my body curled around the medicine ball that is embedded in my stomach. "Great."

CHAPTER TWO

A SHORT DISCUSSION OF MY BROTHER, HIS VOLATILE NATURE, AND HIS DOUBTFUL PARENTAGE

"The tutor hasn't shown up AT ALL?!" says Josh. "I'm going to KILL HIM!"

He slams his fist down on the kitchen table, and the place settings all jump about an inch off the Formica surface. I cower in my chair.

It's Saturday afternoon. My parents decamped for Italy this morning. About ten minutes ago Josh made me recite my haphtarah for him.

"You can't remember *any* of it?" he asked after my third attempt ended in miserable failure.

So I spilled the beans.

Josh was not happy.

"Why didn't you tell anyone?" He slams the table again. "WHY?!" he roars.

I don't respond. Instead I leap from my chair in pure panic and flee out the sliding door to the back deck, heading for the yard.

"COME BACK HERE!"

While I'm running from my brother, I want to share some observations that might shed some light on our relationship, and why, exactly, I'm running.

First, I have a theory about my brother: Either he was adopted or I was, or both. My money is on him. There is just no way my parents could possibly have made him.

To begin with, he is six foot three, easily three inches taller than my dad. Also, my dad has a kind of pearlike shape to him, and the closest he comes to exercise is talking about how he used to play squash thirty years ago—"And I was pretty good, too," he says while my brother rolls his eyes. My brother, on the other hand, is 245 pounds, about 3 percent of which is fat. He holds the Edina High School record for bench press, sit-ups, pull-ups, and squats. He was also undefeated—like, he never lost, not once—in wrestling. He won state. That's how he got into NYU on a wrestling scholarship (he also got a full scholarship to Oklahoma State, a "real wrestling school," as he called it, but my dad told him, How about just a real *school*?). Why Josh is back home from NYU after a semester and a half is a mystery. It's all part of the Mystery of Josh, which I'll get to in a little bit.

"Keep running, Isaac! I'll see you in a few minutes!"

That's him now, shouting to me as he comes down the steps from the back porch at a leisurely pace. I continue running across our broad, sloping backyard, aiming for the low wooden footbridge that crosses the creek, hoping to lose him in the acres of woods on the other side.

To continue: Josh's nose has been broken, like, three times, he has a scar that splits his right eyebrow into two sections, he has a chipped tooth, and his left ear looks like it has been gnawed on, because it has. That happened during a fight with some punk-rock kid from Minneapolis who had a Mohawk. Josh needed a tetanus shot. Mr. Mohawk needed his jaw wired shut.

My brother likes to fight. I mean, he really *enjoys* it. They kicked him off the hockey team for fighting too much. How is it possible to get kicked off a *hockey team* for fighting too much? asked my dad. How is it possible we have a son who plays hockey? asked my mom. Jews don't play hockey.

"You better go faster, Isaac. I'm coming soon," Josh calls after me. I'm almost to the bridge. I twist to look back at him. He's still by the house, doing some warm-up stretches.

I'm not sure about you, but pain bothers me a lot. The *thought* of pain bothers me. Pain doesn't bother Josh at all. He doesn't mind getting hit. I once saw him get in a fight with a big kid during a soccer game. He let the kid punch him first, and the kid hauled off and smacked him as hard as he could. All the kids surrounding them gasped.

My brother started to laugh. If that kid didn't know he was in trouble then, he did a second later when my brother picked him up and slammed him onto the ground.

My mother likes to say that there is absolutely no crime in Edina—"except of course for Josh." He has actually been arrested, for real. It happened after a traffic accident, when Josh was a junior in high school. Some guy, a college student—"some big stupid frat guy," says Josh—rear-ended him and smashed up his brake lights. As Josh tells it, "The two of us then exchanged some words."

They also exchanged some punches. "He came out on the worse end of the deal," Josh likes to say in a matter-of-fact manner, which from someone else would be a pretending-to-be-modest manner.

To be fair, witnesses later testified that the frat boy had attacked Josh first, and the frat boy turned out to be drunk. But when the police arrived, the frat boy was the one lying on his back, moaning and bleeding, and Josh was the guy standing over him with bloody knuckles, swearing at him and telling him to get up. So it was Josh who got cuffed and hauled in. My dad had to bail him out. He was grounded for about a month after that and lost his car privileges.

I'm at the bridge, then over it, stumbling along the narrow, weed-choked path, the marsh grass nearly as tall as I am.

"Okay, Isaac, I'm coming now," I hear him call. I try to accelerate.

Things Josh did in high school besides fighting: drove fast, played music too loud, drank beer and barely tried to hide it, nearly got expelled four times, had screaming arguments with my parents, wore out the patience of a long line of therapists, put his fist through several walls and one thick door, and threw the television through a window.

He's much calmer now that he's twenty, but you can see why I'm running.

I take a branching path, one that roughly parallels the twisting course of the creek. A few hundred yards downstream is a dense copse of trees and vines, the sort of place where I might be able to hide and figure out my strategy. Maybe I can sleep there. Or wait until sundown and then get my bike and ride to Danny Wong's house. They'd have to take me in. Or I could go to the Fitzgeralds' house and use their phone, call my mom, and explain everything. I decide that would be worse than letting Josh catch me.

I stop to listen, panting, and don't hear anything. This is ridiculous. He's not actually going to hurt me. Then I remember the time at Lake Calhoun when the guy bumped into Josh and cursed at him. Afterward, when the guy's friends were dragging the guy off, Josh said to Lisa, "Sorry you had to see that. Sometimes I just get so *angry* . . ."

I start running again.

I guess girls are attracted to Josh's sort of behavior, because he's had a ton of girlfriends, most of whom my parents didn't like (typical question from my mom to my dad: "So, who's this latest little whore?"). I think, but I'm not positive, that they caught him having sex in his room late one night.

Josh will be returning to school this fall. This makes my parents very happy. New plan: to become a lawyer ("So I can sue doctors," he tells my dad).

Last year I finally got up the guts to ask my mom if — considering how different Josh was from the rest of us — well, if he was maybe adopted.

"No," said my mom, "I screwed the doorman at our building in New York."

Here's a suggestion I have for any mothers out there who have a sense of humor like my mother's: Save it. It's gross and shocking, and your son will be appalled. I certainly was. My mom quickly realized that I was disturbed by what she said, but if anything she seemed exasperated with me — like me being grossed out was *my* fault.

"Oh, c'mon," she said impatiently, "Look, somewhere along the line one of our ancestors probably got raped by some Cossack." Which wasn't much better, but whatever. "So just the right sperm hits the right egg" — still very gross; why always so gross? — "and we end up with Josh."

And me?

You know the old Looney Tunes cartoon where the guy finds the frog, and the frog starts dancing and singing show tunes? Except every time the guy tries to get the frog to perform for someone else, the frog just sits there? That frog is my brain. For a certain select group of people the frog will come out and perform. For the rest of the world, and especially when I need him the most, the frog is AWOL. *Rrrrrribbit.* Don't worry, says my mother, you'll bloom. Soon everyone will know how funny and smart you are. But if you've seen that cartoon, you know that the guy ends up putting the frog back into the box and burying it again.

My legs are getting weaker. I trip over a hidden knot of intertwined roots and stumble forward, catching myself with my hands. I pause again, gulping air, listening. Nothing. More running.

Josh loves our little sister, Lisa. He adores her. He's constantly giving her piggyback rides and paying attention to her and buying her little presents, even when it isn't her birthday.

He doesn't love me. He doesn't even like me. When I first learned the meaning of the word *contempt,* I realized that it's what he feels for me. I actually wrote that on a weekly vocabulary quiz for Mrs. Jensen's fifth grade class. "Contempt: what my brother Josh feels for me."

Josh has since made an appearance in several other vocab quizzes as an example for the following words: *Mercurial. Volatile. Ruminative.* And *conundrum.* As in, "My brother is an inscrutable conundrum."

Because that's what he is to me: a mystery. I don't know what he thinks, what he does, who his friends are, where he goes at night when he comes home at sunrise, why he left college, what he's doing home now without a job. He's a mystery, a closed door. And I think most of the time I'm like a ghost to him, someone who barely registers in his consciousness.

The path has taken me back close to the creek, which is about fifteen feet off to my right. The tangle of trees is up ahead of me. I'm maybe twenty seconds away from safety. I look over my shoulder. No sign of Josh. I'm fine.

Then I look to my right, at the creek, and at the lawns that slope down toward it. Josh is there on the other side, jogging effortlessly along on a parallel course with me, relaxed and unconcerned. He waves cheerfully. I stop running. What's the use. Then, with no warning, he alters his course and accelerates and rockets directly at me, as if the eight-foot-wide creek isn't there between us. And it might as well not be, because he's suddenly airborne, and I watch with my jaw hanging open as his leap takes him in an impossibly high trajectory over the water to land practically next to me.

I stare at him, dumbfounded, my chest heaving.

"Don't . . ." I say, pausing to get more oxygen to my brain, "hit me."

But he doesn't hit me. Instead he places a hand on my shoulder. I flinch anyway.

"Isaac," he says, "we have to talk."

CHAPTER THREE

AN UNFORTUNATE PLAN IS CONCEPTUALIZED

"What's the first thing you say up there onstage during your bar mitzvah?" asks Josh.

Above my head, the grass is rising and falling with each step Josh takes.

"Josh, would you please put me down?"

"Nope. What's the first thing you say up there, other than all the Hebrew stuff?"

"I don't know."

The grass is over my head because Josh has me slung over his shoulder and is carrying me back to the house. To be honest, it's actually not that uncomfortable, now that I've stopped struggling.

"What you say," says Josh, "is 'Today, I am a man.'"

"Oh. Right. Which is pretty stupid."

"Yeah, I'd say so. Are you a man?"

"Um . . . no?"

"No, you're not. You're still a boy."

"Thanks."

"It's a simple statement of fact."

"Yes, I'm aware of that."

An orange lawn sprinkler drifts by overhead, followed by an abandoned chewie toy. We must be crossing the Elofsons' yard. Josh could carry me like this for an hour in any direction and the scenery would look about the same: huge suburban lawns, wooded areas, broad, quiet streets, parks, golf courses, more lawns. The Golden Ghetto, one of the wealthiest communities in the country. My parents make fun of it and tell me how sheltered and coddled I am and how much better New York is. But I was born here, and I'll be honest—I like it.

"You know," says Josh, "when our ancestors got bar mitzvahed, it really meant that they were men, that they were ready."

"Yeah, and they died when they were, like, seventeen."

"That doesn't matter. The community saw them as men. They saw themselves as men. I don't think you can honestly say that about yourself."

"Again, thanks."

I spot a new-looking golf ball partially hidden in the lush grass. Dave Erickson must have been practicing his chip shots again, making his way from yard to yard along the creek. No one minds around here.

"And I'm not talking about your voice being low or having hair on your balls."

"Josh . . ."

"I'm talking about being a man, the things that make you a man."

"Yeah, I got that."

I'm not exactly sure what those things are to Josh, but I'm a bit worried I might be finding out.

An upside-down rosebush passes on my right. We're now in our backyard. The swing set comes into view, and then the garden, and then we're walking up the twelve wooden steps to the back porch. From my vantage point I realize that they could use a coat of paint.

When we get to the porch, Josh flips me off his shoulder and deposits me neatly into one of the patio chairs.

"Don't move." He heads to the sliding door and pauses. "You want a lemonade?"

He reemerges a minute later with two tall lemonades, the condensation beading on the glasses. He hands me one, pulls a chair around to face me, and sits.

"Cheers." He knocks his glass against mine.

"I want to make something clear," he says after a sip. "I'm not blaming you."

"For not having hairy balls?"

"You know what I mean. It's really Dad's fault. He's not a bad guy, but I mean, what is he going to teach you? How to identify a Bach recording?"

I wince at the reference. Two years ago I had come home in tears, having learned an important life lesson: When the music teacher plays some classical music and challenges his students to identify it, don't be the kid who eagerly shoots his hand up and says, "That's Glenn Gould playing Bach's *Goldberg Variations.*" And absolutely don't dig yourself in deeper by adding — with the total certainty of someone who's parroting his father — "It's really the best rendition."

The teasing was vicious. It was weeks before I could walk the halls without someone sneering, "It's *really* the *best* ren*di*tion."

"It's my fault," continues Josh. "I've been a crappy older brother."

I don't rush to disagree, and then realize that maybe now is a good time to start doing so.

"No, you've been a . . . good older brother. You really have. You don't have to do anything else. Really."

"No. I should have been there for you, and I haven't because I've been so caught up in my own crap. There are things you need to know. Things I wish *I* had known. Things I wish someone could have taught me."

How not to get expelled? I nearly say, but my instinct for self-preservation wins out.

"I mean, look at you," says Josh.

I look at me.

"When's the last time you did any exercise?"

"I have gym every day."

"I'm not talking about kickball. Or jerking off."

"I don't jerk off!"

"Really? I didn't know you were born without a dick."

"I play soccer."

"Okay, so the last exercise you did was last summer."

"So what? So I'm not a jock."

"Not a jock? You're in the *chess* club."

"I'm *not* in the chess club. I occasionally play chess. Some of the people I play with are in the chess club. It's a false syllogism to suggest that indicates I'm in—"

"Did you just say 'syllogism'?'"

"What? No. Maybe."

"This is exactly my point. You're in the chess club—"

"I'm *not* in the chess club."

"—and you use words like 'syllogism.'"

"What, I'm not manly if I use big words?"

"You still play D&D."

I don't have an answer for that. He sits back and crosses his arms, triumphant: check and mate.

It's true. Danny, Steve, Paul, and I have been playing faithfully for four years, introduced to it by the assistant librarian. The librarian vanished after a few months, at which point our parents sat us down individually for awkward conversations about whether or not he'd ever done anything that made us feel *uncomfortable.* That's when Josh taught me the term *pedophile,* which he described in traumatic detail. But the four of us keep playing secretly. When we talk about it at school — if ever — we use code. We all instinctively understand where D&D players are ranked in the junior high school social hierarchy and that it's probably time to hang up our dice. Still, you don't just walk away from an honestly earned level-nineteen half-elf cleric.

"Isaac," says Josh, "you can't keep being a nervous little kid who runs to Mom for everything."

"I don't run to Mom for everything. Sometimes I run to Dad."

"You know why you're such a smartass? Because you're weak, and scared of everything. You want to keep being a scared smartass?" he says. "Huh?" he adds when I don't respond.

"Hold on, I'm trying to think up a smartass answer."

He snorts and sits back in his chair. "You're smarter than me, Isaac. You're certainly smarter than I was at your age. And you know what you're like? All those supersmart, weakass Jews who got slaughtered by the Nazis."

There it is, finally. I'm surprised it took him so long to get to it. Josh, who my dad says always wants to refight the Second World War. Josh, who transformed himself into SuperJew — the single most effective thing he ever did to annoy my parents — and who used to go around Edina wearing a yarmulke. A black one with skulls and crossbones on it.

"The world doesn't need any more weak Jews."

I'm not sure what an appropriate response is to that, so I say nothing. I sip at my lemonade, avoiding his gaze, watching a squirrel skitter nervously along the branches of the tree that rises above the deck, the leaves making shooshing and rustling noises as he agitates his way along. I can feel Josh watching me.

"How's your lemonade?" he asks.

"Fine, I guess."

"Good."

He takes another drink of his lemonade, observing me, thinking. He's silent long enough that I finally look over at him. His expression makes me even more nervous.

He finishes his drink and puts his glass down, then turns in his chair so that he's square to me. "Isaac," he says, "we've got a very short time until your bar mitzvah."

"I *know*."

"And you know what we're going to do?"

Oh no.

"Josh, all I need to do is memorize my haphtarah."

"We're going to make you into a man."

"Josh, no. Please. I just want to go and watch my haphtarah DVD—"

"You know, in primitive cultures, the boys would have to go on a quest or pass some sort of painful challenge before they could be declared a true man."

"That's fantastic, Josh."

"They'd put them out in the wilderness to fend for themselves, to fight other villagers—"

"We live in the suburbs."

"There's ritual tattooing . . ."

"Great."

" . . . fasting . . ."

"I'm *not* fasting."

" . . . scarification . . ."

"I'm gonna go now."

I put my glass down and stand up. He grabs my upper arm as I try to slide away and swings me back around. He grabs my other arm with his other hand. I squirm. He holds fast.

"Isaac."

"What?" I'm not looking at him.

"Isaac," he repeats. "Look at me."

"Josh . . ."

He gives me a shake. "Look at me."

I look. He's staring into my eyes with an earnest, determined expression, and it's giving me goose bumps. My heart starts to thump.

"It's time, Isaac."

"Oh, God."

"It's time."

"No, I really don't think it is."

"It's time."

"Time for what?"

"Time for you to become a man."

CHAPTER FOUR

THE QUEST BEGINS

"What do you mean, you're not going to make it?!"

My best friend, Danny Wong, calling at 4:23 in the afternoon, his tone incredulous.

"I can't. I can't come."

My tongue feels thick. It's hard to talk.

"It's D&D Sunday! Steve and Paul are here!"

"I know."

"We never miss D&D Sunday!"

"I know!"

Some sweat escapes from the saturated kamikaze headband and makes its way into my left eye, burning it. I wipe at it uselessly with a grimy, sunburned forearm.

"Can't you just ride your bike over? We can wait."

"No, you don't understand. I—"

"Isaac! Are you on your cell phone?"

My brother, shouting down to me from the porch, looking up from his copy of *Guns and Ammo*.

"Why can't you come?" Danny again. "What's going on?"

"I can't explain now," I slur. I feel vaguely delirious. Even holding the cell phone is an effort. "I'm having the weirdest frigging day of my life. My brother—"

"Isaac!" shouts my brother again. He has put down his magazine and is standing up.

"Are you in trouble? Where are you?"

"I'm in my backyard."

"Doing what?"

"Digging."

"You're what?"

"Digging! I'm digging!"

I'm aware that I'm not making much sense. I can see in my head what a coherent sentence would look like, but it would take too much energy to move it from my brain to my mouth.

"Dude, are you wasted or something? You sound wasted."

"No! I'm digging! I'm exhausted!"

Mr. Olsen is staring at me. He's standing in his backyard, which is next to ours, holding a weed whip and staring at me. I imagine he's wondering what I'm doing here shirtless, wearing a headband, and digging a hole in the lawn. And wearing camouflage war paint on my face. He's probably noticing that. I manage a limp gesture similar to a wave. He cautiously waves back.

"I get that you're digging," says Danny. "What the hell are you digging?"

"Isaac, get off the phone!"

Josh is coming down the steps. I turn away from him, leaning on the shovel like a crutch, shoulders hunched forward, head down, trying to finish the conversation before he arrives.

"Danny, I can't talk right now."

"What is going on? What is it you're digging?"

"A fire pit."

"A fire pit?"

"Yes!"

"Isaac! I'm warning you!"

"Um, why are you digging a fire pit?"

"It's part of the Quest!"

"The what?"

"It started this morning!"

"What did?"

"Everything! The Quest!"

"Isaac, are you crazy? Now you just sound crazy!"

"I don't know. I might be. I think I might have sunstroke. Listen—I may not be in school tomorrow."

"What?! Don't blow it now!"

Three weeks left until the end of the year, and I haven't missed a day. Jerry's Ice Cream Parlor is donating a fifty-dollar gift certificate to every student with perfect attendance, and Danny, Steve, and Paul are counting on me.

"Danny, screw the ice cream. I might not even be *alive* tomorrow."

"Dude, what is going *on* over there?"

"It's my brother. He—"

That's as far as I get before Josh tears the phone out of my hand. I can still hear Danny's voice saying, "He what? He what? What's he doing? Isaac?" in the instant before Josh hurls the phone away. I follow its trajectory and note its landing spot, wondering what it sounds like on Danny's end as the phone disappears into the creek.

"I warned you," says Josh.

CHAPTER FIVE

THE QUEST CONTINUES

MERIT BADGE: CAMPING

I can hear the high-pitched whine as the mosquito comes around for another pass. I swat at it lethargically, my palm and fingers thudding slackly against the side of my skull like a glove filled with sand.

I groan.

I roll on my side, groaning some more with the effort, feeling the hard, lumpy ground through the sleeping bag. The tent is hot and stuffy and smells like mildew. I check my watch, my only source of light. It's 11:52 p.m. on the worst Sunday of my entire life.

The Quest has begun.

That's what Josh has been calling it: the Quest.

He first used the term on Saturday, while we were drinking our lemonades on the back porch. He spelled out my choices in stark terms: I could either (a) bravely rise to the challenges that he'd be choosing for me as a rite of passage, and thus seize the Glorious Mantle of Manhood, or (b) he could just go ahead and tell our mom about Yoel and my lies and ruin my life forever.

Glorious Mantle of Manhood, here I come.

"What will we do?" I asked.

"Lots of things. Challenges. Sometimes just hanging out with me, get you out of your shell, give you some actual life experience."

"What will the challenges be?"

"They'll be revealed at the appropriate time."

"Thanks, *sifu* Josh."

I take it the appropriate time was five a.m. That's when Josh violently shook me awake this morning and then yanked the covers off the bed when I tried to go back to sleep. I was still stunned and disoriented when he shoved me out the door for a nightmarish stumble around the block, the headband around my forehead and the war paint on my face, Josh jogging next to me and bellowing abuse.

From what I can tell so far, physical fitness will be a big part of the Quest. After our run there was an agonizing sequence of squats and sit-ups and pull-up attempts and pushups, with Josh standing over me in classic hands-on-knees coach position, deliberately miscounting the number of repetitions I'd completed.

"Why are you doing this to me?" I pleaded.

"It's the Quest, Isaac. We need to break you down before we build you up, shock you out of your normal patterns."

"I think you've done that. Can we stop now?"

"Stop? This is just the beginning, Isaac. We have two full weeks together."

"Josh, we have all summer to do this."

"No," he says, "we have now. I'm going to be busy."

Doing what, I think, but before I ask it he says, "By the time these two weeks are done, you're going to be a transformed person, and you'll be thanking me. You're going to know the pride of real achievement. You're going to have a whole set of new experiences. You're going to learn a lot about the world and yourself. You're going to earn your manhood."

"I don't think I'm going to reach manhood."

"Shut up. All right, you've done nine pushups, and you need to do ten. Go."

"I did ten!"

"GO!"

Around seven thirty a.m. Lisa wandered into the living room, sleepy-eyed, roused by our high-volume discussion of Josh's counting. She stood in the doorway in her pajamas, regarding me as I lay on the floor like roadkill.

"What are you doing?" she asked.

"Murdering me," I muffled into the carpet fibers.

"We're trying to turn Isaac into a man," said Josh. "It's not going very well."

"Oh."

Pause.

"Why is he wearing makeup?"

"Because he's on a sacred quest," said Josh. "He's a warrior."

"Oh, good," I said. "And I was worried that there wasn't a reasonable explanation."

"Shut up, Isaac," said Josh.

I watched Lisa's feet approach until she was standing next to me, her toes about six inches from my face. They seemed to be examining me.

"You look stupid," Lisa said after a pause, her voice coming from somewhere up above.

"Mmph," I said.

Her feet disappeared from view as she walked over me, using my back as a step.

The phone rang. I closed my eyes and listened to Josh talking to our mother, grateful for the break.

"No, it's not even eight yet. No. No, *eight*. Mom, I don't care if it's supposed to be six hours' difference, it's before eight here. Right."

He listened.

"Yes, Mom, we had a massive rager of a party last night and trashed the place. We burned it down."

On the bulletin board is the simple contract my mother made Josh sign before they went to Italy. It has two words: NO PARTIES. There is no sign that says FEED YOUR SIBLINGS or DON'T ABUSE ISAAC. Just a sign that says NO PARTIES.

Josh handed the phone to Lisa. Lisa talked to my mom. Somehow the fact that I was lying on the floor didn't come up. Josh took over the phone again.

"Yeah, he's up. Hold on."

He got down on one knee next to me and held out the phone. "Say hi to Mom."

He pressed the phone against the side of my face and then suddenly drew it back and gave me a look, a look that left no doubt about what boundaries I shouldn't cross. Then he held the phone against my head again.

"Talk," he said.

"Hi, Mom," I mumbled into the phone.

"Hi, sweetie! You're up early."

"Mmm."

"You should see it here, Isaac. It's fantastic."

"Mmm."

Long description of the sights they'd been seeing and food they'd been eating. I half nodded off.

"Isaac?"

"Mmm?"

"You know what I was thinking?"

"Mmm?"

"I want you to call Eric Weinberg."

I was suddenly more awake.

"What? Mom, no."

"I was e-mailing with his mother, and I think he needs some friends right now."

"You're calling me from Italy to tell me that?"

"I want you to call him and invite him over this week."

"Mom . . ."

"Do it this week, Isaac! Is everything else going okay?"

"Yes, but—"

"Is Josh treating you all right?"

Pause.

Threatening look from Josh.

"Yes."

"Good. I miss you, sweetie."

"Mom—"

"Okay, talk to you soon, Mom," said Josh, pulling the phone away from me. "Bye."

He hit the end call button. "Right," he said, "time for some wrestling."

There was wrestling. There was the punching bag. I cleaned the bathrooms. I cleaned the kitchen. I cleaned my room. I cleaned Josh's room. I cleaned Lisa's room. I have a vague recollection of cleaning the gutters. Any complaints were met with demands to drop and do ten pushups. As I slaved, Josh treated me to wise anecdotes about tribal elders and secret journeys and spirit animals and Apache vision quests.

"Spent some time on Wikipedia last night, huh?"

More pushups.

I lugged the firewood from the cellar to the garage, which I pointed out was a task that Josh was supposed to have done weeks ago but had been avoiding. This led to yet more pushups and another discussion about whether Josh could accurately count to ten, which then led to Josh grabbing me by my upper arms, lifting me off the ground until I was nose-to-nose with him, and issuing an elaborate threat that was so intensely gross, I'm still trying to get it out of my mind.

By midday I was exhausted. By midafternoon, as I was finishing mowing the lawn, I had moved into a whole new realm of physical pain and was beginning to understand the whole vision quest thing. I cut the engine and collapsed onto the lawn and lay on my back, breathing slow and evenly, the sun hot on my face and bright through my closed eyelids, the birds suddenly loud after the racket from the lawnmower. I smelled newly cut grass and dandelions and hints of gasoline, and waited for the voices of my ancestors to speak to me, to tell me that things couldn't possibly get worse.

The light darkened, and a voice addressed me. "Get up," said the voice. "Time to pitch the tent."

I lay there for a bit, considering that statement. "The tent," I finally said.

"Yes," confirmed spirit voice Josh.

"Okay. That's what I thought you said."

"And we have to get the fire going."

"Fire?"

"For your dinner."

It was at this point that I began digging a fire pit, had my delirious phone call with Danny, and watched Josh dispose of my cell phone in the creek.

The fire pit I made is about a foot deep and three feet in diameter, and it's tastefully ringed with stones that I lugged up from the creek. I'm sure my parents will love it.

While I was gathering firewood, Josh disappeared into the house. He returned carrying a raw whole chicken, and I realized what he'd meant about dinner.

"No no no no no," I started saying, waving my hands.

"Catch," he said, tossing it at me while I shrieked and leaped backwards. The chicken landed on the lawn with a hollow thump, rolled a few times, and came to rest, covered with bits of grass and twigs and dirt.

"Josh! What am I supposed to do with this thing?"

"Cook it and eat it."

"You're crazy."

"If this was a real rite of passage, you'd have to hunt it and kill it, too."

"A chicken?"

"You get the point."

"I'm not cooking this whole thing."

"No, you don't have to," he said, and sent his big survival knife cartwheeling through the air to land point down in the turf about two feet from me. "Just cut off the parts that you want."

I looked at the nauseating, yellow-pink carcass lying in the grass, the body cavity gaping obscenely toward me, felt the bile rise in my throat, and knew that I had reached my absolute limit.

"I'm not touching that," I said. "I'm not. I'm done. I'm not touching it, and I'm not cooking it, and I'm not going to sleep in this stupid tent!"

"You're done?"

"Yes! This is all completely retarded! I've had it! Running around the block, cleaning the stupid house, mowing the lawn, this stupid face paint. You can do whatever you want—I'm not doing this stupid Quest."

Josh was silent for a moment, then nodded gravely.

"I understand. I respect your choice."

"Good. I'm going inside."

"Of course."

"Stupid tent. Frigging chicken," I muttered, detouring around the carcass as I started walking up toward the house. "Can't friggin' believe this. Sleeping in a tent. Campfire on the stupid lawn. Friggin' ridiculous . . ."

"Isaac," called Josh from behind me.

"What," I said, still walking.

"Will you be explaining to Mom about Yoel? Or do you want me to take care of that?"

I stopped walking and closed my eyes.

By the time I found a stick, sharpened it, skewered the tattered chicken limb I'd hacked off, and actually started roasting it, it was nearly dark. Lisa came out and stood a few feet away from me, watching in silence and eating an ice cream cone.

"Can I have some of that?" I asked.

"Josh told me not to give you any. He says you can't have any sugar."

I slapped at a mosquito and did some muttering.

Lisa turned her attention to the half-blackened, half-raw chicken at the end of the stick.

"Are you really going to eat that?"

"Yep. Want some?"

I extended the stick toward her and she shied away, making a face.

"Gross! Josh!" she squealed, and ran back to the house. I slapped at a few more mosquitoes and continued my low-volume carping.

Mr. Olsen came out as well, a can of beer in hand, watching me from his yard.

"Doing a little camping, Isaac?" he asked.

"It's for my bar mitzvah," I said.

"Huh," he said, nodding, looking somewhat perplexed.

"It's a Jewish thing."

"Right," he said, nodding some more. "Huh." He took a sip of beer. I could see him filing this all away along with the other highly unusual things about the Kaplan family, like us being the only ones on the block with the Obama sign on the lawn. "Huh," he repeated. He watched for a little while longer and went inside.

It's now 12:07 a.m., meaning it's Monday.

Here are some of the diseases you can get from mosquitoes in Minnesota:

- La Crosse encephalitis
- Equine encephalitis, both eastern and western
- West Nile virus

My father had an otherwise healthy fourteen-year-old patient who contracted encephalitis, probably during a camping trip. He presented with a headache and high fever, and then the delirium started and he was dead in a few hours. Those sorts of stories tend to stick in my mind.

I will admit that I've been crying.

Next time my parents call I could tell them. I could tell them, confess everything, and that way Josh wouldn't have anything over me. Except if I did, they'd know I had been lying — one of the most egregious, stupid lies I'd ever told, and they'd be furious and know they'd wasted all that money. Plus, Josh would be right — I'd just be running to them.

There's another noise outside, something rustling around. My heart starts pounding like it does with each new noise, which happens every few minutes. This is my first time sleeping in a tent, and

I'm desperately wishing that I wasn't, and that I'd never watched *Blair Witch* on cable.

I've done some research on the web and diagnosed myself with an anxiety disorder. When I announced this to my parents they just laughed. No, said my mother, you're just Jewish.

More rustling. I hold my breath.

No, said my father, you're just a person who sees consequences. That's not a bad thing.

No, says Josh, you're just a pussy.

He's right. I'm a pussy. I'm afraid of everything. I'm afraid of noises outside in the night, and I'm afraid of my bar mitzvah, and I'm afraid of Kevin Nordquist and Tim Phillips, and I'm afraid of Patty Morrison, and I'm afraid of getting a hard-on in the shower during gym, and I'm afraid I'll never touch a girl, and I'm afraid if I do, I'll throw up or something, and I'm afraid of getting older and of getting sick and dying and of my parents getting sick and dying and of being left alone and of global warming and epidemics, and I'm afraid I'm as weak and useless as Josh says I am and that everyone knows it.

I unzip the tent and crawl out. The grass is damp under my hands, the air cooler than I expected. I half run up the slope of the lawn, afraid to look over my shoulder, scurrying to the door under the deck. Making as little noise as possible, I try the handle. It's locked, but I expected that.

I go to the rock under the bush near the rear picture window. I pick it up and pull out the spare—

Wait a second. Where's the stupid key! No! I feel around in the dirt, searching for it, until my fingers encounter an unseen spider web and I jerk my hand back, shuddering.

I straighten up and nearly let out a scream as I spot the face pressed against the glass. It takes my brain a few seconds to realize it's Josh, cackling at me from the other side of the window.

"Asshole!" I hiss at him.

He doesn't answer. He just holds up the spare key — the one that should be under the rock — and grins, and then points in the direction of the tent.

CHAPTER SIX

MY PEEPS ARE INTRODUCED, MY COWARDLY SHALLOWNESS IS MADE MANIFEST, AND A FANTASTICAL PLAN IS ENVISIONED

"Turn you into a man?" says Danny.

"That's what he says, yes."

"You?" says Steve.

"Yup."

"Good luck with *that*," sniggers Paul.

"Yeah, thanks."

It's the first lunch period, the lunchroom loud with jabbering seventh- and eighth-graders and silverware and thick plastic trays clattering on the hard surface of the long tables, cell phones blooping and ring-toning as everyone takes advantage of the one time during the day when we can call and text. I'm sitting with Danny Wong and Steve Wilton and Paul Schoener in our usual spot among the patchworked territories of students, the Jocks and popular girls and Sk8ters and Happies and so on grouped with each other and talking about whatever it is they talk about. In our four-seat patch we're discussing the Quest. Or at least they are, and I'm grunting answers to them.

"So what else is he making you do?"

"I don't know. It just started."

I've got my elbows on the table, and I'm gingerly massaging my sunburned temples with my hands. It turns out that camouflage paint doesn't have a very high SPF rating. I also have several attractive welts on my face from mosquito bites. Every layer of my body hurts, from my skin to my skeleton.

"Maybe he'll make you get a tattoo," suggests Steve.

"Yeah, of some pubes," says Danny.

High-fives and giggling.

"C'mon, dude, that's *funny!*" insists Danny, punching me in the shoulder. It's excruciating, but I still can't avoid a weak laugh.

Danny Wong: skinny, clear braces, zit patches on both cheeks. Paul: average build, forehead zits, his expression set to Friendly Dog, able to reenact almost every scene from *Monty Python and the Holy Grail*. Steve: taller than all of us, taller than most everyone in seventh grade, but with a pudgy face that makes him look eight years old.

My peeps.

We've known each other and shared the same gifted classes since third grade. I know we'll be solid until that far-off time when college does us part, and maybe beyond then. We're the Not-Thems: not Jocks or Stoners or Sk8ters or Happies or Rockers or the popular crowd or anything, really, other than four guys clinging to each other as we tread water desperately, trying to avoid being bashed against the rocks of the popular crowd or sucked into the nerd whirlpool that's always threatening to engulf us. They can give me all the crap they want, because in the end there's no one else I'm closer to, maybe not even my parents, and that will never change. Ever.

"Maybe he'll get you a prostitute," says Steve.

Excited discussion among the three of them of that unlikely event.

"He'll probably make you eat dog shit," says Paul.

"What?"

"Dog shit. That's what my uncle had to do when he joined his fraternity."

Danny puts down his fork. "Okay, he did *not* eat dog shit."

"He did."

"No. That's not even remotely possible."

Animated debate between Paul and Danny regarding whether that could be even remotely possible. That's what Danny keeps repeating: "That's not even *remotely* possible. Not even *remotely.*" This morphs into a discussion of whether at some point during the Quest I'll have to take a midnight crap in the creek, and whether it would be worse to be bitten in the balls in the middle of the night by a snapping turtle or by some sort of snake.

"Oh, dude, that would *suck!* Could you imagine, you're, like, squatting in the creek, and —"

I close my eyes, lay my head on the table, and tune out.

Yesterday was the worst Sunday I've ever had. Today looks to be making a strong effort to be the worst Monday.

Josh woke me early again and dragged me out of the tent for some predawn sadism. At least this time I got to skip the war paint and headband. Another call from my mom, again asking if I'd called Eric Weinberg.

"Yes, I did," I said.

"You didn't, did you," she said. "Call him. How's the haphtarah going? Josh helping you out?"

"Mom, you wouldn't believe everything Josh is doing."

And then it was time to go to the bus stop, which brings us to the Assholes Who Afflict My Life and Josh becoming aware of their existence, which is exactly what I didn't want to happen.

When it was time to leave, Josh announced that he was going to take the unusual step of walking me and Lisa to the bus stop.

Panic.

"Josh, you don't have to. I think I can manage to put Lisa on her bus and get on mine. I do it every day."

"I want to."

"There's no reason."

"Is there some reason you *don't* want me to do it?"

"No, fine, whatever."

Do not be waiting for me. Do not be waiting for me, I prayed as I trudged toward the bus stop, hunched over from the weight of my backpack, weaving a bit, my legs feeling like overcooked spaghetti. Josh and Lisa were walking ahead of me, holding hands and singing songs.

Do not be waiting for me.

Which of course they were, because they do it every day. We were a full block away and I could see them, Kevin Nordquist and Tim Phillips, dawdling by the open door of the bus, lying in wait for me while pretending that they weren't.

I do not like being bullied, but I can live with it. What I really didn't want was Josh to *see* me being bullied, because I knew exactly how it would play out—Josh would witness whatever was about to happen, and the stone gears would start to churn inside his thick, scarred skull, and he'd get *ideas*: Isaac being bullied = Isaac needing to stand up for himself = a perfect challenge for the Quest: to confront the bullies.

I do not want to confront the bullies.

But then, about a hundred yards away from the bus, Josh stopped.

"You're on your own from here. I don't want anyone thinking you're a pussy," he said to me, and kissed Lisa on the cheek. I breathed half a sigh of relief, which turned into an explosive *huuuuuuh* when Josh gave me a whack on the back to send me on my way.

"I'll see you when you get home. Be ready to study."

Please go home now, I thought, beaming the request out of the back of my head at Josh as I hobbled toward the bus. *Please turn and go. Don't stay and watch.*

"Hi, *Isaac*," said Kevin as I got close enough, saying it like my name is Ass Hair. I stared at the ground and tried to move past them into the door, but Tim shoved me into the door frame and I banged my knee on the first step, which set off a chain reaction of me stumbling forward and my heavy backpack flopping over my head and jerking me further off balance, and then I tried to recover and instead ended up in an awkward, crunched, half-squatting position at the base of the bus entrance. Kevin and Tim skipped up the steps, cackling. I pulled myself up, my face burning, and reflexively turned to see if my brother was still there.

He was, his body half-turned to me as if he had started to walk home and then stopped to watch. He was too far away for me to read his expression, but I knew he was disgusted with me. Then, without a wave, he turned and walked off.

Since then the day has had a veneer of normalcy: furtive passing of dirty homemade manga drawings between me and Paul in homeroom; furtive sidelong glances at Ellen Healy's growing boobs in English; similar behavior in social studies. The only difference between today and other days is I can't properly move my limbs, and I can't stop worrying about what surprises are waiting for me when I get home.

"Dude, you all right?" Danny is gently shaking me by the shoulder.

"Mmm?" I sit up, wiping the drool off my mouth and the table.

"Were you asleep?"

"No. Maybe."

"You don't look so good."

"You look like shit, dude."

"You look like if shit could take a shit."

My peeps.

"Thanks, guys."

"Dude," says Paul, "what if during your bar mitzvah you throw up and crap your pants?"

"Would you please?"

"Oh, man, do you remember the YouTube thing with Weinberg?" says Danny, as if we haven't been discussing that very thing every day since it happened.

"Oooooh!!" say Paul and Steve, reacting to the memory with renewed horrified glee.

"The way he's, like, *blaarrgh!*" says Steve, acting it out, "and then he's, like—" He hits the table with his open hand to illustrate Eric's now-legendary faint.

"Yeah, he's totally like, *bleeehh,*" starts Paul.

"Baaarrrff!!" adds Danny.

"RRraaaalph!!" retches Steve, everyone getting into the act.

"Dude, that would totally *suck* if you did that!"

"That'd be the worst!"

"In front of all those people like that?"

"Heeaaavvve!!"

"Haarrrrrrgghhh!!"

"Bllaarrrgggggaaahh!!!"

"Could you just—"

"Rrraaaaaaaaaahh!"

"Huuuurrrrggg!"

"Booooooooorrrhhuhuhuh!"

"ALL RIGHT ALREADY!!" I shout.

"Geez, dude, you have to chill out."

As we're walking out of the dining hall we spot Eric Weinberg and fall silent. He's sitting alone near the windows at the end of one of the tables, a pallid, solitary example of how cruel life can be, his gaze fixed on the tabletop as if wandering lost inside the dense, squiggly, bacteria-like pattern on the surface. No one is within a dozen seats of him. If you squint, you can just about see the poisonous cloud of doom above his head.

"Man, look at him," whispers Danny.

"You know what he should do? Move. Move to another state," says Paul.

"I think I'd just kill myself," says Steve.

"C'mon, let's go," I say. They've all slowed to a crawl, and I try to urge them forward, fearful that Eric is going to notice me. And just as I'm thinking it, his head turns slowly toward us and his eye line floats up from the table, unmoored and unfocused, as if searching for a dim, distant light in a dark cave, some promise of hope in the endless night, and what he finds is me. I can see the stages unfolding: his eyes acquiring me and focusing up, the moment of recognition, his eyebrows raising and lips parting as he draws in a breath to call out to me — and then I'm looking away, rejecting him and his desperate neediness.

Next to me, Steve makes a wet, bubbling fart noise with his lips. Danny shoves him, and we all stumble away, giggling. I'm a terrible person.

In the hallway we pause. "Everyone's in for tonight, right?" says Danny, lowering his voice and looking around furtively. The make-up D&D session. We all nod. "You're not going to miss this time, right Isaac?"

"I'll be there."

"You sure?"

"Positive. I'll be there."

"And you're coming Thursday to my birthday party, right?"

The annual tradition: Danny's birthday party at a local pizza place.

"Of course."

The mention of the party sparks something in Steve's head. "Dude."

"What?"

"Your parents are both gone, right?" he says.

"Yes."

"Dude," he says, "you should have a party!"

It stops Paul and Danny dead in their tracks. Obviously they think this is a fantastic idea. None of them know about the no-party contract.

"Dude."

"Dude."

"Dude! Girls and booze!"

"Invite Heather Paulson! She'll friggin' sleep with anyone!"

"Invite Sarah Blumgartner."

"OOOOH!!!!!"

Hideous Sarah, fellow tribe member, another troll at the elf party. She never leaves me alone, which is a source of great hilarity for my friends.

"Gotta have a party," Steve says.

"Dude! Think of the tail!"

"Let's get wasted!"

"We could get weed!"

"Think of the pussy!"

"Weed, dude!"

I look at my friends. Baby-faced Steve has pizza sauce in the corner of his mouth. Not one of us has ever smoked a cigarette, or even *seen* a real joint. I've had a few sips of gloppy sweet Manischewitz wine on Passover. Paul once French-kissed with his second cousin.

"We'll totally get *laid*," says Danny, whispering it.

I pause for a moment, as if I'm actually considering the idea.

"Yeah, maybe I will have a party," I say, nodding, and they cheer and we high-five, because we all secretly know that our fantasies about weed and getting wasted and having sex are no more real than fighting Orcs and that we're perfectly safe, because we never will have that party.

CHAPTER SEVEN

MY GOAL AND THE TROLL

The instant we've parted ways I check my watch, curse, start race-walking. I have to hurry or I'll miss my daily moment of happiness, and I really need it today.

I move as quickly through the halls as my rubbery legs will let me, keeping myself at a pace just under that which would draw the attention of a hall monitor. I pass the basketball courts and the music room, then cross the wide common area near the auditorium, walking along the endless glass display case with its rows of hockey trophies and framed magazine covers indicating that our school was once again selected as one of the top ten in the country. As I hurry along I keep an eye out for danger: the Assholes and their crew; or worse, Sarah Blumgartner, who lurks around here and will lock on to me like a remora if she spots me.

I make it to the corner near the auditorium just in time and assume my customary position, leaning casually against the dark brown brick wall. Hands in pockets today? No, out. No, one hand in, the other arm hanging at my side. Slouch a bit more. Good.

My brother has goals for me. I have goals for myself.

Or at least one goal.

And here she comes now.

Her name is Patricia Morrison.

She's rounding the corner from the hallway that branches off about thirty feet from where I'm standing. Her locker is number C-138, and every day she goes from there to Mrs. Halgren's English class at this time, sometimes with friends, sometimes alone. Today she's alone. I'll have about twenty seconds to look at her: ten as she approaches, and then another ten as she disappears from view.

She has sandy blond hair that falls straight to her shoulders, and perfect skin. She is slim but not skinny. She's athletic but not a jock. I've seen her smile—a great smile, absolutely great—and she's cool, but not mean cool, not one of those vicious popular girls, walking around with their copies of Gossip Girl and The A-List books. A few following-in-her-wake-in-the-hallway research sessions have confirmed that she smells good. Her eyes are grayish blue, or at least I think they are, because I've never really been close enough to get a good look.

I've never spoken to her.

Not once, not in four years.

I am embarrassed to admit this.

I've known her, or at least watched her, since I was in third grade. I saw her one day during recess, playing foursquare, and it was like someone flipped a switch. You know that really old song by the band the Police, called "Every Little Thing She Does Is Magic"? Listen to it. It pretty much says it all, especially the part where he talks about feeling like a total idiot and not being able to talk to the girl he's in love with.

I have never told anyone—anyone—how I feel about Patty.

So, my goal. My goal is to talk to her. That's all I have to do, talk to her. Have a conversation of some sort. I decided at the beginning of the semester that I would do it before summer vacation, no doubt, no way out. Of course, I made that same decision last semester and the semester before and the semester before that, and so on and so on and so on, back to the day I first saw her. And now here I am, standing in the hallway each day, waiting for my big chance. I'm not exactly sure what form that chance will take, but here are some potential scenarios I've been working through:

- She drops something. I pick it up. This naturally leads to talking.
- She is walking with someone I know. This is unlikely. Our social circles don't overlap in the least. But somehow she is with someone I know, I greet that someone, and talking with Patty follows.
- There is an incident: maybe a fire, or a wall collapses, or a rabid dog, tornado, flood, geologically unlikely earthquake, crazed shooter, et cetera, and I pull her to safety. Again, talking.
- I say hello to her as she passes. This is the least likely scenario of them all.

She's getting closer. I deepen my slouch and try to look at her while giving the impression that I'm looking elsewhere. Josh, I've noticed, looks very cool when he stands this way. I'm hoping that, at the very least, I've been registering somewhere in her mind, slowly building up an unconscious impression so that when we do finally talk, she'll already be thinking, *Hey, it's that cool guy.*

Here she comes. She's passing. She's past. She's walking away.

I sigh. None of those scenarios will ever happen. There will be no fire, no building collapse, no dog, I'll never say hi to her, she'll never drop anyth—

And then she drops her textbooks.

The world goes slow motion.

My heart begins to pound like it wants to leap out of my chest and run away. It's here. It's happening. It's now. Now is my chance. Now. All of this is racing through my mind before her books have even hit the floor. They're hitting now, splaying open to random pages, and she's turning, realizing what's happening, and I have to go help her *now now now,* but I can't, I'm stuck to the wall and the floor, but then I manage to push myself up from my slouch and I'm taking a step—

"Hi, Isaac!"

NOOOOOOO!!!!

Sarah Blumgartner looming in front of me, blocking my path with her braces and big nose! *NOOOO!!!*

"What are you doing? Are you going to math now? Did you do the homework? Did you figure out number seven?" she's saying, her movements mirroring mine as I dodge back and forth, trying to get around her or at least see past her explosion of thick, wiry, Airedale terrier hair.

"What? Uh, I just—I need—" I splutter, watching Patty gather her books, and now—*NO!!!* Someone's helping her! *ARGH!* It's Tim Keavy! Tim Keavy, with his blond hair and nice sweaters, retrieving the books and saying something as he hands them to her, something that makes her giggle. *ARGH!*

"ARRGH!" It escapes from me before I can stop it.

"Whoa. Are you okay?" says Sarah. "You're acting, like, psycho."

"What? I'm fine!"

Now Tim and Patty are talking. They're laughing and smiling and talking and walking off together. *NO, NO, NO!!*

"Hey, are you ready for — what are you looking at?" She twists to follow my gaze.

"Nothing. Nothing at all."

"Oh."

Patty is vanishing with Tim, along with any hope I'll ever have of talking to her. I realize that Sarah is still standing in front of me, expectant, grinning stupidly at me. "So, are you going to math?"

OF COURSE I'M GOING TO MATH, YOU IDIOT! AND NO, I DON'T WANT TO WALK WITH YOU, AND YOU'RE RUIN-ING MY LIFE!

"Yes" is what comes out.

"Great. Let's go."

I grind my teeth as we walk together, Sarah babbling on about whatever. I had one chance, and she destroyed it. I'd be talking with Patty right now if Sarah hadn't materialized like a Semitic night-mare. Without a doubt.

"So I'm, like, totally tripping about my bat mitzvah," she's say-ing, but I'm not paying attention, because I've spotted Patty up ahead. She's not with Tim anymore! She's stopped in the hallway, talking to two other girls, kids swirling past on either side! She's talking to . . . who is that . . . Gina Ueland and . . .

Kelly Thorenson!

I *know* Kelly Thorenson!

It's my *second chance!*

"Are you?" Sarah says next to me.

"Whu?" I say.

"You know, freaked out."

"Uh, no. Not really."

"You're not?"

"Not what?"

"Freaked out."

"About what?"

"Your bar mitzvah?"

"Oh, yeah, totally freaked out, totally . . ."

Patty's conversation with Kelly Thorenson is ending. They're saying goodbye! I have to get to them!

"Isaac, what's going on?" says Sarah, once again twisting around to figure out what I'm looking at. "You're truly acting psychotic."

"Nothing. I have to use the bathroom."

"I'll wait."

"No, I'll catch up with you."

"Okay. Well . . . I'll see you in math."

I duck into the bathroom, count to ten, peek out the door. Patty is still talking with Kelly. Sarah is gone. No excuses. Here it is. My second chance. I'll just say hello to Kelly and start talking. Just say hello. *One, two, three, go. One, two, three . . . Go. Two, three, go. Go. Go. GO!*

Of course I don't.

Maybe tomorrow.

"Dude, I can't believe this."

"Danny, I can't help it! It's my brother!"

"You said you could make it! We're all here again!"

53

"Isaac," calls my brother from the other room, "we're not done yet. You've got ten seconds to get off the phone."

"Danny, can we do it tomorrow?"

Danny talking away from the receiver: "He wants to do it to-morrow." Groans, catcalls. Steve shouting, "Don't be such a pussy!" in the background.

"Seriously, Isaac, this sucks," says Danny.

"You think I want to do this? Look, I promise that we can meet tomorrow."

"For sure?"

"Yes, for sure. I'll go—"

"Ten," says Josh, hanging up the phone for me.

CHAPTER EIGHT

SON OF THE 613

I got home at three fifteen, and Josh was waiting for me when I came in. He was holding the Xbox.

"Kiss it," he said.

"Kiss it?"

"Yes. Kiss it goodbye, because this is the last you're seeing it for a while."

He put the Xbox on the top shelf of his closet, paying no heed to my keening and wailing. Then, equally deaf to my explanations that my friends were expecting me, he sat me down in front of the computer in his bedroom to practice with the cheesy bar mitzvah DVD my parents bought.

Except for the brief phone call from Danny, we've been sitting here for two full hours, surrounded by an audience of Navy SEALs and Marines and Israel Defense Forces commandos who stare at us grimly from the posters that cover the walls. My sister watched for a while, until she got bored and wandered off. I tried to wander off. Josh wasn't having it.

"I want to show you something."

He rolled up his sleeve to indicate the tattoo on his shoulder, a Jewish star with some Hebrew writing in the middle.

"You know what this says?"

"Kiss me, I'm Catholic?"

"It says six hundred and thirteen. That's the number of commandments there are. You know what it means to be a bar mitzvah?"

"I get a pen from Pop-pop."

"It means you're a son of the commandments. A son of the six hundred and thirteen."

I wait.

"Which means you better take this shit seriously, dumbshit."

Ah.

"Again," says Josh.

I groan and start hacking my way through my haphtarah for the thirtieth or four hundredth time, Josh reminding me when I forget sections and interrupting to correct my pronunciation. I have to hand it to him; for a guy who nearly flunked out of school, he knows his biblical Hebrew. He can read it for real, not the slow, pulling-teeth, sounding-it-out way that I can.

My parents are not very good Jews. They'll say it themselves.

Mom (serving pork chops): Jesus, we're terrible Jews.

But when I was young they still tried to keep up appearances and raise us correctly. It all fell apart around the time I was eight. It was Passover, when you're not supposed to eat any bread or even have it in the house. Instead you enjoy delicious, wonderful matzo, which is like toasted cardboard, if that cardboard was made with a substance that removed all flavor not only from your mouth but from your memory itself. I walked into the den, and my dad was parked in his favorite chair, eating a bratwurst sandwich. On rye toast. A triple-decker. Pork on bread. It was like opening up his closet and having a dead body fall out. I was horrified.

"What?!" said my dad. "I'm *hungry!*"

And so they stopped pretending. Which is when Josh decided to go in the other direction and do the SuperJew thing: the yarmulke, synagogue every week, keeping kosher, making us light the Sabbath candles. I don't want anyone to know I'm Jewish. Josh wanted everyone to know, so they could make fun of him, and then he could punch their lights out. He even had peyes, the little sidecurls, for a while. It all worked: It drove my parents insane.

Imagine Josh stalking around Jew-free Edina like that, glowering at people.

Imagine now that you are a well-meaning, innocent exchange student from somewhere in rural Germany who had somehow never met a Jew. Excitedly approaching the beyarmulked Josh in the common area of the school, seeing an opportunity to finally unburden yourself of the crushing weight of your country's collective guilt and shame (which, yes, you should share). An opportunity you've been awaiting for your entire sixteen years. Little knowing that your counterpart, a suburban Jew, had likewise never met a real live German and had also been waiting his entire life for such an encounter, but with a very different agenda, one apparently involving a German person and a German-person-size garbage can.

Well done, Josh, my father said later, you've just turned that young man into a Nazi.

From my mother's reports I gathered that she saved Josh from expulsion through some lengthy diplomacy with the school administration and skillful wielding of the phrase "descendant of Holocaust survivors." Which, by the way, is not true at all—it was the Russians who slaughtered our ancestors.

After a while Josh got tired of being SuperJew—my guess is because he ran out of people stupid enough to tease him for it. But even now when it's time to read the blessings at Passover dinner, we all turn to him.

I finish my haphtarah.

"Jesus," says Josh, "maybe we can lie, tell them that you're turning twelve so they'll postpone it for a year."

CHAPTER NINE

AN UNEXPECTED NIGHTTIME OUTING

MERIT BADGE: UNDERAGE VISIT TO BAR

I'd been worrying about what I'd have to blacken for my evening meal, but instead Josh stood up and announced that we were having pizza.

He lets me sit with him and Lisa at the table as we eat. He listens with an indulgent smile as Lisa tells him all about her day and what she did and the project she's working on and the book she's reading and about Debbie Frank's new dog, a poodle. He ignores me completely, other than to tell me to clear the table and do the dishes before he gets up and walks off.

A little past ten and we're watching *The Ultimate Fighter,* that show where they put a bunch of MMA guys in a house and they beat the crap out of each other.

I once asked Josh if he'd thought about fighting in the UFC. He revealed that he'd actually fought in some local events, lying about his age to get in.

"What?! What happened? How'd you do?"

He'd looked at me, confused, like I'd asked if he was potty trained. "How'd I do? I *won*."

"So why not do the UFC?"

"I don't know," he said. "It just sort of takes the *fun* out of it." He seemed genuinely sad.

At the moment I'm settled into the big overstuffed recliner chair, my overtaxed muscles cramping into rocks. Lisa is asleep in her room. So far Josh hasn't mentioned the tent, and I'm not about to bring it up. The day seems to be drawing to a relatively uneventful end.

Then Josh checks his watch and stands up, turning off the TV with the remote.

"Let's go."

"What? Go where? To bed?"

"No. We're going. Come on."

I follow him out to the car, which is parked in the driveway. The night air is chilly, and I pull my jacket tighter.

"Josh, where are we going?"

"Hear some music."

"Music?"

"A band."

"Are you serious? What about Lisa?"

"She'll be fine."

"What if she wakes up and we're gone?"

"I left a note. She has my cell number." He's climbing into the driver's seat. "Get in."

"I don't want to hear music, Josh!"

"It's part of the Quest. Get in."

• • •

We take the highway toward the city, the skyline growing as we approach.

"Where are we going?"

"Downtown."

"Downtown Edina?"

He laughs.

"Downtown Minneapolis. A club."

My anxiety grows. Downtown? The city? I've only been in the city a few times, always during the day. True, Temple Israel is nearby, but we always get there in the protective shell of the car, go straight inside, and return in the car again, all without interacting with any dangerous characters or influences. There are weird people downtown. Things could happen. I feel like he's telling me we're going to Baghdad. I shift uncomfortably in my seat.

"Are you scared?"

"No."

"Well, stop looking like it."

We drive on the freeways, cloverleafing from one to the next until we're pointing at the skyscrapers, and then we're leaving the freeways to pull into what looks like a warehouse district, old brick buildings flanking the streets, rising up five or six stories. The upper windows are dark, but here and there on the sidewalk level are restaurants and bars, some with small groups of people standing outside, talking and smoking. It all seems very foreign and wrong and threatening to me.

Josh is steering, looking ahead, but he seems to sense what I'm feeling. "We've got to get you to New York," he says. "Get you out of Edina."

"No, no, we really don't."

"Yeah, we do. Let you see what a real city is like. You're freaked out by this? This is like a toy city. And Edina?" He shakes his head.

He sounds like my parents. They're always telling me that when I go off to college I'll go to the East Coast and understand. When I tell them that I don't want to leave, that I *like* Edina, they give each other a certain look, a look I've come to realize means, *How did we raise a child like this?*

In civics we were learning about the immigrant experience, and there was an essay by a woman whose parents were from China. Thirty years they lived in America, she said, and they still never considered it home, always believing that at any moment they would move back to their *real* home. *That's my parents,* I thought.

Josh turns onto a smaller, darker, less trafficked street and parks at the curb.

"I think we should just go home," I say as he's stepping out of the car. It's the third or fourth time I've said it in about ten minutes. It has the same effect on him as the earlier repetitions: nothing.

"C'mon," he says.

"No. This is stupid. I'm not going."

"Okay."

He shuts his door and walks off. I sit there for a moment and catch sight of myself in the mirror, then sigh in exasperation and climb out of the car and follow him. He's thirty feet away already and holds the key remote over his shoulder and locks the door without looking, not slowing down or turning to see if I'm behind him.

He disappears around the corner and I scurry to catch up, feeling vulnerable outside the bubble of strength and confidence he projects. When I round the corner I get a brief jolt of panic as I search for him, then spot him in the short line of people waiting to get into a club that's halfway down the block.

When I get there he's reached the doorman, a big guy with a shaved head and a leather jacket. They seem to know each other, doing that jock greeting that guys like them do: the soul handshake that turns into a quick off-center embrace, their left hands thumping each other once on the back, their gazes bored and expressionless and focused elsewhere, just in case someone might get the wrong idea that they actually like each other or have any friendliness inside them at all.

Josh registers my presence next to him and says, "Let's go," and steps through the door ahead of me. I glance at the doorman, who pays no attention to me, his dead-eye gaze already shifted to the next customer in line.

In the vestibule between the double doors I ask Josh how he got in.

"Do you have a fake ID?"

"Don't need a fake ID here," he says, and opens the next set of doors.

The noise that greets us is so loud, it feels like a physical barrier thumping against my chest. It takes me a bit to organize the distorted sound into parts that resemble music. The room is dark and crowded, people pressed up against the bar and gathered in front of the stage, where the band is tearing through some sort of metal-punk hybrid song.

I hang back as Josh shoulders his way to the bar. I get a few curious glances from people and I quickly look the other way, afraid of eye contact, wishing I were home. Josh reemerges with a beer. I know that he drinks, but this is the first time I've ever really seen him do it, and there's something almost shocking about it. Josh goes right past me, holding his beer just like an adult does, confident and relaxed like it's the most natural thing in the world. I tag along as he makes his way toward the back, wondering if he's forgotten about me entirely. He finds an open spot and stands there facing the stage, sipping the beer, nodding distractedly to the music and scanning the crowd. I plug my ears.

And that's what we do for the next several songs: me standing there grimacing with my fingers jammed in my ears, feeling stupid, Josh totally ignoring me.

After a while I start to get used to the situation, relaxing a bit, maybe even enjoying the music a little. It's not so bad, really. I'm in a club with my older brother, listening to music. Has Danny, Steve, or Paul been to a club like this? No. To be honest, this is sort of cool. Everything will be okay.

And that's when I notice the guy coming straight at me from my right.

He's big, as big as Josh, a fierce-looking punk with a red Mohawk and a motorcycle jacket and spikes and studs and big black boots, marching with purpose directly toward me, his fists clenched, looking like violent death personified.

I feel a rush of terror and adrenaline and turn toward Josh for help, but it's too late — the guy is just a step away, and now he's on top of me, but then he's brushing past me and I realize it's Josh he's heading for and something horrible is about to happen.

CHAPTER TEN

IN WHICH THE MYSTERY OF JOSH DEEPENS

MERIT BADGE: ATTACK BY PUNK ROCKER

There's no time to warn Josh, no time to even shout something, before the punk jabs out a stiff arm and gives Josh a brutal, jarring shove on the shoulder.

The impact jolts Josh sideways a step or two, beer erupting from the bottle he's holding. Josh pivots in surprise, his face registering bewilderment and then instantaneous fury, and I feel my knees nearly buckle from the fear of what's about to happen. And then Josh's expression changes again, shifting from angry incomprehension to recognition, then a huge smile, and then he and the punk guy are embracing and pounding each other on the back and laughing.

I watch them as they have a shouted conversation, a conversation punctuated with enthusiastic fist bumps and high-fives, the two of them leaning close to scream in each other's ears over the music. Josh points to me and says something, and the punker nods, then leans over and shouts, "What's up, little dude?" and offers me a hand. I'm not sure whether to slap it or shake it or bump it, and there's an awkward moment where I try to do all of those things at once, and finally the guy just grabs my hand, makes it into a fist, and does the fist bump for me, he and my brother laughing at me. Humiliating.

They talk a bit longer, do more bumps and high-fives, and then the punk walks away, patting me on the head as he passes. His rings hurt my skull.

As I watch him go the band finishes, and suddenly I can hear again. I turn back to Josh.

"Who was that guy?"

"Him? That's just Patrick."

I watch Patrick vanishing into the crowd, pausing to greet someone else.

"He looks like that guy you told me about, the one you got in the fight with. The one who bit your ear off."

"He is."

"What?!"

"Yeah, that's him. Not a bad dude, really."

He's distracted again, looking around at the crowd, looking toward the bar, like it's no big deal that he just ran into the guy who bit off half of his ear and whose jaw he shattered.

"You're friends now?"

"Yup."

I shake my head, adding another item to the Mystery List. Now that the band has stopped, the house lights have come up and I can see the rest of the crowd. Everyone looks like college students or older, and they all look like they could be drunk or high or I don't know what, and the atmosphere feels charged and unstable, like an orgy or a riot could break out at any second. I have to pee, but I'm

66

afraid to go to the bathroom, envisioning someone grabbing me and making me smoke pot or something.

"Josh, can we go now?"

"Not yet."

"I have to pee."

"So go pee."

I twist around, looking for the bathroom, then spot it. Someone pulls the door open, and I briefly get a clear view inside, where a guy is standing at a urinal, peeing. I decide holding it is a better choice.

I look at Josh again. He's checking his watch.

"Why are we here?" I ask.

"Part of the Quest. So you know what it's like. So you know how to behave in a place like this."

Right. Of course. Just the skill I need for my bar mitzvah.

Josh is examining me.

"What?"

"Clothes," he says, like he's added something to a list.

"What? What about them?"

He's not looking at me or listening—back to scanning the crowd.

"Is this a dive bar?"

He chuckles. "A dive bar? Clearly you've never been to a real dive bar."

"Um, I've never been to *any* bar. I'm *thirteen*."

"Stop looking around like everyone is going to murder you. These are not meth dealers. They're all normal people. They go to school or have jobs."

"Like the guy who bit your ear off."

"Hmm." He thinks about it for a moment. "No, I think he's a meth dealer."

"Jesus."

"Look, relax. Act like you belong here. You act confident, like everything is cool, like you're supposed to be here, and no one will bother you. Remember that. That's a good general rule."

You hear that, everyone? When you're thirteen and you're in a bar and it's near midnight and there's drug dealers with Mohawks who bite people's ears off, just act like you're supposed to be there, and everything will be fine.

"Josh, I'm not sure that—" I begin, but he's walking off abruptly, heading back toward the bar. I can see him as he steps up to it and addresses the bartender.

A she. An attractive she, wearing a tight tank top, her dark hair drawn back in a ponytail. I didn't notice her before, and realize she must have just started her shift. And then I realize that she's why we're really here.

They're talking. They know each other. They more than know each other. He's holding her hand across the bar, and she's laughing, shaking her head. Even from where I am I can see her say *no*, and then *no* a few more times, still laughing, and then *no* again, growing more serious. Josh says something. I can see her saying *Josh . . .*

She breaks off and takes someone's drink order. She's still talking with Josh as she pours a drink and gets someone a beer, shaking her head and frowning as Josh says something back to her. Another guy tries to get her attention, and Josh holds out his hand to him without looking at him, gesturing for him to wait. The guy says something back to Josh, and now Josh turns, and I'm getting nervous again. Josh says something. The other guy takes a step back, holding up his hands, mollifying Josh. Josh is still trying to talk to the bartender. She's trying not to talk to him. The guy Josh threatened is rolling his eyes, sharing a laugh with his friends, like, *Can you believe this guy?* I don't blame him.

Josh, I can see the bartender say, pointing at him, and then she launches into what looks to be a lecture, cutting him off with an open hand or a finger in the air each time he tries to interrupt her. Then she finishes and turns from him to a customer, all smiles again, and it's like she's slammed a door in Josh's face. The conversation is over.

Josh spins away from the bar and stalks toward the exit and disappears through the doors. It takes me a second to realize that he's leaving for real and he's leaving me behind. I start toward the door, and suddenly the room seems crowded again, people blocking my path and slowing me down, and I have to fight my way through. I need to catch up to Josh, and I need to pee, and it's like a nightmare where your feet are sinking into the ground and you can't move forward. I detour around a fat guy and squeeze through a tight circle of girls, mumbling apologies as I go. I hear someone say, "Check that kid out," and I try to speed up, only to run into a herd of guys heading from the bar, one of them slopping beer on me from a pint glass when I bump into him.

"Hey, watch it!" he says, and I squeak some more sorries as I backpedal away and bump into someone else. Rough hands grab my shoulders and spin me around, and Patrick the Meth-Dealing Punk's face looms in front of my own.

"What's up, li'l dude!" he bellows, his acrid breath stinking of liquor and what I guess to be a cheeseburger and fries that are de-composing in his stomach. "Your bro's, like, friggin' awesome, dude! He's the friggin' shit! He's, like—"

"I gotta go!" I say, and I mean it in more ways than one. I go around him and get another jarring pat on the head, his rings making a knocking sound on my skull.

I swim upstream through the hordes of people coming in the front door and finally make it outside, gulping for air.

Josh is gone. For a moment I can't remember if we came from the left or the right, and I'm lost and unprotected and have to pee so bad I almost want to wet my pants.

I pick a direction, realize it's the wrong one, and double back. I make it around the corner and spot the car with relief. Josh is sitting in the driver's seat, waiting.

I open the passenger door and lean in.

"I have to pee," I say, hopping from foot to foot.

He doesn't respond, just gestures roughly toward the wall behind me.

Cursing, I find the spot farthest away from the pool of illumination cast by the street lamp. I'm picturing being caught in the sudden blinding light from a police cruiser, like on *Cops,* and it takes me forever to start peeing and then forever to stop. A car goes by and honks. I cut off the flow and zip up and racewalk back to the car, my face flushed.

Josh puts the car in gear before I've even closed the door and accelerates away from the curb, still without saying a word.

"You were going to leave me in the club," I say angrily as we pull onto the highway. He doesn't respond. I sit back in my seat and cross my arms, mad.

We drive in silence until we get home. When we pull into the garage I follow him wordlessly to the door to go inside.

"Where do you think you're going?" he says.

"Asshole," I mutter, repeating it as I trudge out of the garage, walk around the side of the house, into the backyard, and climb into my tent.

CHAPTER ELEVEN

"I'm gonna get expelled. I'm going to get expelled. I'm going to get—"

"Isaac, would you shut up, already? You're not going to get expelled."

"I have perfect attendance!"

"Had."

"I was going to get a fifty-dollar gift certificate to Jerry's!"

"Ice cream is bad for you."

"Where are you driving us? What are we doing?"

"You'll see. C'mon, it'll be fun."

Oh, God.

CHAPTER TWELVE

THE ARRIVAL OF LESLEY MCDOUGAL

Merit Badge: Love at First Sight

I had figured that after our late night I'd be getting a reprieve from my early-morning workout session. I was wrong. Josh dragged me from the tent at six a.m. for our run and calisthenics and wrestling, mostly him tossing me around while I lay there like a rag doll. This led to threats of more pushups unless I put forth some real effort. More effort was forthput.

Standard hostage-situation conversation with parents, Josh looking on to make sure I stuck to the script. More urging from my mom to contact Eric Weinberg deflected. Comments from her that I sounded tired again.

At breakfast Josh was texting with someone on his phone, and then he made a call.

"You can't do it tonight?" he said to whomever he was talking to. "What about the weekend? Seriously? All right, we'll do it today."

As Lisa and I were walking out the door, Josh told me to wait. I waited.

"I'll drive you to school," he said.

Um . . . okay.

Then we got in the car and he went the exact opposite direction, and I commenced freaking out.

We get on the highway, Josh responding to my panicked where are we goings with an equal number of you'll sees. Wherever it is, it's taking me out of Edina and out of school and out of the running for fifty dollars' worth of ice cream.

We're off the highway now, on Lake Street, heading toward Uptown, another no-go area for me: boutiques and bars and used bookstores and punky kids, and what I'm pretty sure are gay men who have shaved heads and handlebar mustaches. As I peer fearfully out of the window Josh pulls the car up and parks at the curb.

"Out," commands Josh.

Out we go. I employ my standard half walk/half jog that I need to keep up with Josh on the sidewalk. I whine. He ignores.

As we near an old movie theater I notice a girl leaning against the wall by the doors, smoking a cigarette and watching us approach. Josh doesn't seem to see her. She's about his age, I figure, and she seems vaguely amused, her eyebrows raised just slightly, a suggestion of a smile on her face. She's wearing skinny black jeans and Chuck Taylors and a T-shirt with an illustration of a dancing girl on it and the words THE BEAT, and it all looks just right with her slim frame and pretty face and bright red hair, which falls in tight curls to her shoulders. I like her. I don't know why.

When we draw even with her, Josh stops dead and regards her in silence. I stop as well, waiting, not sure what's going on. She returns his gaze and takes a drag from her cigarette.

"I thought you quit," he says finally.

"I thought you left," she says in response, smiling, and flicks the cigarette aside. Then she turns to me and smiles warmly.

"You poor guy. Has it been terrible, being his little brother?"

I stammer something, not sure what to say.

"I thought so. Here, c'mon," she says, offering me her elbow. "C'mon," she says again when I hesitate, and so I link my arm with hers.

"Let's go shopping," she says, and we walk arm in arm down the sidewalk, Josh following behind us. And that's how I fell in love with Lesley McDougal.

"Dude, where were you?!"

"Danny, I'm sorry."

"You promised you were going to be there! We waited an hour!"

"I know. I'm sorry."

"I called you, like, five times!"

"I told you, Josh threw my cell phone in the creek."

"I e-mailed you!"

"I didn't have time to log on."

"Well, what the hell happened? What were you doing?"

"Uh . . ."

CHAPTER THIRTEEN

THE DETAILS

MERIT BADGE: PRODUCT

That night I lie awake in the tent, stroking my forearm where Lesley's skin had touched mine. I can still feel the warmth of her arm. I'm wearing the shirt I was wearing today, and I pull it up and hold it to my face, inhaling the faint aroma of tobacco and her perfume.

Patricia Morrison seems like a distant, foolish memory.

On top of my long dresser in my room is a messy stack of new clothes: four pairs of jeans, eight new T-shirts that have bands like the Clash and the Ramones on the front, or doodles that Lesley called "design elements." I also have a new belt, several three-packs of boxer-briefs, a pair of black high-tops, and boots that are sort of like combat boots "but really much more all-purpose and without all those racist skinhead connotations." This last was from the salesperson at one of the stores, a guy Lesley seemed to be friends with.

It's safe to say I'd prefer to drink a large glass of warm mucus rather than have to shop for clothes. But I would happily spend the rest of my life shopping if I could do it with Lesley.

"I'm Lesley," she announced as she was escorting me down the sidewalk, "and I'll be your stylist today. How great is that?"

"Um . . . pretty great?"

"Exactly. Are you mentally prepared to have your mind blown by sheer fun-ness?"

"Um . . ."

"Say, 'I'm mentally prepared to have my mind blown by sheer fun-ness.'"

"I'm mentally prepared to have my mind blown by sheer, uh . . ."

"Fun-ness."

"Fun-ness."

"Right on. All right, here we are."

I won't bore you with the play-by-play of the actual consumer experience. To me it all went by in a fuzzy, joyous blur. She led me into one store after another, laughing and joking as she loaded up my arms with clothes until they towered over my head. She was funny and wise and genuine and completely unintimidated by my brother, and she listened to what I said, as if it never dawned on her to notice how dumb and awkward and hideous and hopeless I am. And because she was somehow able to pretend that I'm actually worth talking to, I started to think that maybe I was, and I managed to put together real sentences with all the words in the right order and not make the usual fool of myself. The frog sang, or at least hummed quietly.

She knew everyone at the stores. She'd walk in and announce some variation of "Hey, [name of gay hipster clothing salesperson], this is my BFF Isaac, and he's supercool and needs the clothes to match his inner coolness."

The very first store we went into, she leaned into the dressing room when I had my pants half off. I nearly collapsed into the corner, desperately trying to cover myself up, but she didn't apologize or cover her eyes or react at all, except to say, "Nice legs. How are those pants working for you?" By the end of the day, I was changing with her in the dressing room with me, as if it was completely natural that an attractive nineteen-year-old girl I'd just met that day was seeing me in my underwear.

"Two words for you," she said at one point, looking at my white Hanes undies. "Boxer briefs." So we got the boxer briefs.

Things I learned about her: waitress right now, not going to college because she plans to move to Hollywood and become a stylist for movies and fashion shoots and TV. That's the person who selects all the clothes for the stars to wear, and they have to have really good taste and know what they're doing, and they can make really good money and it's glamorous and cool.

"Are you enjoying being my guinea pig?" she asked.

"I love being your guinea pig."

Josh hung back, content to observe and make the occasional comment or just roll his eyes. Sometimes he'd disappear entirely for a stretch, reappearing at checkout time to put the clothes on my parents' credit card.

"Josh," I said as I watched him ring up the first sale, "you sure this is okay?"

"Nope," he said, signing the receipt.

A few times when I came out of the dressing room I saw Josh and Lesley talking quietly. Sometimes she seemed to be teasing him, or just listening intently. Once I saw her place her hand on his shoulder. Other times I'd catch her watching him, following him with her eyes, her expression wistful.

I know, okay? I'm not an idiot. I might be in love with her, but she's in love with him. But he's not in love with her, and I don't know why. Maybe he was at some time in the past.

I pieced together that she works at the diner next to Jerry's, near downtown Edina, the place where Josh used to be a line cook.

"The first day I worked there we just started talking," she said, "and we just kept going and ended up sitting in a park, talking until about two in the morning."

I tried to visualize my brother having that much to say to anyone.

"So you guys have been . . . *friends* since then?"

She nods. "Friends."

"Friends?"

"Friends," she repeated, in an and-now-we're-done-with-this-subject tone of finality. "That shirt isn't working for you. Next."

I followed her out of the dressing room. We were in a store with exposed brick walls and cool light fixtures. Josh was hunched in a modern-looking chair in the corner, his thoughts somewhere else.

"I worry about him, you know," said Lesley, looking over at him. "I worry about the decisions he makes."

"Like what?"

"You know, what he's doing. I think it's a bad choice."

I stared at her, not sure what she meant. Her expression changed.

"You don't know what I'm talking about, do you." She sighed and looked over at Josh again. "Josh . . ." she said, shaking her head.

At one point we passed a jewelry shop, and Lesley gasped and said, "You know what? We should totally pierce your ear! Not here, though—I'll do it."

"Um . . ." I said.

"No," said Josh.

"Why not?" said Lesley. "He'd look supercute with an earring."

"I would?"

"*Super*cute. You're cute already, so you'd be supercute with an earring."

Let me be clear: No female who's not my mother's age has ever called me cute. It's unimaginable to me that someone might see me in that way. I know she was probably just being kind, but I was flooded with a sensation I can hardly describe, a warm maple syrup combining love and joy and ecstasy, a feeling so euphoric that my eyes teared up and I had to turn from her to hide it.

"We're not piercing his ear," Josh ruled.

"Okay," said Lesley. Then a moment later, when Josh wasn't looking, she pulled me close and whispered, "*Super*cute. But if you do it, you have to promise to let *me* do it, okay? I'll do it right."

"Okay," I said, my face flushed.

"Promise?"

"I promise."

We reached the car and Josh opened the trunk, tossing in the bags of clothes. My heart sank, the euphoria ebbing away as I realized my time with Lesley was coming to an end. I started to stumble through a thank-you to her, my usual awkwardness returning to paralyze my tongue, when she interrupted: "Hold on, we're not done yet. You still have to get your hair cut."

We went to an actual salon, the kind of place that smells like flowers and doesn't have a candy-cane barber's pole. Josh has a simple approach to his hair: He just gives himself a buzzcut with my parents' ancient hair clippers. He seemed uncomfortable in the salon, hovering over the hairstylist's shoulder as the stylist turned my head this way and that, fussing as he planned his strategy.

The hairstylist's name was apparently Tao, and all I can say is, he was exactly what you would expect at that sort of salon. Both he and Lesley agreed that my hair was (a) luscious and (b) thick, and Tao informed me that (c) it also had wonderful root structure. Josh made faces.

"Just don't make him look too . . . you know," he said to Tao.

"Gay?" said Tao.

"Right," said Josh.

In the end the volume of my semi-Jewfro was reduced by about two-thirds or more. Lying in my sleeping bag, I run my fingers over the hair on the back and sides, which is now very short, and then over the spiky terrain on top, the result of the Product that Tao rubbed in as a final touch. According to Tao and Lesley, Product is very important, and there is now an expensive tube of the stuff in the bathroom. Josh made his grimace/sneer face when Tao was smearing the stuff around the crown of my head, but Lesley told me to use Product, so I'll use Product.

I fall asleep still smelling perfume and cigarettes, and dream of Lesley.

CHAPTER FOURTEEN

THE MINOTAUR

"Isaac! Wake up!"

I open my eyes and sit up, confused and dull headed. I'm still in the tent. It's dark. My Lesley-scented shirt is still in my hand.

"Wake up!" repeats Josh, and my eyes are seared by the painful stab of a flashlight beam. I twist away, squinting, holding my hands up to block the light.

"What's going on?"

"Time to get going!"

I stumble along after him. We cut through the Olsens' yard, the Johnsons', the Patricks', the Schwartzes', the erratic line of the creek to our left. The moon is bright enough that we don't need the flashlight. I check my watch. It's 2:43 a.m.

"Where are we going?"

"You'll see."

He picks up the pace, jogging now, and I run to keep up with him, running through the backyards, dodging the dark shapes of trees, passing silhouettes of swing sets and jungle gyms and volleyball nets and lawn furniture, our footsteps nearly silent on the grass, then clomping loudly over the narrow wooden footbridge behind the Schwartzes', the creek gurgling beneath us. A patch of trees, a field, another backyard, people whose names I don't remember, a security light blinking on as we pass, our shadows sweeping hard-edged against the lawn. Everything like a dream. I look at my hands, because they say you can't look at your hands when you're dreaming. I wonder if this is what it's like to be stoned. I say, because nothing is real and it doesn't matter, "Who was that girl at the bar?"

"Just some girl."

"Why did you leave school?"

"I needed a break."

"What's your decision? What did Lesley mean?"

"What?"

"She said you're doing something."

"She talks too much. She didn't mean anything."

"You're going back to school?"

"Yep."

"Who is the girl at the bar?"

"Just some girl. Come on," he says, and I race to follow.

I'm not very happy with our destination.

"Josh," I whisper, "there's three dogs in there."

"Really? He used to always have four. Oops—there's the fourth."

He indicates the fourth dog, which has come meandering lazily around the corner from the side of the house to join its pals in the fenced-in backyard.

"Rottweilers, man," says Josh. "Those are mean-ass dogs. Smart, too."

"Josh, those things weigh more than I do," I hiss.

"Oh, yeah, easily," says Josh, speaking low. "They'd eat you and probably not even notice it. Plus, Nystrom's got the shotgun."

"What?!"

"Shhh!!"

We're lying in the brush at the top of a rise that looks down on Mr. Nystrom's yard. This was our destination. The house looks like it was plucked from some other, very different community and deposited in Edina—a low, one-story ranch, the paint peeling on the back wall, shingles missing from the roof, the gutter pulling away from the roofline like someone had tried to hang from it. A harsh flood lamp illuminates the yard, which is mostly dirt with a few patchy areas of crabgrass—except right in the middle, where there's a ring of low, ragged bushes surrounding a circular planter, on which is perched a statuette of a naked cherub playing a harp. From here it looks to be about a foot tall.

"So there it is," says Josh. "That's the challenge. You figure out a way to get in there, remove the statue, and bring it home."

"Now?"

"No, you've got until Mom and Dad get back. Consider that the central challenge of the Quest. That's the Minotaur you have to slay."

"Josh, that's the dumbest thing I've ever heard."

"The central challenge, Isaac. You can't consider yourself a success until you've achieved that goal."

As we watch, the fourth dog comes and sniffs at the bushes, then urinates on them. Two of the other dogs are sprawled out, apparently asleep. The third is sitting, looking out beyond the chicken-wire fence into the night, occasionally opening his massive mouth to pant. He doesn't look smart. He looks blank and stupid, even for a dog, a mindless machine designed to reduce statuette thieves into a pile of dog turds.

"There's no way," I whisper.

"Sure there is," says Josh. "I personally stole that statue, like, five times, and the first time I was younger than you are now."

I examine the yard. I am now very much awake, my earlier dreamlike reverie completely gone. Now we're just sitting in the woods in the middle of the night, sticks poking me in the ribs, and looking at the dogs that will be eating me.

"How am I supposed to get in there?"

"Wait till the dogs are asleep or inside, grab the statue—"

"And carry it back over the fence? While I'm climbing?"

"No, first you throw it over the fence."

"*Throw* it? I don't even know if I can *lift* it!"

"Look, figure it out. That's the challenge."

"It's stealing!"

"It's borrowing. You'll deliver it right back to him."

"Josh, what's the point?"

"The point? The point is being a man, Isaac. Conquering your fear, facing danger, dominating the powers of nature—"

"Getting eaten by a dog . . ."

"Look. It's *supposed* to be dangerous. That's the whole idea. I'd rather have you fight a bull or break a horse or hunt a frigging lion or kill a Minotaur. But what we've got is this—four fat-ass rottweilers crapping in some crazy guy's yard. That's what you've got to beat. This isn't defeating the Xbox, Isaac. Or winning the stupid game you play with Dad, the guess-why-the-dude-is-sick game."

"It's called differential diagnosis, Josh, and Dad says I'm pretty good—"

"'Dad says I'm pretty good at it,'" he says, mocking me. "Who gives a shit? This is *real*. The central challenge, Isaac. The key to the whole thing."

"Josh, that old guy is crazy. Everyone knows that. You ride by his house on your bike and he'll scream at you. Even if I do get past the dogs, he'll kill me."

"Nah. Dogs'll get you first. AWOOOOOO!!!"

I jump at the unexpected noise as Josh throws his head back and howls. The dogs are instantly up, converging into a boiling, four-headed knot of muscular black fur and flashing teeth as they bark and snap blindly in our direction. Josh is already up and running off, and I follow his cackling voice through the woods, heart pounding, picturing those dogs surging over the fence and pursuing us under the night sky.

"Josh, please, not again."

"What, you didn't have fun yesterday?"

"Josh, I can't—would you turn down the music?—I can't miss two days of school in a row!"

"Sure you can. I did it all the time. Hey, look—cows!"

"You do understand that I have to go to school?"

"This is a different kind of school. C'mon, buddy, move it!" He honks his horn at a slow-moving truck. The truck changes lanes to let us pass.

"Is Lesley going to be there?"

"No." He steps on the gas, and I'm jammed back in my seat as we accelerate past the truck. "This is going to be a little different from yesterday."

CHAPTER FIFTEEN

STANDOFF ON THE ST. CROIX

MERIT BADGES: GUNS, MOTORCYCLES, PERSONAL ENDANGERMENT

"Isaac, I swear, you either jump or I'm going to throw you off."

"I'm not doing it!"

"Jump!"

"No!"

I'm bleeding and trying not to cry. The edge of the cliff is about twelve inches in front of my bare toes, which is about ten feet closer than I want it to be. The blood is oozing from a big scrape that runs the length of my right shin, a souvenir from the treacherous, slippery climb up here. Beyond the edge of the cliff and a long way down, the river rolls and swirls past, the surface dark and oily. I'm in a semi-semicrouched position, leaning forward slightly, my knees bent, hands out to the side and a bit to the front—a compromise between standing straight up and being where I want to be, which is in a full knees-down hands-on-the-ground pose. Each time I try to sink down into that, Josh puts his hands under my armpits and pulls me upright. We've been at this impasse for what seems like hours.

So yes, today is a little different from yesterday.

Yesterday I went shopping with Lesley and got a haircut. Today I went firing assault rifles and crashing a motorcycle with an inbred survivalist freak, and now Josh is going to throw me to my death from a one-hundred-foot cliff above the St. Croix River.

"I'm seriously going to throw you off, Isaac."

"I'm not doing it!"

"Isaac, do you understand how key this moment is? How important this is to the Quest?"

"What, dying?"

"No, growing a pair and jumping."

"I could die!"

Behind me I hear Darrell the inbred survivalist freak murmur some sort of comment to his freak nephew Craig. They both laugh. I try to ignore them.

"Isaac," says Josh, "this is exactly the time you need to pull yourself together, face your fear, and jump."

"It's, like, a hundred feet down, Josh!"

"Actually, it's probably closer to about twenty-six feet, depending on the water level," says Darrell. "We've had a considerable amount of precipitation, though, so I imagine it's less of a drop. On the other hand, with the increased water volume the current'll be stronger when you land."

That's how Darrell says everything, always in totally assured expert lecturer mode, using terms like "subideal" and "considerable amount of precipitation," like what he really wants to say is, *Let's get this straight: I have a mullet and bad teeth and I'm a mechanic, but I'm still intelligent.*

"You should just jump. Just don't think about it and jump."

That's nephew Craig, chiming in with his helpful advice in his flat tone. He's standing behind me and to my left, arms wrapped around his bare, bony frame, his big, rabbity teeth chattering. He's already jumped three times so far.

It doesn't help that he is only twelve years old but is both taller than me and already knows how to ride a motorcycle and fire a gun, and did both things like they were second nature, like he'd been doing them for years and couldn't figure out how anyone could have grown up differently. He figured out pretty quickly that he hates me.

Backing up: Josh woke me in the morning from a nightmare where I was being torn apart by dogs. So tired during our a.m. workout that my dream world and awake world blurred and blended together, the dogs still snapping and tearing at me as I stumbled along the road. I thought of Lesley then, trying to hold her image and the sound of her voice in my head, and it made me stronger.

And then we somehow ended up in the car again, not going to school, and drove way out past the end of civilization until we were on a dirt road that ended up in a clearing in the woods. In the middle of the clearing squatted a cabin that was the setting for every movie ever made about people who take a dirt road to a cabin in a clearing in the woods and get hacked apart by inbred freaks who want to wear their skin.

"No," I said as the car rolled to stop near a muddy, beat-up pickup truck that was parked at a random angle to the cabin. "You've got to be kidding me."

"Nope. We're here."

As we got out of the car two hunting dogs came trotting around from somewhere around back and began baying and yelping at us, chins pointed toward the sky, hopping back and forth on their hind legs, flashing me back to my nightmare. Then the screen door opened and banged shut, and the person who would turn out to be Darrell emerged, wearing cutoff jeans and a gray army T-shirt, beer can in one hand, shouting at the dogs to shut up.

"*Hey*-ey!" he said as he approached, and gave Josh a big hug and a few paternal slaps on the cheek, like Josh was his long-absent and much-larger son who had returned to the freak roost after looting and pillaging some distant villages. There was some quick back-and-forth banter, mentions of mutual friends, and inquiries about how they were doing, while in the background nephew Craig emerged from the front door in a T-shirt that reached to his knees, rubbing his eyes like he'd just woken up. Why wasn't he in school? Was he homeschooled? Did he just tend the barrels where they render the fat from the victims? While I was pondering that, Darrell looked me up and down, grinning, and said to Josh: "Yep, pretty much like you described."

While I was trying to figure out what, exactly, that meant, Darrell cracked the beer, managing to spray me directly in the face, and said to Josh, "So, where would you like to begin? Bikes or guns?"

Guns it was.

Introductions done, Darrell said, "We're going to go retrieve the firearms," and then he and Craig went back into the murder cabin to do that.

"Josh," I hissed as soon as they were inside, batting away the dog who kept jabbing me in the balls with his nose, "I want to go home!"

"What? What are you talking about?"

"I want to leave! I'm missing school!"

Josh seemed genuinely taken aback.

"Isaac, I set this up specially for you. Darrell is taking time out of his day, doing this as a *favor*, because I asked him to."

"I don't want to ride a motorcycle, Josh, and I don't want to shoot guns."

"You don't want to—I can't believe this. I go out of my way—"

"Especially with these freaks. Don't you know any normal people?"

"Well, yes, *Mom*, I know plenty of *normal people*. Darrell is a *normal person*. He used to work on my bike."

Did I mention Josh had a motorcycle? Of course Josh had a motorcycle. For a while. And then he didn't. I never found out what happened. I don't think things ended well.

"I want to leave."

"We're not leaving. I thought you'd be *psyched* to do this. This is the *fun* part!"

"The *fun* part?"

"It's friggin' *motorcycles* and *guns*, Isaac. It's about as close to the definition of fun as you're going to find!"

"Maybe our definitions of 'fun' are slightly different."

"Oh, for God's sake. You're about to start lecturing me on the accident statistics, aren't you."

"Shut up," I said, because I had been.

"What is it that you'd rather be doing? Sitting in math class? Don't answer that."

"Josh, I just don't—"

"You were certainly psyched to do the whole *Queer Eye* thing yesterday—which, believe me, I wasn't so hot on."

"That was different."

"Are you gay? Is that it?"

"NO!"

"Look, you can just tell me."

"Josh, shut up. I just don't think I'm a motorcycles-and-guns type of person."

"Oh, no shit? But that doesn't mean you can't at least know how to do it, know what it's like. That way, you see some dude on a bike, you can say, I know how to do that. Or you hear some jackass going on about guns, and you can think, big effin deal, I've done that. He's got nothing on me."

"Do you know how pissed Dad would be?"

"That's exactly the point. You'd never get to do this with Dad, never, never, never, never. Christ, I wanted to give you a chance to do something like this, and thought it was something special that we could do together. Because once I'm gone you're not gonna get another chance."

So we ended up in a field that had plywood targets set up against a hillside. I had to get a lecture from creepy Darrell on how to shoot and the importance of the Second Amendment, and then they all had a great time, an orgy of *weeYOOOO*ing and cheering and *BANG BANG BANG POP POP POP BLAM!* as they worked their way through a lovely sampler plate of shotguns and pistols and assault rifles. Darrell shoved guns in my hands and I took my turns, flinching with each shot and weirded out and miserable, and, yes, sulky and pouty and uncooperative so that Josh would know just how miserable I was. Pretty soon he was shaking his head and making snide comments, and they were all snickering, and finally they all gave up on me and my half-assed shooting and I faded into the background, eventually just taking a seat on the ground a dozen yards behind them, wanting to go farther away but not wanting to draw more attention to myself.

You wouldn't like guns so much, I had muttered to Josh earlier — "'If you'd ever seen a child with a bullet wound,'" finished Josh for me. "Do you know what would be great? If you had an independent thought in your head that didn't come directly from Dad."

While I sat there on the ground I watched Josh interacting with Craig. That's who he wants as a brother, I thought, the two of them talking about guns and motorcycles and the NFL. Josh gesturing with his hands, describing some fight, Craig looking at him worshipfully. Maybe he could teach Craig my haphtarah.

After a lot more *WEEEYOOOO*ing and gunfire and male bonding and Craig using the 20-gauge to transform a passing crow into a puff of black feathers — they're really smart birds, you know; they use tools — the ammo was used up, and Darrell said, "Ooo*kay!* Let's ride some bikes!"

Which we did. And I crashed. I crashed within seconds of starting my very first ride, crashed with all of them watching, crashed exactly when I didn't want to crash, the front wheel rocketing skyward and throwing me onto my ass.

Everyone ran to the bike to make sure it was okay.

I got up and limped in circles, swearing loudly and rubbing my leg, not because I'd hurt myself but because I wanted to make it look like I had, at least a little bit.

Josh watched me for a few moments and said, "You're all right." It was a command. So I made some faces and swore a bit more and kind of dialed back the limp, fading it out after a few more circles.

Then Josh sighed—another check mark in my failure column—and said, "Screw it. Let's just go to the falls."

Which is where we are now, the whole horrible day building to this moment, with me standing up on this cliff, a gun-flinching, motorcycle-crashing, non-cliff-jumping coward.

"Jump."

"No.

"You know," volunteers Professor Darrell in his serious voice, "in these sorts of situations it's important to dominate one's fears."

Giant pine tree, fall and crush him now.

"Oh, shut up," I mutter.

"He looks like he's gonna start crying," observes Craig.

"Isaac, one, two, thr—"

"No."

"All right, if he ain't gonna go, I'll go again," says Craig, and he gets a running start and brushes past me as he rushes to the cliff edge and launches himself into space.

"WeeeeYOOOOOoooo!!!!" he says on the way down before splashing messily into the river.

"You see how easy that is?" says Darrell.

Just because your nephew is retarded, I have to be retarded too?

"All right, go," said Josh. "I mean it."

"No."

"Go!"

"I don't want to!"

I am aware of Darrell watching the exchange, waiting to see who is going to win the contest of wills. He thinks this is funny. I see Josh glance over at him and shake his head subtly, inviting Darrell to share in his disgust, the four hundredth time he's done that today.

Can you believe what a pussy my little brother is? I want to kick both of them in the balls.

"All right, then," says Darrell, "guess I'ma go. WEE-YOOOOoooo!!!" *Splash.*

"Isaac, this is one of those times when you can either stand up and be a man or be a failure."

Now I *am* crying, my eyes welling up.

"I don't care."

"Isaac, we have to leave and go home in about twenty minutes. And before we go, you are gonna jump off that cliff."

"No, I'm not going to." My voice has that thick, slurry sound you make when you're talking through your tears.

"Yes, you are."

"No, I'm not."

"Just jump!"

"No! No! I'm not going to!"

"*I'll* go."

A female voice. I turn, hurriedly wiping my face, and my heart does a backflip.

"Lesley," says Josh, "what are you doing here?" His tone is not of the *What a wonderful surprise!* variety.

She shrugs. "You said you'd be here."

She's wearing a bikini top and cutoff jeans. She looks incredible. She shifts her gaze to me and smiles and says, as if everything was normal, as if I wasn't standing there with tears and snot gleaming on my face, "Hi, Isaac."

Then she says to Josh, "You know, you shouldn't make him jump if he doesn't want to."

"Yeah, well, he's too much of a pussy to—"

"WEEEYOOOOO!!!" I whoop, cutting him off, and before the thinking part of my brain can step in, I'm airborne over the river and then plunging toward the swirling water.

Jesus I'm *still* falling Jesus why did I do this Jesus why did I—

I scramble back up the path, wet, cold, exhilarated, alive. *Alive!* HA HA HA HA *HAAAA!* When I get to the top I'm going to rush straight into Lesley's arms for a celebratory hug and—Where is she? She's gone. Josh and Darrell and Craig are there. Lesley isn't.

Darrell is clapping as I get close. "Thatta boy!" he says, and gives my hair a muss before I can pull my head away.

"You see what you can achieve when you focus?" he says while I'm twisting around, trying to find Lesley. "You understand now the power of confronting—"

"Where'd she go?" I say to Josh.

"Who?"

"'Who?' Lesley!"

"She left." He's fuming about something.

"Why?"

"Sounds like someone's got a bit of an infatuation," says Darrell in his wise, amused elder voice. *Boulder, roll down the slope and flatten him.*

"Did he really jump?" says Craig to Josh, like I'm not worth talking to.

"Yeah, he really jumped," I say to Craig. "Why'd she leave?"

"I was thinking you were gonna be too much of a pussy to jump," says Craig.

"Thinking? Wow, big step for you," I say. "Why did she leave? She drove all the way out here and just left?"

"Definitely infatuated," says Darrell, nodding his head and grinning. *Meteor. Bear. Frozen shitcube from a passing airplane. Anything.*

"Josh, why did she leave?"

"She just left."

"What did you say to her?"

"What did I *say* to her? What's it to you?"

"What, it's like she's his friggin' girlfriend or something," says Craig to Josh with a hopeful smile, waiting to be rewarded for his great joke. Instead Josh turns his head and just looks at him, a deliberate, blank-faced, dreadful moment that makes Darrell hurriedly interject, "Craig, whyn't you come over here for a bit?" For a few seconds I almost feel a glimmer of affection for my brother.

"Okay," I say, "I jumped off the stupid cliff. Can we go home now?"

CHAPTER SIXTEEN

INVESTIGATION

MERIT BADGE: ELECTRONIC ESPIONAGE

We say our goodbyes at Taylors Falls and leave Darrell and Craig there. Josh doesn't say anything about my jumping, like it didn't count. It's a long way to drive in tense silence. After a while I fall asleep.

We're cold and formal with each other during haphtarah practice. I don't mention anything about the day, and he doesn't bring it up. We might as well be unrelated, Josh just a grimly professional hired tutor.

When he gets up to use the bathroom, he leaves his cell phone on the desk. The instant he is out the door and down the hallway I grab the phone and start scrolling through his call history. Outgoing, outgoing, outgoing, outgoing, to someone named Trish. Lots of them—days of them—with only a few incomings from her.

Lots of incomings from Lesley, especially over the past week. A few outgoing.

I pause and listen for Josh. I don't hear anything.

I go to his text inbox, but it's empty, and so is his outbox, everything scrubbed clean. There's one text in his drafts file, a fragment of a message to Trish — "Unfair? How bout u? Y can't u" — and then it stops.

There are other calls, names I don't recognize. The most recent call from Lesley was at 3:23 p.m. today, one of a cluster that he never answered.

I get up and go to Josh's doorway and lean out into the hall. The bathroom door is still closed. I step back into the room and stare at the phone, at Lesley's unanswered call.

What I should do is put the phone back down. Instead I press the call button.

Lesley answers.

"I hope you're calling to apologize."

I nearly drop the phone in a rush of terror and excitement and jab the end call button, then race back to put the phone on the desk, hop away from it, and stand frozen in frightened-squirrel pose, arms hugged close to my sides, fists together under my chin. From down the hall comes the sound of the toilet flushing and then hand washing.

The phone rings. I jump. More frozen squirrel. *Ring.* I scurry back to the desk and stand over it, dart my hand out, pull it back, repeat, then snatch up the phone and hit end call. The phone falls silent midring.

I put it down. The phone and I regard each other, neither moving.

It beeps. New text.

WHAT RU DOING? it says.

The bathroom door is opening. Here he comes. I fumble with the phone and accidentally hit reply, then have to work my way back to select Lesley's message and figure out how to delete it. Josh is coming down the hall, three steps from the door. I highlight the message, delete it, put the phone back in its place, and leap into my seat just as he is rounding the corner into the room.

"Did my phone ring?" he says as he sits down.

"Yeah, but they hung up," I say.

He picks up the phone, sees who it was, makes a face, and puts the phone down again.

"All right, let's keep going," he says.

• • •

ISAAC, SERIOUSLY, YOU HAVE TO CALL ME BACK BECAUSE WE WERE WAITING FOR YOU AGAIN AND YOU DIDN'T CALL. ARE YOU COMING TO MY B-DAY PARTY? ARE YOU DEAD?

D

Yitzhak, I hope you're okay. You missed it: Jensen threw a total shit fit today at Darrick Prince. I took notes in math if you need them :)

Sarah

CHAPTER SEVENTEEN

PURSUED BY THE TROLL

I eat in silence while Josh and Lisa talk. After dinner I do some homework. Josh watches TV. There's a terse message on the answering machine from Danny, and several more e-mails from him, but somehow I keep putting off calling him back.

At nine fifteen I'm doing math homework in the kitchen when the phone rings. Josh answers.

"That depends. Who's calling? Oh, yeah, hey, Sarah! How are you?"

He looks over at me, grinning. I mouth *No!* to him and wave my hands violently.

"He sure is," says Josh. "Boy, am I glad you called. We were just talking about you. He's sitting right here. He's been hoping you'd call."

I bury my face in my hands.

"Here," he says, holding the phone out to me, then knocks it against my skull several times until I snatch it from him.

"Hello?" I say.

"Hi, Izzie!" says Sarah. She's one of the only people besides my mother who call me that, which is what happens when you've had

Passover dinner together every year since you were born. "Are you okay? I was just wondering if you needed those notes from math."

She goes on. I answer with as few syllables and as little emotion as possible. All the while, Josh is pantomiming all sorts of perverse acts.

"What? Condoms? Of course I can lend you some condoms!" he announces in a loud voice, just before I say goodbye and hang up. He finds this very funny.

"I would not touch her if you paid me a million dollars," I say, fuming.

When I'm done with my homework I shower, and then go out to the tent without being asked.

But tonight, when I fall asleep, I have a plan.

CHAPTER EIGHTEEN

THE REBELLION BEGINS

MERIT BADGE: BREAKING AND ENTERING

1:15 a.m.

Out of the tent, moving quietly across the backyard, detouring toward the edge of the lawn, where the illumination from the security lights is weakest.

This time I go around to the front door. Josh's window faces toward the rear, and he's less likely to spot me this way. Plus, I had loosened the bulb in the fixture on the front porch, the one that would normally light up automatically because of the motion detector.

The key fits and turns in the lock. I had remembered that my dad kept a spare in his office junk drawer, along with ancient cuff links and strange fraternity pins and campaign buttons for someone named Dukakis. I pocketed the key in the morning, my plans already forming.

I close the door behind me slowly, slowly, then stand quietly, listening for any sounds. Nothing. I reach under the hallway table and find my father's shoes, feeling in the left one for the small flashlight I'd put there.

I keep the flashlight off for now. First to the kitchen and the refrigerator, easing the door open, slipping a hand in and holding down the little button on the inside so that the interior light doesn't go on. Quick rummaging for the pizza box. I sit on the floor with the lights off, next to an off-kilter rectangle of moonlight coming in through the sliding doors that go out to the back porch. I eat the pizza cold, wolfing it down, the cheese hard and waxy.

Then downstairs, fast walk in the dark to my parents' bathroom, shut the door, turn the faucet on to a slow trickle, and give myself a head-to-toe sponge bath with a washcloth.

Then upstairs again, naked except for the towel wrapped around my waist, staying on the right side so the stairway doesn't creak. I stand at the entranceway to the hall that leads to Lisa's room, Josh's room, and my destination: my room. Josh's light is off. I move cautiously down the hall, noiseless on the carpet.

Twist the door handle and open my door in a smooth, slow motion, *shoooosh* as it brushes over the carpet, *shoooosh* as I ease it shut, the tiniest of clicks as I twist the handle back into place, then off with the towel. I squat to place it over the bottom of the door to block out any stray photons, straighten, feel for the light switch, flick it on, turn, and shriek like a girl.

"What are you doing in the house?" demands Josh. We're in the living room, where he herded us after all the excitement. "How did you get in here?"

"What are you talking about? What is he doing in my *bed!?*"

"Dude, seriously, I can, like, go sleep on the sofa or just split."

This last slurry bit is from Patrick. As in punk-rock Patrick from the club, Patrick the Ear Chewer.

"You're not sleeping on the sofa," says Josh to Patrick, who WTF is he doing in our house?! To me: "You're going back outside."

"I'm not going back out there!"

Patrick is wearing black boxers and one black sock. Now that we're not in a dark club and he's not covered in several layers of studded leather, I can see that he has a lot of tattoos of the skull/demon/naked-lady variety. His Mohawk lies completely limp down over his shoulders, like a deflated sea urchin. Even with his boxers on he's wearing more than me. I'm holding a sofa pillow in front of my crotch.

I was not expecting to turn on the light and find him splayed out on my bed, his mouth wide open and his eyes only half-shut, like he was dead. That's what caused the shrieking. Then I turned and tried to run out of my room, remembering too late about the whole shutting-the-door business. By the time I had unscrambled my brain and managed to find the doorknob and yank the door open, Josh was already out of his room and yanking *Lisa's* door open — "Because I thought all that high-pitched screaming was her," he said. Then she did start screaming, because of Josh nearly pulling her door off the hinges, then I came running into the hall and ran right into Josh, which was like running into the door but more painful.

So now here we are, Josh furious at *me* for being inside.

"You're going back out."

"No!"

"I could go sleep in the tent," suggests Patrick.

"You're not sleeping in the fucking tent, Patrick. Isaac is. And *do not frigging touch those.*"

Patrick quickly pulls his hand back from the shelf with our mother's prize collection of Chinese snuff bottles.

"Sorry."

"What is going on?"

Lisa is standing in the doorway.

"Nothing. Go to sleep."

"Who is that?"

"This is Patrick."

"Hey," says Patrick, waving at Lisa.

She looks at him, expressionless.

"Go back to bed," says Josh.

"What's he doing here?" asks Lisa.

"He's staying here for a few days."

"A few *days?*" I say.

"Why is Isaac naked?"

"Go to bed!"

"You said 'fucking.'"

"Lisa . . ."

There's a meth dealer with the Grim Reaper tattooed on his chest sleeping in my bed, and Lisa is upset that Josh is swearing.

"Lisa, please go to bed," says Josh. Please, he says, which he's never once said to me in his life. She goes.

"All right," he says to me, "put some pants on and let's go."

"No."

"Put some pants on, and let's go."

"No."

Patrick is doing the tennis-match thing, head twisting back and forth as we have our standoff.

"Isaac . . ."

I can see what's going to happen next. He's going to grab me, pick me up, stuff my clothes on, toss me out the door, and humiliate me. Patrick's presence makes him even less likely to budge. I feel helpless and angry, and I'm still shaking from the shock, but I also feel half crazy, like it being two in the morning and having Patrick there makes anything possible, and I don't want to back down. I want to win somehow.

"You want me to go?" I say. "I'll go."

I toss the pillow to him and march past him, out of the living room, and through the house to the kitchen and the sliding doors.

"Isaac," I hear Josh say from somewhere behind me, but I keep going. I slide the door open violently enough that it bounces a third of the way closed again, and I turn sideways to step out onto the porch. The security light blinks on, and I can see my own naked shadow as I accelerate down the steps to the lawn.

"Isaac!" Josh is calling to me in a strained half shout, the kind of voice you use when you want to be loud but can't. I'm halfway across the lawn, and I turn and walk backwards, seeing Josh and Patrick crowded at the kitchen doorway.

"Isaac!" says Josh again, and I salute and turn back to face the tent at the edge of the yard.

"Damn!" I hear Patrick say—two syllables: "DAY-um!"—and he starts laughing. Josh says something to him but I don't catch it, and then I can hear the door closing roughly and the click of the lock.

Naked on the lawn under the moonlight. Two fists up over my head in triumph.

CHAPTER NINETEEN

IN WHICH REBELLION PROVES TO BE SOMEWHAT ADDICTIVE

MERIT BADGE: JOURNEY TO THE GREAT UNKNOWN

Climbing out of the bathroom window is harder than I thought it would be, especially in my tight new jeans and with my new belt buckle scraping against and almost getting caught on the window frame. I make it, though, and drop to the ground without hearing any seams give.

If I time it right, it should all work out—Josh should be making breakfast for Lisa right now, giving me enough time to get to the garage, retrieve my bike, and be on my way. After a while Josh will start wondering why it's taking me so long to shower and change after our morning exercise session. Maybe he'll even be concerned. He'll knock and say, *Isaac? Are you in there? Are you okay? Isaac?* I can picture his face now as he realizes that something's wrong, that maybe he's pushed me too far and I've collapsed, and he'll open the door and rush into the bathroom to find me—but I'm gone. And then he'll see the note on the mirror, written in my mom's lipstick: I'M GOING TO SCHOOL.

I was hoping for a brighter, bolder red, but the brownish color was the only one I could find in my mom's makeup drawer. Either way, it should get my point across: any surprises today are coming from me, not from him.

I'm pedaling now toward Tracy Avenue. There's a surprise for Josh right there, in case he decides to come tearing after me and kidnap me for another one of his stupid plans: he's not going to find me on the road to school, because I'm not actually going to school. At least, not yet.

Patrick didn't stir when I went into my room this morning to get my clothes. He looked very comfortable on my bed, especially the way he was facing the wrong direction and had his feet mushed onto my pillow.

I check my watch. Plenty of time. I figure it will take maybe twenty minutes or so to get where I'm going. I'll get there, just stay for about ten minutes, and then ride back to school. Worse comes to worst I'll be a few minutes late for homeroom. And my brother's right: What are they going to do? Expel me?

In the end it takes me twenty-seven minutes to get where I want to go, not counting the three minutes I need to lock my bike, and then the other three minutes I take fanning myself and wiping my face before I accept that I'm not going to stop sweating and I should just go in.

I fidget by the brown sign that says PLEASE WAIT TO BE SEATED until the hostess notices me, glancing over at me from behind the long counter with a quizzical expression on her face. She's about fifty, I'm guessing, and fattish and unfriendly.

"Can I help you?" she says.

"Um, I just wanted to . . . I wanted some breakfast."

She looks at me just long enough for it to get uncomfortable, then says, "You're alone?"

"Yes. It's just me."

She's still eyeing me suspiciously as if she's trying to decide whether to give me a table or call the authorities.

"You're going to be eating?"

"Yes," I say. "I have money," I add, in case that's the sticking point.

"You want to sit at the counter?" she asks grudgingly.

"I got this one, Jenny," says a voice from my left, and it's like the sun has just come out.

Lesley doesn't say a word to me, just gives me a sly grin when she turns her back to Jenny to grab a menu, a look that says, *You and I are a team in this conspiracy.*

She leads me across the restaurant to a booth in the back corner. She glances over at me as we walk, taking in the clothes that she selected for me.

"I dig your outfit," she says.

I look at the pink striped shirt that's part of her uniform. "Yours, too," I say.

We arrive at the table and I sit. "Here you go, sir," she says, handing me the menu.

"I think I know what I want."

"Oh, good. I like a man who knows what he wants."

"Can I get French toast?"

"Of course. Coffee?"

"Uh . . . yes, please."

She raises her eyebrows and smiles, but doesn't say anything as she writes on her little waitress pad. "I'll be right back."

I watch her walk away and I look around the restaurant. I think it's a chain, a step or two above a Denny's and a step below a real restaurant. There are just a few customers sitting in some of the booths. I'm the youngest one by at least fifty years.

"I know what you're thinking," says Lesley as she places a coffee in front of me. "How did I get such an awesome job?"

Then she puts a second cup on the table and slides into the booth opposite me. "Cheers," she says, and knocks her cup against mine and takes a sip.

She watches as I try mine, then wordlessly slides the cream and sugar toward me. I add some cream and a packet of sugar, wanting to add another but deciding against it. I take my time stirring, thankful for something to focus on, because I didn't expect that we'd have this much time face to face, and I suddenly can't remember what it was I had rehearsed saying. Everything seems very quiet. When I figure I've done about as much stirring as I can get away with, I take another sip and put the coffee down hurriedly. Lesley, again without a word, picks up another packet of sugar, tears it open, and dumps it in my coffee.

"Someday I'll take you to a place where they make actual coffee," she says.

"Thanks," I mumble, because I'm not sure what else to say.

She sits leaning forward with her elbows on the table, both hands holding her coffee cup. I expect her to say, *So, to what do I owe the pleasure?* Or, *Shouldn't you be in school right now?*

Instead she says, "Tell me everything."

So I do.

I start drinking my coffee and tell her about Josh and the Quest. She listens silently, getting up a few times to give people their checks or refill their waters and to get my French toast, but after each interruption she sits down and nods at me to continue. I tell her about my parents and Lisa and school and the Assholes and Patrick and my bar mitzvah and worrying about crapping in my pants during my haphtarah. I even tell her about Patricia Morrison. There's a point when I'm talking about Josh and what a turd he is to me that I get a little teary but don't want to wipe my eyes because that would draw attention to it, and she pulls out a napkin from the dispenser and hands it to me in one smooth move, all the while nodding and listening, just like she did with the sugar, and I talk and drink coffee and talk and drink coffee and by the time I've told her about pretty much every experience in my entire life I realize that I'm speaking very quickly and gesturing emphatically and fighting an urge to get up and run laps around the dining room.

Finally, I fall silent.

"Maybe we do decaf next time?" she says.

"Yeah. Yeah. Yeah. Yeah, maybe."

Tap tap tap tap tap on the table with my fingers.

"Am I a freak?"

"Only enough to make you interesting."

She smiles and gets up to help some customers, resting a hand briefly on my shoulder as she passes. My heart, which is already redlining, goes a bit faster.

When she comes back and sits again, I ask, "What happened yesterday?"

"Your brother and I," she says, "have a very complicated relation-ship."

"Did you ever go out?"

She laughs. "No."

"Did you ever want to?"

She sips her coffee and looks at me.

"One of us did," she says.

"What happened?"

She smiles.

"You're sure nosy."

"Sorry."

"Your brother has bad taste in women," she says.

Well, clearly, if he never went out with you, I think of saying. Cool and clever, or like I'm *trying* to be cool and clever? *Well, clearly, if he never went out with you.* I could say it with a shrug or looking off into the distance or looking right at her over my coffee. No, casual, while bringing my coffee up to my mouth, right now. *Well, clearly, if he never . . .*

"Well, that would, well, clearly, if you, if he, clearly—"

"You know," she says, interrupting me and saving my life, "I think in some ways he might be one of the closest friends I have. And I'd say I'm the closest friend he has."

I put my coffee back down. There's an inch of liquid at the bot-tom, a distorted white oval reflecting on the glossy surface from one of the lights. I can't quite identify what it is I'm feeling, and then I realize it's jealousy—and I'm not sure if it's because I'm jealous of his attention or hers or both.

"I think he hates me," I say after a bit, still peering into the depths of my coffee, jiggling it so that the reflection shimmers.

When she speaks it's more of a breath, so quiet I can barely hear it. What I think she says is, "Not as much as he hates himself."

"What?"

She smiles again and shakes her head. "Nothing."

More customers are coming in now, bunching up by the entranceway. I can see her attention sliding away and want to hold on to it.

"Why did he leave school?"

"Lesley," says Jenny from behind the counter.

"I'm coming," she says. I'm not sure she heard me.

"Do you know why—"

"Why don't you ask him?"

"You said he was doing something you didn't like. You said—"

"Lesley," repeats Jenny.

"Sorry." She's standing up. "I'll be right back."

I wait for a while, watching her seat customers, take orders, bring water. It's getting more crowded. She passes me several times, twice saying sorry or smiling apologetically, and then starts brushing by, too busy and focused to say anything. I should leave—I know it—but I'm hoping she'll sit down with me and talk some more, and so I linger until it feels like I've suddenly crossed the Awkward barrier, and then when I stand up she's disappeared into the kitchen.

I wait a bit longer by the table for some more awkwardness, then walk slowly to the front register.

"Where's your check?" says Jenny.

"Uh . . ." That's what people do, they get the check from the waitress, and that's how you know what to pay. I don't have a check.

"I got it," Lesley says, and swoops in once again, shouldering

114

Jenny aside to punch numbers into the register. My hero. I make feeble protesting noises but she won't have it.

"My treat. Sorry I got so busy." She's waving to a table as she says it, letting the people know she sees them. I'm embarrassed that I stayed so long, that she basically had to kick me out.

"No, that's okay. Thanks. Well . . ."

She stops scribbling on her waitress pad and looks up at me, and suddenly I have her full attention again.

"I'm really glad you came today, Isaac," she says, grasping my hand as she says it. "C'mere."

She pulls me into a big full-body hug. It feels great, but I'm not quite sure where to put my hands, and they end up resting uncomfortably around her hips.

She leans back and looks at me. "You know what I want you to do?"

"What?"

"Have confidence in yourself. Okay?"

"Okay."

"Good. Now go. Fly, little bird! Go, be free!"

She spins me around and swats me on the ass and sends me out into the world with a stupid grin on my face. I get my bike unlocked and peer in through the window, hoping for a wave, but she's busy again, and so I get on my bike and ride to school.

Or partway to school. Sort of.

CHAPTER TWENTY

A TALMUDIC DEBATE OF THE HIGHEST ORDER

MERIT BADGE: SHINER

"So which one is it, Josh?"

I bat at his huge forearms, trying to move them out of the way, get his hands out of my face.

"Is it commandment 370, to break the neck of a firstling cattle" — swat — "if it's not redeemed?"

"Isaac, are you going to shoot in, or are you just going to friggin' talk?"

Wrestling in the backyard. It's the afternoon of my Lesley Day. Josh shoving me away with his giant paws, pushing against my head, me attempting to swim past his arms and shoot in for a takedown. Meanwhile, I friggin' talk, enjoying it as Josh gets more irritated.

"Is that your favorite commandment, Josh? Or is it number 402" — swat — "that an uncircumcised not eat of the heave offering? No?"

Yes, I did some Googling of the 613 commandments today. Among other things I did. I'm sure those 613 commandments were very important, back when high technology meant a goat. Now they just seem stupid.

"Why the hell are you so chipper, Isaac? You get an A in algebra or something?"

"Something like that. And it's pre-calc. I finished AP algebra two years ago."

"Good for you, Melvin. You're dropping your hands again. Stop dropping your hands."

"What is the 'heave offering,' anyways?" I say.

"I'm gonna heave you on your ass in a second."

"You don't know what a 'heave offering' is, Josh? I thought you were the Jew expert."

"You know what you should be concentrating on, Isaac? Not moving like a homo."

I dive for a leg and end up face planting into the sod.

"You almost got him, little dude!"

Patrick, watching from the porch, drinking from a forty-ounce bottle of malt liquor. *Buuuurp.*

I spit out a mouthful of grass and dirt as I get to my feet. I go after Josh again.

"I thought for sure you'd know, Josh."

"Hands!"

"I mean, it's your tattoo, after all . . ."

I shoot for a leg again, do another face plant.

"Jesus, Lisa could do that takedown better than you."

When I walked in the door this afternoon I was greeted by a wad of workout clothes rebounding off my forehead.

"Welcome back," said Josh. "We're gonna work more on your wrestling."

He didn't refer to this morning's daring escape at all, which was sort of annoying. I changed, and we went out back. Oh, right—first there was a minor detour so I could snake out the clogged upstairs toilet and mop up the overflow from the bathroom floor.

"Josh," I said, holding up the cause of the clog in a yellow-gloved hand, "there was a sock in the toilet."

Josh grabbed the offending item—no glove for him—and marched out to where Patrick was sitting on the back porch. Josh hurled the dripping sock at him, like he'd done to me with my workout clothes.

"What are you, retarded?" he said as Patrick blinked at the sock, which had splatted off his forehead and landed in his lap.

"You never seen a flush toilet before? No wonder your landlord booted you."

"Whoa," said Patrick. "*That's* where that got to."

In addition to clogging up the toilet, Patrick has managed to leave the freezer door open so that the interior now looks like it's lined with thick white fur, and to park his ancient Toyota Camry directly on top of the flower bed that sits next to the driveway. I think he's also been playing with my Gundam figures, too, because somehow the Thief Zaku figure is now missing an arm.

So now Josh and I are in back, tussling. And I'm needling. And he's getting pissed off. It's great.

"So, Josh, remind me, which is the one about not eating the sinew of the thigh? Have you been observing that one?"

"Isaac, shut up and focus."

I can see the indicator on the annoyance meter creeping into red. Part of my brain is tapping the other part on the shoulder, saying that provoking Josh is a game with a pretty certain outcome. But I still feel intoxicated and giddy, a halo effect from today's clandestine meeting with Lesley. And from the other things I did today. So I taunt him, my wimp's revenge as he twists and bends my limbs in the wrong directions.

"We're lucky we can still hold on to our Canaanite slaves forever, huh, Josh? I think that's number 199."

"Stop being a little bitch."

(Headlock.)

(Me, muffled): "Are you carrying out the laws of the sprinkling of the water?"

"There're five-year-olds who wrestle better than you."

(Slam. Hip throw. Josh on top, squeezing the air out of me.) "Whuzza one . . . about . . . the clusters of grapes?"

"Shut up. Don't just lie there like a faggot, get out."

He hoists me back to my feet so we can lock up again. We're in that classic wrestling pose, one hand clamped behind each other's head, the other hand on each other's upper arms, Josh bent over and jerking me around and testing my balance.

"Hey, Josh," I say, our foreheads pressed against each other's, "I figured it out. I know which one is your favorite commandment: number 72."

"Isaac, what the hell are you talking about?"

Quick shift of grips, swapping hand positions to the other side.

"You told me to take the Jew stuff seriously. You're the one with the tattoo of the commandments. Don't you know what commandment number 72 is?"

Arm shift again. Battle for position.

"Not to stuff your brother's head up his ass?"

"Not to get a tattoo."

Arm shift. Loud *BONK.*

"Whoa," says Patrick.

I'm now looking up at the clouds as they float past. I think the *bonk* was the sound Josh's elbow made as it collided with my skull.

"Ow," I say.

"Oops," says Josh. "Okay, haphtarah time."

• • •

ISAAC—MY PARTY IS TONIGHT. YOU'RE COMING RIGHT? DANNY

CHAPTER TWENTY-ONE

ANOTHER MIDNIGHT OUTING

MERIT BADGE: POOL HALL

Josh is talking to a real live Black Person.

Not a black person like Wayne Billings at school, who's adopted and whose parents are both white, or even Ben Riser, whose parents are both black but who acts even whiter than Wayne Billings or even me. No, the man Josh is talking to — talking to in a relaxed, casual manner, both of them leaning against the pool table or on their pool cues between shots, talking quietly like they know each other — is Black. City Black, like you see on TV, or in a rap video. He's about twenty-five or thirty, I'd guess, and about six feet tall and slim and athletic looking. He's wearing a dark T-shirt and jeans and what I think is called a porkpie hat on top of his shaved head. So far his expression has stayed in a narrow range between very serious and light scowling. His skin is very dark. I somehow feel like he's familiar, or that I should know him, but I'm realizing it's the TV thing — he's the Black Guy who would be at the pool hall on a TV show. I'm just realizing now that I've never once spoken with someone like this, and I feel oddly jumpy and awkward, like I'm in the presence of a celebrity.

I'm trying not to stare at him, but I'm not sure where else to put my eyes — the room feels jam-packed with hazards, visual land-mines that I could set off just by looking at them: the three scuzzy-looking men drinking beer out of bottles and shooting pool at the table nearest Josh; the man three stools to the right of me with his gaze fixed on nothing, idly rotating his shot glass on the bar with his fingers; the bartender, who looks like Jabba the Hutt's unattrac-tive brother; the booth with the four American Indians in it, their expressions impassive.

We've been at the pool hall for about ten minutes.

During our afternoon study session I actually made it through my haphtarah with only a few errors, and Josh looked at me and said, Not bad. He also repeated, Why the hell are you in such a good mood this afternoon?

No reason, I said. Just happy. And I was. Am. Despite the black eye I'm now sporting from the "accident" at the end of our tussling session. When I complained about it to Josh he shrugged, dismiss-ive, almost confused by my concern. For Josh, having a black eye is sort of the natural order of things — the days you walk around *without* your face marked up are the rarities.

I'm not supposed to be here at this pool hall. Not just because it's a pool hall and I'm thirteen. I'm supposed to be — or supposed to *have* been — at Danny's birthday party. For some reason I kept forgetting to tell Josh that it was coming up, and then sort of forgot about it, or at least didn't think about it. And then after Torah prac-tice Josh said, "A man should know how to play pool, right?"

Sure, I said, not mentioning that Danny has a pool table and we play all the time.

"So after dinner I'll get a sitter for Lisa, and we'll go play some pool," said Josh.

And being the new me, I said, "Cool."

I have to call Danny, I thought, *and tell him I can't go to his party. I just can't.* The new me can't go to a pizza parlor tonight for a birthday party, even if it's ironic. Not after today. *So I should call Danny,* I thought. Then I didn't. *I'll explain everything tomorrow.*

Josh and I got into the car and drove to I'm not exactly sure what part of the city — it's not Uptown, and it's not Downtown; it's just weirdtown, a dim, lonely stretch with low buildings that seem to be either Taco Bells, auto supply stores, thrift shops, or just boarded up.

Please don't stop here, I thought, and so of course that's where we stopped.

Now I'm sitting on the very last barstool, my back to the bar, sipping a Coke. Josh seems to have forgotten about the pool lesson. Instead I'm watching him and Durwin play. That's the Black Person's name, Durwin. When we walked in, Josh scanned the room and grimaced, as if he wasn't finding the person he was hoping to see. Then he and Durwin spotted each other at the same time, Durwin standing at the pool table across the hall, tilting his head back almost imperceptibly in greeting, Josh responding the same way. I followed Josh to Durwin's table, and the two did the manshake with chest bump like Josh had done with the bouncer at the club, Durwin still holding the pool cue as he delivered a few light thumps to Josh's back.

"Durwin, this is my little brother, Isaac."

"'S'up, baby," said Durwin in a soft voice, holding a fist out to me. I was determined to avoid another handshake fiasco like I'd had with Patrick the Ear Chewer and had been internally rehearsing all the likely greeting scenarios as we approached, so I managed to pull off a flawless fist bump, trying at the same time to mirror Durwin's neutral, distant expression.

"Yeah, you all right," he said approvingly as our fists touched, as if he were able to peer into my soul through the contact points of our knuckles. I felt a sudden bloom of pride, along with the realization that I really, really wanted Durwin the Black Person to like me.

I'm staring at him now in fascination as he plays pool, watching as he walks in a fluid, unhurried pace around the table, lines up his shot, sinks it, and floats to the next position. I realize that this is the real lesson of tonight, not pool practice. I catch myself trying to imitate Durwin's expression — the subtle downward curve of the mouth, the slight furrowing of the brow, and then that far-off look to the eyes, like he's here but not here completely, because he's got several deadly important things on his mind, probably involving guns, and by the way, don't fuck with him because he's dangerous. Josh looks dangerous, too, like a walking bar fight, like a car crash, but Durwin makes it look cool, like it's less his main defining characteristic and more an interesting side note.

For some reason I've always wanted a British Friend. Maybe it's because of the Harry Potter movies. I saw them and decided that I wanted a British Friend, someone named Thomas or William, and he'd have pale British skin and British manners and a British accent that makes everything sound sophisticated and intelligent and innocent all at once, and I used to fantasize about what that would be like, acting out both sides of our conversation. *'Ello, Isaac, bloody wonderful to see you.*

Now that I'm watching Durwin play pool, though, I've concluded that I desperately want a Black Friend, maybe even more than a British Friend.

'S'up, baby.

Nothin', baby, 's'up witchoo.

I take another sip of the flat, watery Coke, the ice melted to little slivers. I'm trying my best to do like my brother told me: Act like it's totally natural to be here, slouching against the bar. When I feel it's safe, I take furtive peeks around the room, avoiding eyes, especially careful not to look over my shoulder at the horrific bartender. The walls are paneled in fake wood, like the Schwartzes' basement. The bar sticks out like a tongue halfway into the center of the room, splitting it into two halves, stools fringing the bar in a U shape. There are tables and booths on the side near the entrance, more booths and seven pool tables on this side. In the back there's a real pinball machine, and someone is playing an arcade game, shooting at targets with a plastic pistol. There's country and western music playing from a jukebox near the pinball machine, and the clicks and knocks and dull thuds of people playing pool, and the low murmur of conversation, but somehow the place feels silent and still, like everyone is waiting for something.

Josh is definitely waiting for something, checking his cell phone for the fourth time since we got here. Whoever was supposed to be here is late, and they haven't called yet. Just as I'm thinking that, Durwin, who's leaning over to line up another shot, says, "You know she ain't gonna come."

She. Not Lesley, I'm guessing. The girl at the bar. Trish?

Josh grunts and puts his cell back in his pocket.

I glance over at the Indians. I have a clear view of the one facing me on the outside of the booth. He's watching Josh and Durwin, and I try to guess at what he's thinking. Is he sizing them up? Four of them against Josh and Durwin? As I'm wondering that, the Indian shifts his gaze over, and for a moment our eyes meet and I look away, feeling a thrill of terror. *Hello, sir, are you perhaps Dakota Sioux? I once made a Dakota beadwork coin purse for a school project. I have also attended an Ojibwa drum ceremony, in case I've guessed your tribe incorrectly. Either way, I have studied your proud and tragic history and feel nothing but respect and please don't kill me.*

When I hazard another look his focus has shifted back to Josh and Durwin, his expression bored. Durwin, swinging around for another shot, notes the man looking at him and gives him a tiny nod.

"What's up?" I hear Durwin say. There's no challenge or aggression in it, but no fear, either, just a simple greeting. The Indian nods back in response, also free of aggression. I immediately put Durwin's move right into my mental file of behaviors I want to master. I'm already planning how I'll practice in front of the mirror—the "what's up," the nod, the effortless delivery. I'm learning a lot tonight.

One thing I'm learning, in addition to how much I want a Cool Black Friend, is that Josh is absolute crap at pool. He stalks around the table like he's just kicked its ass, and looks good when he leans over to aim, and then he takes his shot and the balls just go off and do their own thing. This makes me happy.

When Durwin heads to the bathroom, Josh walks over to me.

"You doing okay?"

"Yeah."

"You want another Coke?"

I shake my head, no. I do, but this would require further interaction with the hideous bartender, and I don't want to remind him of my presence.

"Is Durwin a drug dealer?" I whisper to Josh.

"Durwin? Oh, yeah."

"That's what I thought." I lean back, disappointed by that news, too, but also excited. "What kind?" I ask.

"What kind of drug dealer? What does he deal? Everything. Weed, hash, meth, heroin, X, roofies . . . He's killed a few guys, too, guys who fucked with him."

Holy shit.

"Jesus, Isaac, don't stand there with your jaw hanging open. You look like a retard."

CHAPTER TWENTY-TWO

DURWIN THE DRUG-DEALING KILLER

MERIT BADGE: BLACK FRIEND

This time when they play I *really* can't take my eyes off of him. Durwin, sighting down his cue at the ball, the same concentrated expression he would have before pulling the trigger. Durwin, coolly sinking the eight ball, finishing the game. Durwin, who deals drugs and kills people.

I decide this: He deals to a very select group of customers who are consenting adults and responsible for their actions. He also, I project, really just deals marijuana, high-end organic stuff. If he has killed anyone, it's because his hand was forced, and the killee was undoubtedly a violent predator who got what he deserved. Durwin is an honorable drug dealer.

After Durwin has beaten my brother again and he's gathering the balls and reracking them, he glances up at me, eyebrows raised, and makes a little gesture with his head. I freeze. What is that? Does he want something? Did I do something wrong? Should I not have been looking at him? Should I say hello?

"You play?" he says.

I babble something that must have added up to *yes*.

"Okay, why don't you break."

I miss the triangle of balls completely on my first try, hitting the cue ball with a glancing blow that sends it spinning pathetically away like a wayward planet, slowly drifting toward the side bumper.

"Sorry," I say, and add what I want to be a laugh, but which comes out as two separate, turdy *heh heh*s. Behind me, Josh snorts. Durwin's expression barely changes as he traps the cue ball and rolls it back to me for a second try.

I reset the ball. I never knew that when people talk about having sweaty palms it's a real condition.

"You have to hold your arm steady," Josh is saying. "Use more chalk."

Oh, screw you, Josh.

I lean over and sight down the cue at the cue ball. Durwin is standing to the side of the table, his expression impassive. The music has stopped. The entire bar is watching. The three scuzzy guys have stopped playing and are watching me. The people in back playing video games are turned this way. Bartender the Hutt is frozen, half-eaten pork hock interrupted in its journey to his gaping maw. The drunk at the bar has shifted his attention from his shot glass to me. Even the Indians are standing, peering at the drama unfolding on pool table number seven.

"Don't mess up," says Josh.

Have confidence in yourself, says Lesley.

I slam the stick into the cue ball and it rockets straight into the cluster with a heavy *CLACK,* the other balls exploding outward to cover—well, to cover much of the other half of the table in a pattern that spells a mediocre but let's-live-with-it break.

I look up. The music is still going. Pool players are still pool playing, video gamers still video gaming, Indians are still silent in their booth. One looks asleep. No one is paying any attention at all.

Durwin nods. "All right," he simply says.

After that we play mostly in silence, except for Josh, who won't shut up: "You're holding the stick wrong. That's the wrong shot. You have to be lower. Bank it. No, the three ball. Cut it here. Bad angle. Hit it softer. Hit it harder. Morespinlesssspinthatballtherethispocket." And for some reason, the more he talks, the better I start to play, like I have an enchanted pool cue that is powered by Josh's contempt. I'm sinking shots that I have no right even attempting, glorious, right there in front of Durwin, one after the other, which only makes Josh even more exasperated, until finally Durwin chimes in and says, "Leave the boy alone. He play better than you."

I look up at Josh, grinning. He opens his mouth to respond, which is when his phone rings.

"Crap," he says, looking at the display. "Hey, Mom."

I glance over at Durwin. It's possible that there are traces of amusement on his face.

"What are you doing awake?" Josh is saying. "Mom, no one's answering the home phone because I turned off the ringer. Lisa's asleep."

Charlie Brown parent voice faintly audible from where I stand. Josh's eyebrows go up in surprise. He glances over at me sharply. Uh-oh.

"Yyyeah," he's saying, dragging the word out, playing for time. "An e-mail? From the school. They sent you an automated e-mail. Uh-huh. Yeah, he was sick again today." He glares at me and mouths, *What the fuck!?*

130

Muhmuhmuhmmrmuh, says my mom, her words indistinct but her strident tone very clear.

"Because I didn't want to worry you! No, he's fine, the fever's down. He's sleeping now. Like you should be. What is it, five in the morning there?"

More talking from my mom while Josh shakes his head at me and covers the mouthpiece and whispers, "I'm going to kill you."

Now I'm almost certain that Durwin is amused. It's wonderful.

"What? Yes, Mom, that's *exactly* where I am," says Josh, with the irritated sarcasm you use when someone has asked you something completely absurd. "I'm in a *pool hall.* I'm *playing pool* while Isaac is sick and he and Lisa are home alone. Mom, I'm watching TV. Yes, okay. Fine. Bye."

He cuts off the call and turns to me.

"You skipped?!"

"I was going to tell you . . ."

Behind me, Durwin makes a sound that might be a chuckle. He's on my side.

"You can't just skip, Isaac!"

"You mean, like the past two days?"

More chuckling from Durwin. Josh is getting his wide-eyed nostril-flaring pursed-lips expression, meaning the explosion isn't far off.

"Isaac," he says through clenched teeth, and then his phone rings again. "Crap!" he says, then checks the display and his expression changes completely. "I gotta take this," he says. "You're dead," he adds before he hurries toward the door, phone at his ear.

131

I sneak a glance at Durwin, who's smiling and shaking his head as he chalks up his cue.

"We still playing?" is all he says.

I now have a Black Friend.

It's clear that we've bonded, that I've earned his respect with my minor naughtiness. I am playing pool with a Black Man, a dangerous Black Man who has killed several people who frigging deserved it. He's right there, and I'm here, and we're playing pool together. I try to mimic his fluid, languid movements, his casual expression, trying to be as natural as Josh was so that if someone new walks into the bar they'll see me and Durwin playing together and notice our unforced, easy friendship and wonder at it. Every so often when I sink a shot he murmurs something, one of his "Yeah, you all rights," or a simple *Mm hmm,* and each utterance fills me with a sensation almost like what I felt when Lesley called me cute, a glow of sheer pleasure.

"Been brawling?" he says out of nowhere when he's lining up a shot. It takes me off-guard and at first I'm not sure if he's even talking to me, and then not sure what he means, then finally get that he's talking about my black eye.

"Uh, no. I'm not, I just, heh heh," I blurble, then kick myself for missing the opening. He continues playing, the same mixture of melancholy and menace returning to his face. *You blew your chance, kid,* is what he's thinking.

For the next minute we play in silence while I try to think of ways to reopen the conversation. Then he takes me by surprise again: "You like the Clash, huh?"

The Clash. The Clash. Quick! What does he mean!? Why is he talk-

ing about the Clash? What does that—my shirt! I'm wearing a Clash shirt!

"Oh, yeah, I like them," I say. They're okay. "But, you know, I really like Li'l Wayne."

"Mmm," he says.

What am I saying?

"Yeah, Li'l Wayne, Fitty, Jadakiss . . ."

"Mmm."

Seriously, what the hell am I saying?

"'Course, Jay-Z is, like, the classic stuff."

"Mmm."

"And Biggie."

"Mmm."

I don't know what's happening. I can't stop it. Usually I can't get my mouth to work, and now I can't stop it, and I'm afraid of what's going to come out next.

"I get a lot of stuff from my friend James," I hear myself explaining, surprised to be describing a friend that I didn't know I had. *Don't say anything more. Don't speak. Don't—*

"He's black too."

Oh, God.

It falls between us with a heavy, wet thud, and lies there like a dead thing, like a sack of excrement. My black friend, my imaginary Black Friend. I've ruined everything.

But my real Black Friend doesn't seem particularly surprised or offended, just registering the information as if I'd said that I'd heard it might rain tomorrow. While I hold my breath he finishes chalking up his cue and takes his shot, and we're back at it, playing pool, and when he misses an easy one and scratches I go way out on a limb and say, "Nice shot," and he chuckles and says, "They can't all be magic, baby."

Once he says that, we're in a groove, and I get to work on building our relationship to a new level with a few more comments, little teasing things when he misses that get a smile or a chuckle each time: "That's amazing. Is that part of some long-range strategy?" "You *have* played this before, right?" "Are you luring me into a trap?"

Soon he's making comments back: "You know that white ball's supposed to stay on the table."

By the end of the game we're both chasing the eight ball around the table, each of us somehow unable to sink the damn thing, and we're both laughing and giving each other crap with every failed shot. And then finally, I do it—I win. I win. It's an easy shot, yes, just a little nudge to put the eight ball in the corner pocket, but I do it, and we do the soul shake and he gives me a thump on the shoulder with the other hand. *It's just like a movie,* I'm thinking, *the bonding moment, when—*

Josh comes stalking back.

"We're going."

"Now?" I say.

"Yeah, now. Durwin."

"Josh."

Hand bump. Durwin's face has returned to its former impassiveness. He turns to me. "Isaac."

We do the hand bump, and then Durwin starts pulling the balls out of the side slot and placing them on the table, the fun over.

"See you," I say to my Black Friend.

"Bye, now," he says.

I stay for a moment, hoping for more. Then Josh says, "Hey, Durwin, what do you do? Graphic design, right?"

Durwin, herding the balls around and capturing them with the rack, says, "Yep. A lot of branding, logos, that sort of thing."

"My brother thought you were a drug dealer and a murderer."

I'm on fire. I'm drowning. I'm falling. I want to bash in my idiot head with one of the pool cues or force-feed myself the eight ball. I want Durwin to look up, to snort and shake his head at me so I can smile and shrug back at him, because we're friends and have a deeper understanding, but he doesn't. He barely changes his expression, just raises his eyebrows for a moment and nods a few times as he arranges the balls in the rack.

I should say something, but my voice is jammed sideways in my throat.

"Let's go," says Josh, and pulls me away.

CHAPTER TWENTY-THREE

CAUGHT

"What are you doing skipping?"

"Why did you tell him that?!"

"I asked you, what are you doing skipping?"

"You made me look like an asshole! You're the one who told me he was a drug dealer! Fifteen!"

"That was twelve."

"It was fifteen! Sixteen, seventeen . . ."

The instant we walked out of the building: "Drop and give me fifty." I didn't argue.

The concrete is cold under my hands. There's a blackened blotch of gum on the pavement, aligned with my right cheekbone, approaching and receding with each pushup, and I time my breathing so that I'm not breathing in at the bottom of each repetition. I make it to twenty and have to stop, resting on my hands and knees.

"Keep going. Eighteen."

"Twenty."

"Eighteen. Go." He puts his foot on my tailbone and shoves me forward.

I start doing more. "You're such an asshole. You told me he was a drug dealer."

"Why'd you believe me?"

It takes me several pushups to untangle the stupidity of what he said.

"Because you *told* me!"

"Maybe you shouldn't make assumptions about other people."

This is worse. Making a fool of me was bad, but now pretending it's a life lesson is worse.

"You lied to me. That's what I learned from this, that you're a liar. Thirty."

"That was twenty-seven. Stop resting. Go. Go! Twenty-eight. Twenty-nine —"

"Thirty-two!"

"Thirty. And who's the liar? I thought you were going to school. That's what you wrote on the mirror, right? Whose lipstick was that, yours?"

I'm silent, concentrating on my counting.

"Why'd you skip?"

"Forty-two."

"That's thirty-nine."

"It's forty-two! He could be a drug dealer. He looks like a drug dealer. He looks mean."

"Mean? Durwin?"

"He does! His face!" I do an approximation of Durwin's expression.

"He's a black guy. They all do that. What, you have a crush on him?"

"Shut up!"

It comes out louder and angrier than I thought it would, practically a bark. It's the worst sort of anger, the kind where someone catches you doing something shameful and stupid. Because that's exactly what it is, a crush, and because I made a fool of myself in front of Durwin and I know it. I drop back down and finish the rest of the pushups, powered by my rage, adding five extra ones just to shut Josh up, then get up and walk to the car ahead of him.

It's half raining now as we drive away from the pool hall, the drops settling on the windshield as a thin mist. We don't seem to be heading in the right direction.

"It's after eleven," I say. Josh doesn't answer.

"Are we going home?"

"Not yet. Part two of the evening."

"Where are we going?"

"To see someone."

"I'm tired, Josh."

"So go to sleep."

I slump down in the seat and turn away from him, looking out the window.

"Why'd you skip?" he says. "Isaac."

"I don't know."

"What do you mean, you don't know? What'd you do?"

"Nothing."

"Nothing?"

That's one thing I've definitely been learning from Josh: how to be sullen and nonresponsive.

Why did I skip school? The same reason I skipped Danny's birthday party. Because I was in a bubble, a magic bubble, and inside the bubble was Lesley. Outside was everything else. I wanted to linger there just a little bit longer, cradled by that warm euphoria, fearful that if I moved, the membrane would rupture and reality would come flooding in and I wouldn't be immune to the laws of the universe any longer. Like the moment before opening the shower door on a frigid winter morning, dreading the blast of icy air and the bite of the tiles as you step onto the cold floor.

What did I do all day? Nothing. I rode my bike. I sat by the creek. I stopped by the library and Googled the 613 commandments. I went and peered into Nystrom's yard, at his four attack dogs and the statue, and thought, *No frigging way.*

"Isaac," says Josh, "I know we took a couple of days there. But you can't just skip school like that."

"You did. You did all the time."

He doesn't say anything for a moment, and then mutters, "Yeah, well, I'm a fuckup."

The way he says it reminds me of what Lesley said about him, and for a moment I take a break from hating myself and hating Josh to wonder how much *Josh* hates Josh.

"I want to go home."

"I told you, the Quest continues. We have someplace to go."

"Where?"

"Go look at some tits."

CHAPTER TWENTY-FOUR

IN WHICH TITS ARE OBSERVED, LEADING TO FURTHER UNHAPPY RESULTS

MERIT BADGE: TITS

I'm looking at tits.

I'm looking at tits while trying to look like I'm not looking at tits.

We're in the dressing room of a strip club, and it's even worse than the pool hall in terms of where not to look, because there are bare tits and bare ass cheeks and private parts covered with tiny triangles of fabric everywhere, swirling about me, and I feel dizzy from the sheer effort of the look/don't look thing and the totally surreal I-can't-believe-this-ness and from all the thoughts banging around against each other in my head.

I don't know where to start. We pulled up to a curb on a side street, and Josh issued fragmentary instructions over his shoulder as he tromped ahead of me on the sidewalk: Just be cool, everything will be fine, I just need to talk with someone, just be cool, figured you should come along, see what this is like, just be cool, just be cool. Then we reached a door that looked like nothing and Josh banged on it and a huge—HUGE—black guy leaned out, had a quick conversation with Josh, and let us in. A hallway, a turn, thumping music growing louder and fading, another turn, then holy shit that woman walking toward us is just wearing a thong and high heels, then Josh nodding to another HUGE guy standing next to a door, and then we're through the door and in the dressing room and Josh is greeting several of the strippers and kissing cheeks, and now he's standing against the opposite wall, talking earnestly with a woman (girl? woman?) who is putting on her dress as she speaks.

I am just inside the door, leaning against the wall, thinking *invisible, invisible, invisible.* The room has a floral carpet and big mirrors and long vanity tables that stretch along both sides. There's a doorway at the other end, and women go in and come out. Lockers?

The lights are fluorescent. The room smells something like cinnamon and sweat and flowery deodorant. The women look like the porn stars Danny and Steve and Paul and I watch on the Internet, too much makeup and those weird fake tans and boobs that look rubbery solid. Their makeup makes them seem older than they are. Some of them are very, very pretty. *Stop looking at her.*

It's very busy and crowded and feels like a restaurant kitchen, a constant stream of strippers going in and out the door to my left, checking themselves out in the mirrors, bumping into each other, chatting, laughing, the room loud with their conversations and music playing through bad speakers, interrupted periodically by a soft *splutch* of static and then a man's voice announcing things like, "Crystal to the floor. Crystal and Dani to the floor."

The music club felt wrong, the pool hall wronger, the guns and bikes wrongest, and this wrongest-est.

Invisible. Invisible.

Nipples, nipples, nipples.

I can't wait to tell Danny, Steve, and Paul about this, if they'll believe me.

The weirdest thing: When Lesley brushed against my arm I felt a charge that went right through me and jabbed me right down there. Here there are boobs and asses and naughty bits, and I don't feel anything like that. Everyone is so businesslike and distracted that there's nothing sexy about it at all. On the other hand the urge to look is overpowering, because, hey, tits.

Josh is still talking. Once again I have the impression that he's totally forgotten that he brought me along or that I even exist at all.

At first the invisibility spell seems to be working, because either no one notices me or they just don't care that a thirteen-year-old boy is standing in their dressing room. But then I start seeing the glances as they move past me, the quizzical expressions, the frowns. I catch at least one exchange of raised eyebrows. They know I'm looking. They *know*. I shouldn't have looked at all. I should have kept my eyes closed! I shrink down against the wall and start examining my fingernails like there's a vitally important secret message written on them.

"Excuse me."

At first I don't realize the voice is directed at me.

"Ex*cuse* me," repeats the voice, more stridently. I look up. One of the women is standing directly in front of me, arms folded across her boobs, her head tilted to the side, chin sticking out.

"Who the fuck are you?" she demands. She has very dark hair and sparkly purple eye shadow. I think she's about twenty.

"*Who* the *fuck* are *you?*" she says again, because instead of answering I'm standing there with my eyes wide, making dying fish movements with my mouth.

"What are you doing here?"

I look for Josh for rescue, but he's immersed in his conversation. Incoherent sounds coming out of me. *Aggle flaggle klabble,* like the little girl in *Knuffle Bunny. Blaggle plabble.* It's full on now, total panicked brain lockup, the sweating, the pounding in my chest, the trembling. The frog has left the building.

"What is this fucking kid doing in here?"

She has a very penetrating voice, cutting through the chatter and music. More faces and nipples turning toward me, the nipples quickly eclipsed behind hands and forearms.

"Seriously, who is this kid?"

"He's with me, Terri," says Josh from across the room. Terri twists and spots him.

"Josh? Who is he?"

"He's just my brother."

"I don't give a shit. I don't want him staring at my boobs."

Her words have shredded whatever remained of my invisibility cloak. All the eyes and nipples in the room are staring at me accusingly. Robes are being hastily put on and tied, the herd realizing there's a sneaky, underhanded hyena in their midst.

"Jesus, Josh," Terri is saying, "it's bad enough that I've got to deal with some middle-aged asshole rubbing his hard-on against me. Now I've got some ten-year-old looking at me and jerking off!"

I was not jerking off! I don't even have a hard-on! But the words never make it out of my brain. I'm dying from shame and embarrassment, all these women thinking I was standing there and jerking off when I wasn't, although admittedly I might have been maybe storing up some images for a future session, and they all look like they know it.

"I'm getting Jake," announces Terri.

"You don't have to get Jake," says Josh.

"I'm getting Jake," she says, poking a finger at Josh, and stalks off, I'm guessing to go get Jake.

I flee.

It's the panic thing, just like I did with my brother in the kitchen at the beginning of all this—sheer unthinking flight. *"Run away! Run away!"* like the knights in *Monty Python and the Holy Grail.* I think I hear Josh calling after me—*Isaac, wait!*—but I keep going, head empty, running down the hallway, following our path back out to the alleyway, except someone has swapped the hallways and there's no exit where I expect it. A turn, another turn, running fast, my fear growing even stronger. I have to get out of here—now. This way? No. Next. No, not this way. The hallway blurs in front of me, tears filling my eyes. The music louder, then an open doorway ahead of me, strippers going in and out. I get to the doorway and realize it's the entrance to the main floor.

It seems immense. I can see the stage, which hugs the wall and then juts out to a pole, and then hugs the wall and juts out to another pole again. Strippers are gyrating to loud music. Groups of men around small circular tables, watching, talking, drinking. Further on is a bar with topless women behind it. All the illumination in the room seems pooled around the tables and the stage, the walls disappearing into the shadows.

"There he is." Terri's harsh voice, slicing through the pulsating beat. I look over my shoulder and see her, see her finger jabbing in my direction, pointing me out to a sweating, dough-faced man with a combover. Jake.

He's coming toward me, filling the hallway.

I look out across the floor. There, beyond the bar, is the exit. I dart out into the room, trying to squeeze around and between the dense tables, tripping over unseen legs. I think I hear Josh shouting again but don't turn to look. A server is coming toward me with a tray of drinks. I change directions toward the safety of the shadows along the walls, hoping to vanish into the cool darkness and slip away unnoticed. Then I get close and feel a surge of revulsion. The shadows are alive and writhing with movement, like a nest of snakes. There's a banquette along the wall, men filling every space on it, their legs spread, heads tilted back, while the strippers grind on top of them like they're humping. I stumble along, repulsed, the banquette an endless line of men, men who look like my teachers or my neighbors or my father, their eyes closed or riveted on an ass, mouths open, licking their lips, some scrunching their faces up like they're coming.

Three carpeted steps down to the main floor, girls dancing on the stage to my left, the rectangle of the bar in front of me, the exit just beyond that. A man staggers away from the bar, into my path, his back to me, and I push him aside angrily, feeling him yield and totter away, saying, "Hey!" But I'm already at the exit, darting past another massive doorman, up the steep steps to the street, the music fading and light changing as I make it to the sidewalk at a full run and plow right into Lesley McDougal.

CHAPTER TWENTY-FIVE

FLIGHT

I'm on the back of her Vespa and we're flying through the streets.

She smells of clove cigarettes and of some sort of perfume and of her. I can feel the warmth of her torso radiating through her white T-shirt, the outline of her bra visible through the fabric. My hands are resting on her hips, and I'm incredibly conscious of them and incredibly conscious of my crotch and of the tiny space between my crotch and her rear end, a space that despite my best efforts disappears each time we go over a bump, leading to a moment where I'm involuntarily grinding against her, and then immediately reposition myself, wiggling back guiltily on the cracked vinyl of the Vespa seat.

Do not get a boner.

Strands of her hair have escaped the confines of her helmet along the lower edge, and the wind whips them back to tickle my face. The scooter vibrates and hums beneath us. The rain has stopped but feels like it might start again, and we're traveling in a tunnel of lights that smear and streak by: streetlights, neon, cars. Her neck is pale and freckled and delicate and beautiful, and once the idea of kissing it crosses my mind I am not able to uncross it. It's almost overwhelming.

Do not get a boner.

When I nearly ran her over outside the bar there was a confused moment of What are you doing here? and What's going on? and Did Josh bring you here?! And then I interrupted my own incoherent explanation and just said, "Please, I want to leave."

She hesitated, looking at the strip club entrance and then back at me, and decided. "Okay," she said, and I climbed onboard.

We pull to a stop at a light, the wind noise dying for a moment. "Lesley," I say, "can I stay with you? I don't want to go home."

And she says, "Okay."

CHAPTER TWENTY-SIX

THE ARMS OF A WOMAN

MERIT BADGE: SLEEPOVER

I do not want to sleep.

I'm so tired. My thoughts blur and wander, my eyelids weighted down and closing in gentle slow motion, then opening again halfway to focus on the parallel strips of light on the ceiling from the venetian blind. I'm afraid to sleep, afraid that if I do it will all go away, and I don't want this particular now to end, ever.

I don't want to sleep because she's next to me on the futon. She's lying on her side, her back to me, wearing nothing but her T-shirt and some flannel boy boxers, the elastic rolled once at the waist. The sheet is bunched up and forgotten down by her feet—our feet—and if I roll on my side and scootch back to the edge of the futon I can look down at her pale and perfect legs, the freckle on her right thigh, the shamrock tattoo on her calf.

Nothing has happened. We haven't had sex or even kissed, although she did kiss me on the forehead. Although it's not like I thought for a second that we were going to do anything. Although maybe I was hoping. Although I knew that was impossible and ridiculous. Although hope springs eternal. Although I don't even feel horny. This is better than horny, better than anything. What I feel like is that I'm hearing every beautiful song I've ever heard, all played at once. I feel like I'm floating in those songs, that I am those songs. I'm lying in bed next to Lesley McDougal and the universe is perfect. I feel that way even when her cat steps on my face for the third time and I have to push it off the futon again, its body soft and yielding like an accordion, making it hard to move.

I don't want to fall asleep, so I shift positions, turning slowly to my side so as not to wake her. I can see her ribs, delicate through the shirt, rising and falling with her breath, up, down, see the pattern of her vertebrae, the curve of her pelvis, and I reach out my hand and hold it an inch from her surface, feeling her warmth.

The ride on the Vespa lasted forever and was too short. We pulled up in front of a four-story apartment complex in Uptown, dark brown bricks covered with ivy. She parked the Vespa at the curb and we climbed off, and she took a moment to turn and stand there, helmet under one arm, and look at me, smiling and shaking her head. Then she just said, "C'mon."

The building was old and dark and smelled old and dark: dark floors, dark wood trim on the walls. I followed her up two flights of stairs, neither of us saying a word. It's after midnight and I'm at a girl's place and no one even knows where I am.

"It's just a studio," she said when we entered her apartment, and I nodded, not sure what that meant, although it sounded apologetic. It was one big room with a small kitchen at the far end, and a door to what turned out to be the bathroom. A kitchen table, a futon sofa, bookshelves that were just planks of wood on cinder blocks, and that was it for furniture. There were some laminated

ID cards on lanyards hanging from a peg on the wall. FILM CREW, they said. There were paintings on the walls. She saw me looking at them.

"I painted those."

"They're nice."

She smiled. "You're nice. You hungry? I'm hungry. Want some cereal?"

She sat me at her vintage table, the chairs mismatched, and poured me a bowl of Cap'n Crunch—as illicit in our house as a bong—poured herself one, then sat.

"Well?" she said.

I started telling the story sleepily as I ate, details coming out in disordered splotches, hopping around in time: We were at the strip club, I played pool, there was this guy at the pool hall, Indians, pushups—then interrupted myself again, like I'd done outside the strip club.

"Who," I said, "is Trish?"

She was pouring more milk into her bowl as she spoke. "The devil," she said through a mouthful of cereal. "She's screwing, like, a dozen married guys. At *least*." Then it occurred to her who she was talking to and she put the milk down, looking up at me guiltily.

"Jesus, I'm sorry," she said, and reached out a hand to place it on mine. "I keep forgetting how young you are."

"I'm not that young."

"Okay."

"I'm not."

"Okay."

My dad is seven years older than my mom, I wanted to say, *and you're only about six years older than me. That's not that big a difference.* But of course it is.

"I'm not stupid," I said instead.

"Didn't say you were."

She patted my hand and released it.

"You look a wreck, Isaac. Bedtime."

"You said you were going to pierce my ear."

"If you want to, I will. But some other time. We need to sleep."

"I want to talk more."

"I'm tired, too," she said, and stood to put away the milk and cereal. It was like at the restaurant when she got busy and her attention slipped away.

"She's a stripper?" I said as I watched her put her bowl in the sink.

"Was. Is. Sort of. She still works the bar there sometimes. Can I clear?"

"She's . . . his girlfriend?"

"She's lots of people's girlfriend," Lesley muttered.

"But his, too."

"Was," she said, depositing my bowl and spoon in the sink as well.

"Not anymore?"

"Right. Except that's where the problem is. I don't think he gets that part." She looked at me. "C'mon, let's shower."

I had the very briefest meteor-flash of a fantasy that maybe she meant shower together, which of course she didn't. She led me into the bathroom and gave me a towel and handed me a new toothbrush that was still in its plastic packaging. "Gotta have a few extra around for all the strange men like you that I bring home," she said, and I said "Ha ha," even though I suddenly got jealous, thinking of times that maybe she does do that.

I took a very quick shower, seeing myself from above, a shot that included me naked in the shower with Lesley just a few feet away from me on the other side of the bathroom door. The shower was an old-fashioned tub with a cloudy plastic curtain, the water splashing through the gap onto the tile floor. I kept the shower running while I peed so that she couldn't hear it. Before I turned it off I quietly opened her medicine cabinet and looked inside: a jumble of toothpaste, aspirin, deodorant, shaving cream, girl razor, and a torn-open box of tampons, which made me feel a little embarrassed. I think I was looking for condoms. I didn't find any, which made me feel better.

When I turned off the shower I could hear her on the phone.

"Kidnapping him? Really, Josh? *Really?* Josh, you took him to a *strip club.*"

Pause.

"Josh, you come over here and I'll pepper-spray you, and then I'll call the cops, and then I'll pepper-spray you again."

Pause.

"Yes, I will deliver him safe and sound, with his honor intact."

Pause. She started to laugh, entertained by something he said.

"You're gross, Josh. G'bye."

She lent me a T-shirt and some cutoff sweatshorts. When she emerged from the shower she wasn't wearing a bra under her T-shirt and I had more of the boob issue that I'd struggled with all night, the trying to look without looking. If she cared, she didn't show it. She just said, "Help me get the futon set up."

Before she rolled over and went to sleep she gave me that peck on the forehead. "If I start snoring, just elbow me." Then she turned, shifted around for a bit, and was still.

She's not snoring now, just breathing quietly. My hand hovers over her shoulder, follows the topography of her side, moves slowly down to her hip, not making contact. It glides now to her lower back, then slowly traces the path of her spine, pauses between her shoulder blades. I'm two-thirds asleep, the borders of reality blending and mushing, my hand sinking toward her like a leaking helium balloon until it comes to rest on her back. I can feel her heart beating through the palm of my hand. She doesn't move or react for a moment, and then she takes a deep breath in and lets it out like a sigh, shifts a bit, and is still again, and I think, *I should move my hand, I should move it,* and then everything blurs and dilutes and spreads and I'm asleep.

CHAPTER TWENTY-SEVEN

THE MORNING AFTER

MERIT BADGE: WOODWORKING

It's light when my own snores wake me up. It takes a few seconds for all the parts of my brain to return from wherever they went and reassemble themselves, awareness coming back to me in small units: I'm not in the tent. I'm at Lesley's, meaning it wasn't a dream. She's not next to me anymore in bed. From what I hear, she's sitting at the table, quietly reading the paper. I'm spreadeagled on my back. I'm wearing the T-shirt and cutoff sweatshorts she lent me.

I have morning wood.

Oh my God.

I'm lying here on my back with a hard-on, which I'm sure I had when she woke up. I roll on my side and go fetal to camouflage my condition, and realize that the sheet is over my lower half, which it wasn't when I went to sleep, meaning that maybe she noticed my bonerness and tried to save me the embarrassment by covering me up, which is worse. Also bad: I have to pee, like *now,* and I'm hoping things will sort of calm down down there and I'll be able to get up and run to the bathroom. For now I pretend I'm asleep and hope she doesn't realize I'm up, in both senses of the word.

I hear the newspaper rustle. "You want some eggs?" she says. I don't think I'm fooling her.

"Uh . . ."

"I'll make some eggs."

I take advantage of when she turns to the stove to scurry to the bathroom—*she totally knows*—and then have to do the waiting thing until my plumbing is in the correct state for peeing. I take advantage of the time to punch myself in the head a few times and bite my fist, trying to replace my embarrassment with physical pain.

I camouflage my peeing with the shower again, then realize once I'm in there that I don't have any clothes to change into. Which is when the bathroom door opens partway—panic—and her hand pokes through the opening, holding my pants and another T-shirt. Then she leans her head in, her eyes squinted shut.

"Hey," I say, hands cupped over my personal parts.

"I won't peek," she says. She holds up the T-shirt blindly. It partially unfurls, and I can see that it's the English Beat T-shirt that she was wearing the first time we met. "I'm lending you one of my favorite shirts, so don't get it dirty, right?"

"Okay."

"Want me to lend you some undies?"

"Uh, no."

"I've got some great pink ones with lots of lace."

"No, thanks."

"Okay. You're either gonna have to recycle or go Canadian, then."

"I'll go Canadian."

She suddenly opened her eyes.

"How you doing in there?"

"HEY!"

I can still hear her laughing after she closes the door. After a few moments I start to laugh too.

We eat breakfast together and talk. I don't know what we talk about. We talk about everything. We talk in an easy manner, no rush, lingering over our food, laughing and joking, and I think, *This is what it's like. This is what it's like to spend a night with your lover*—that's the word that comes to mind, *lover,* a sophisticated word for sophisticated people—and wake up in the morning and break your fast with that person. It's the daylight, waking version of what I felt last night, everything timeless and perfect. It's only been about eight hours since we collided outside the strip club, but it feels like that was weeks ago. If she saw me with a hard-on, fine, I don't care. She saw me naked. I don't care. I like it. It's not even about sex. As we're talking, I see it, understand it, understand something I never understood or felt before: I *want* her to see me, to know me in every way. I want to be able to reveal myself completely to her and have it be all right.

She's showing me the various film-crew badges she has and telling me about how she's saving up to move to LA, when she glances at her watch and says, "Unless I'm crazy, it's Friday."

"Yes."

She smiles at me, eyebrows raised.

"No," I say, realizing what she means. "No, I don't want to."

"I told your brother I'd take care of you."

"He keeps me out of school all the time. Can't I just . . . stay?"

"I have to work."

156

I slump down in my chair and play idly with my fork, tapping it on the plate.

"You're adorable like that," she says.

I look up and she sticks her lower lip out, imitating me.

"I'm not pouting."

"Yes you are. It's cute."

"Okay, I'm pouting."

She reaches out with her fork and gives me a very gentle poke on the hand.

"Hey."

I do some more nonpouting.

"Hey," she says, poke-poking.

"What."

"I really enjoy hanging out with you, Isaac. You're good company."

"Really?"

"Yes. Really. I'm very comfortable with you for some reason. You're easy to talk to. You and me"—she does the two fingers pointing back and forth between our eyes thing—"we've got that connection, whatever it is."

"Yeah?"

"Yeah. You think I'd take just any man home?"

I smile and blush.

"C'mon, I'll give you a ride to school."

And so I make my arrival at Edina Junior High School on the back of her Vespa, clinging tight to her, hoping that the entire student body is lined up to see me. They're not, though, because I'm late and everyone is in homeroom, and Lesley is running late for work, too, so our goodbye is hurried and awkward and I don't get a chance to say any of the things I had prepared. We pull up to the curb, and I just hop off and hand her the helmet, and she gives me another peck on the forehead, then makes a shooing motion with her hand. "Go, go!" she says.

I reluctantly start walking backwards, but she's busy fastening the extra helmet to the seat and not even looking at me, so I finally turn and go.

"Wait!" she says from behind me, and I turn eagerly. She's gesturing for me to come back, and I do, practically sprinting, visualizing an intense embrace. Instead she's holding a tube of product.

"Can't let you go in like that."

It's heaven, the twenty seconds she spends fussing over me, her fingers running through my hair, and I have to fight to keep myself from reaching up and placing my hands on hers.

"There. Go! Fly!"

Another swat on the butt like at the restaurant, and I fly, soaring on golden angels' wings toward the waiting entranceway to school. The bell that signals the end of homeroom rings a welcome as I pass through the doorway, a completely transformed Isaac from the last time I was here: triumphant, confident, invincible, the hero returning. Right into the most horrific, humiliating day I've ever had.

CHAPTER TWENTY-EIGHT

REJECTED BY THE HERD

I'm so deliriously happy. I'm happy as I walk into the entrance, happy as I make my way down the hall, happy as I reach my locker, and happy as I spot my peeps near the trophy case.

And then I become unhappy very, very quickly.

"No, seriously, what the hell are you wearing?" Danny says.

He's not saying it as a joke or to tease me. He's saying it with an edge in his voice, like I've offended him.

"I'm wearing. Clothes."

It's been about a minute since I walked up to them and got stunned silence in response to my greeting. No one has even said anything about my black eye. Steve's mouth is literally hanging open, like I just told him I'm gay or that I'm his father, or both.

"What is this shirt? Who are the Beat?" says Paul.

"It's just a shirt," I say, and smile.

"Is that . . . gel?" says Steve.

"Yeah. Here." I lean my head forward for them to touch. No takers. I straighten up. They watch me silently.

"What?" I say.

The three of them exchange glances, then look back at me, and then I understand: I've betrayed them. I'm leaving them. I'm better than them. That's what the clothes say.

"Look, I have some new clothes, I got a haircut. It's still me," I say.

No one answers. I can see the suspicion in their eyes, the resentment, and all my prior happiness is suddenly drowned by a helpless fear that I never saw coming, a queasy panic that my friends might abandon me.

"You see this?" I say, grinning, pointing to my eye, hoping to redirect everything back to the path it should be on, the one where we're all friends. "My brother hit me."

What, for dressing like an art fag? Why, because you think you're one of the Jonas Brothers? How come, because you . . . ?

But no one makes any joke or says anything about it. Instead, Danny says, "Where the hell were you last night?"

"Danny, I'm really sorry, I just . . ."

"Just what?"

"I was going to call you."

"It was his birthday party," says Paul. "We've been talking about it for weeks."

"I know, but—"

"You blew us off three times in a row," says Steve.

"My brother—"

"I called you, like, fifty times," says Danny.

"I told you, my brother threw my phone in the creek."

"I called your home phone, too. And e-mailed."

"I know, I just . . ."

They stare at me like I'm a stranger.

"I didn't mean to miss your party. I was going to call."

Nothing.

"Can we just play this weekend? I promise, promise, promise I'll be there."

They're all silent, glancing at each other.

"What."

"We're starting a new game."

"A new map? A new campaign?"

"Yes."

I'm not sure where to start asking questions.

"Well . . ."

"We *already* started," clarifies Steve.

We all stand there, the next part obvious, but no one wanting to say it out loud. Finally I do, hoping the answer will somehow be different: "Without me?"

"You should have called me back," says Danny, and then he turns and walks away, and Paul and Steve go with him.

I'm literally shaking as I walk to the next class. I sit in my seat, staring at my desk, trying to calm myself down. I'll talk to them at lunch. I'll talk to them and make everything better. But when I take my tray to our table they're not there. And they don't come. Which means they all talked about it and decided to eat outside.

There's part of me that's able to believe that it was unintentional, that they just forgot to tell me where they'd be. That's what I tell myself as I walk the perimeter of the school, looking for them. Then I spot them on the grass by door seven, and then Paul sees me and says something to the other two, and they get up and walk in the other direction.

The rest of the day I am a tooth chewing on tin foil. I'm trapped in a room where a thousand fingernails squeal over chalkboard walls. Everyone in the school can sense it, I know. Everyone can see me now, can see that I've been abandoned and rejected and shamed. I'm burned by eyes glancing at me and my new clothes, my idiot clothes, my idiot hair, people whispering and smirking. Even Sarah Blumgartner looks at me with derision: I pass her in the hall and she stops dead, staring at me, and then covers her mouth as she laughs.

I was right this morning: I *am* a different person now, but different in the wrongest way; I'm John Slenkar when he jumped into the middle of the dance floor during Spring Fling and started break dancing, thinking he was cool when everyone was laughing at him.

Eric Weinberg notices me. He stops as we pass each other in the common area, stops and stares at me and doesn't divert his gaze, almost in surprise, like I've joined his wraithworld and we're fully solid to each other while everyone else is transparent vapor. I drop my eyes and turn away.

I've gotten too excited, run too far away from the herd, rolled in the wrong grass and drunk the wrong water and shed my camouflage and I don't smell right anymore, and the herd is rejecting me. And now that I'm visible and smell wrong for the herd, the predators pick it up, and my day gets far, far worse.

CHAPTER TWENTY-NINE

THE BULLIES ARE CONFRONTED. OR CONFRONT

MERIT BADGE: PUBLIC HUMILIATION

"Hey, faggot!"

I fumble with my backpack, my desperate desire to zip it closed making it take twice as long. All around me kids are streaming out of the school, heading home for the day.

"Hey, faggot!"

It's all of them, the whole group, the Assholes and their Associate Assholes: Bill and Jason and Kurt and Guy and Tim and Kevin.

"What's up, faggot?"

Nice clothes, nice hair, what a faggot, what a faggot, Jewboy, faggot faggot faggot.

The zipper is jammed and there're too many books in there, but I throw it over my shoulder anyway and start walking. So it bursts open, and two-inch-thick textbooks spew forth and *thump thud thump* onto the pavement, slipping from my hands when I try to gather them up, my haste again undoing my efforts. I'll have to drop my books and bag and make a run for it, but while I'm trying to decide what to do they've already surrounded me, grabbing at my backpack and jerking me to a halt.

"Leave me alone!" I say, and immediately wish I hadn't.

"Oh, leave me alone!"

"What a faggot!"

"Leave me alone!" they all mimic, a chorus of them mocking me, whapping me on the top of the head with open hands.

"Nice bag, dumbass," says Tim, and yanks it out of my hands.

"Give it back!"

Why say that?

"You want to make me?" he says, the others jeering and laughing. "Come on, come and take it."

How is it a circle of kids can form so quickly? There's suddenly a dense wall around us, layers thick, everyone crowding in, people shouting, "Fight! Fight!"

Tim pushes me, saying things, pushing me more. He's got me by the shirt, Lesley's shirt, and it's starting to rip.

"Don't wreck my shirt!" I say, and again it's the stupidest thing I could possibly say at the moment. He spins in a circle, pulling me to stumble along, the shirt tearing further. He hurls me to the ground, and I get up again and he pushes me. I want to punch him, to tackle him, but I'm powerless. The tears are coming, and I don't want them. The crowd around us feels thousands deep, every single student there, faces fascinated or eager or pitying or hungry, and then I see them: Steve and Paul and Danny, just watching, not doing anything to help. My peeps.

And then I see *her:* Patricia Morrison, staring at me with the same excited curiosity as the rest. The first time I've ever registered in her consciousness, imprinted in her brain as a victim who deserves what he gets because he's too weak.

And then I see *him:* Josh.

I think for a second that I've imagined it, but no, he's standing in the back of the circle, towering over everyone, his arms crossed, his expression completely dispassionate.

"Help—" I breathe before Tim tackles me to the ground and scrambles on top, sitting on my chest. He's saying stuff to me, horrible things, but I can barely hear him, and he's slapping my face. He's spitting on my face now. I know Josh taught me how to get out from this, but I'm paralyzed, pathetic. Tim spits in my face some more and slaps me, and again, and I don't do anything. I know that Josh is just watching and judging me.

Then Tim stands up, bored with me, fresh out of ways to humiliate me. More taunts delivered from an upright position, gleeful cackling from his cronies, other kids saying things. My life is over. Even Eric Weinberg wouldn't talk to me now.

"Get up."

Josh stands over me.

"Get UP!"

His huge hand gathers up a fistful of my already-ruined shirt and lifts me roughly to my feet. The seams making tearing noises.

"Get your books."

I go to retrieve my books, head down. Kids are dispersing or lingering, not sure what the arrival of the golem means. Danny and Steve and Paul are gone. Patricia is gone. Tim and the Assholes seem to sense that Josh isn't a threat to them, and they're still nearby, darting close to talk smack to me and then retreating, and then repeating it again. Josh doesn't pay them any mind, because he agrees with them, and it makes them bolder, showing off in front of him, still calling me a faggot, an asshole, a pussy. And then Tim says, very clearly, "Stupid Jew."

What it is, I realize, is that he somehow doesn't get that Josh is my brother.

Josh absently reaches out and grabs Tim by the upper arm and spins him around to face him. There is a long two seconds where Tim and Josh are looking at each other, Tim with a face caught in the transition between scornful snarl and surprise — how dare this guy grab me! — Josh with a calm expression that says, *Look at me. Look at me, because I want you to understand that what's about to happen is very intentional.* Then he slaps Tim across the face.

Not a slap, an open-hand blow to the side of the head, Josh's palm nearly the size of Tim's skull. The impact is so loud that I make a coughing, gaspy sound. It's a lazy, relaxed swing for Josh, but it literally knocks Tim to the ground. His eyes glaze for a moment. He's propped up unevenly on one hand and one elbow, looking at Josh, stunned.

Everyone is frozen. Me. The Assholes. Any kids left in the immediate area. We're all rigid and wide-eyed and terrified, me maybe more than anyone, because I know Josh, know what he's like when the rage shuts off his brain.

Tim starts to cry.

I don't feel any satisfaction or triumph, no sense of revenge. I just feel more frightened and want it to stop.

"All right," says Josh, "let's go."

He grabs me, no more gently than he treated Tim, and starts marching me away.

Behind us, Tim blubbers the inevitable cry of the helpless victim, the very cliché I probably would have blurted if I'd been able to speak: "I'm going to *sue* you! I'm going to tell my *dad!*"

Josh stops.

"Wait here," he says, turns, strides purposefully toward Tim, accelerating as he goes: *step step stepSTEPSTEP.* Tim doesn't even try to scramble away, because he still can't believe it, can't believe this full-grown man would actually do anything else. Josh grabs him by the arms and lifts him effortlessly until they're nose-to-nose, like he's done to me.

"Where do you live?" he says. *"Where?"* He gives Tim a shake. "I want to go home with you right now. I want to meet your dad. Because I'm going to fucking KILL HIM."

Tim is bawling. The other kids are bawling. I am bawling. The earth has cracked open and Satan is here.

Josh drops Tim. Tim collapses on the ground. Josh stalks back to me and says, "Let's go."

How do you walk away from something like that?

If you're Josh, you just do, like nothing much happened, your little brother trailing after you.

He leads me to the parking lot. The car is there. He opens the back door and tosses my bag and my books in, not in any special hurry. I can almost hear the sirens drawing closer. If you're a grown-up, you can't just hit a kid. You can't, even if the kid deserves it. Dozens of other kids saw what happened. Maybe a teacher did, too.

But there are no sirens. No police arrive. Josh closes the rear door, gestures with his chin for me to get in, gets in next to me, and starts the car. Some kids are gathered at a respectful distance, watching us, but no teacher comes running out of the school, saying, "Stop! Stop! I saw you!"

We drive out of the parking lot, no one hindering us. But that can't be the end of it. Not even Josh can get away with something like this.

When we get home, the house is on fire.

CHAPTER THIRTY

FIRE

The only thing Josh says to me as we're driving, not looking at me: "I taught you, like, fifty times how to bump and roll out of the mount. *Fifty times.* You could have dumped him easily."

That's it. That's when we really do start hearing sirens. Sirens that are following us. Someone called the police. They saw what happened and dialed 911, and now Josh is going to jail. It sounds like they've sent the entire department—so many sirens, horns blaring, the racket going from zero to one hundred in what seems like seconds.

I twist and look behind us and feel like gagging. There's a cop car right on our tail, lights flashing, squawking the horn.

"What the hell?" says Josh.

"You have to pull over!" I say, my heart thumping. "Pull over!"

Josh swears, then pulls off to the right—and the cop car accelerates by us, and as we're about to pull away from the curb again a fire truck appears and roars by, then a second and a third.

We follow them down Valley View and watch them take the right turn that we have to take. They're still ahead of us, leading us to our block.

"Where are they going?" says Josh.

To our house, it turns out.

We get there just as the third fire truck pulls up and stops. Firemen are already clambering out of the other two trucks, grabbing tools that look like medieval weapons, shrugging beat-up yellow oxygen tanks onto their backs. Lisa and Patrick are on the front porch. Patrick is talking to one of the firemen, gesturing, the fireman nodding and trying to move into the house, eager to disengage from Patrick and get to the job at hand, waving at other firemen to follow.

"Oh, for Christ's sake," says Josh, parking the car half on our lawn and hopping out, leaving the door open behind him. Lisa spots him and comes running across the yard to meet him, yelling, "The stove! The stove was on fire!"

I catch up to them as one of the cops steps in front of Josh, saying, "Whoa, big guy, can't go in there right now." Then he says, "Hey, are you Josh Kaplan? Man, I used to watch you wrestle. You were a*maz*ing . . ."

Lisa is still babbling about how the skillet caught on fire because of the sausages that Patrick forgot about and how it spread to the wood countertop when he dumped water on it and the countertop started to burn and there was smoke and flames and she called 911. I can see through the open front door. It looks smoky in there. Patrick is coming over now, saying, "Dude, I'm soooo sorry . . ."

It doesn't take long for the all-clear signal. They lead us through the still-smoky house to the kitchen. All the sliding doors and the door to the garage are open to help air the place out. I don't want to be around Josh, but I'm curious enough that I stay for a bit. We

170

gather around the stove as one of the firemen goes over the details with Josh and describes what they did, which is pretty obvious: The countertop that borders the stove has a big blackened patch on it, a patch that is also covered with white powder from the firefighters' dry chemical extinguishers.

"When you have a grease fire in a skillet like this," the firefighter says to Josh, who nods in annoyance, the hurry-up-and-finish-because-I-already-know-what-you're-going-to-say nod, "you don't want to put water on it. You just want to cover it—"

"With the lid, yes. I *know*," says Josh, glaring at Patrick, who is scratching the back of his own head and grimacing.

As soon as the firefighters start to file out, I slip out the door to the back porch. Patrick is still apologizing to Josh, who looks like he's considering rebreaking his jaw. As I leave, Patrick points to me and says, "What happened to him?"

"That one?" Josh says. "I went to his school to make sure he wasn't skipping, and . . . screw it. Don't even get me started with that pussy."

CHAPTER THIRTY-ONE

IN WHICH SAGE ADVICE IS RECEIVED FROM AN UNLIKELY SOURCE

MERIT BADGE: DEFIANCE

I sit by the creek and cry. I think *blubber* is the right word. I sit there and blubber and hate myself. Then I climb into the tent and lie there and blubber some more, until I'm puffy-eyed and blubbered out. Josh is right. I could have fought back, but I didn't, I just lay there weak and useless. And that's what I am—weak and useless, and everyone at school knows it.

While I'm lying on my back, staring up at the roof of the tent, I hear someone approaching. *Go away, Josh,* I think. Then there's a sort of poofy thump as a hand knocks on the side of the tent like it's a door, the whole tent shimmying. I also hear some sort of crackling noise.

"Hey," says a male voice. It takes me a second to realize it's Patrick.

"Hey, little dude," he says, "you in there?"

"What."

"You in there? You awake?"

I let that one pass. "What do you want?"

"Can I come in?"

He fumbles with one of the enclosures.

"That's the window," I say.

"Oh," says Patrick. "Where's the friggin' front of this thing? Oh, here."

He finally manages to get the front partially unzipped, and it flops open, his lean, pockmarked face framed by the irregular aperture.

"I brought snacks," he says, holding up a bag of chips, which explains the crackling noise I heard before. He puts the bag down. "I also got these," he adds, now holding up two cans of beer.

"I don't drink beer."

"Oh. Oh, okay. Well, more for me, I guess."

He's still filling the frame of the tent, nodding at me. I don't know what else to do, so I just lie there looking back at him. After a few moments of that he says, "You gonna come out and talk, or you gonna make me sit here like an asshole?"

We sit on the grass, looking out beyond the creek. Patrick doesn't say anything at first, concentrating on a beer and the chips. I note that he's also brought along the rest of a six-pack.

"You're sure you don't want one?" he says, spraying me with a few soggy spit wads of chewed-up Doritos.

"I'm good."

"'Kay." *Slurp.* "Man, I had to get out of there. Your brother is pissed at me, boy. Damn." He pauses to drink, then stuff some more chips in his mouth. "Got a temper, that guy. But he's solid. I love him. He's like my brother. I mean, you know. Not like you and he are brothers, but in here." He knocks a fist against his chest.

You can have him, I want to say, but decide to go with silence. More slurping and munching.

"You know, Josh, he kicked my ass once."

"Yeah, I heard."

"Yep. You know his ear? That was me."

"I heard."

"I mean, I ain't proud of it or nothing. I was getting my ass handed to me. I mean, that boy can *fight.*"

I go back to silence. If that's where this talk is heading, I'm going back to the tent. I'm sick of Josh and how he can fight and what a big tough guy he is. I don't care.

"I mean, I don't think he's ever gotten his ass kicked," Patrick says.

I tease a blade of grass out of the lawn and examine the part at the bottom where the green turns to pearlescent white.

"Probably not even as a little kid, if he ever was a little kid."

I nibble on the soft root, waiting for Patrick to finish so I can be alone again.

"If you wanted to learn how to fight? He'd be, like, the most awesome teacher you could have."

I toss the grass away. "Yes, I *know,* okay?"

"Whoa. Don't get all heated up. You sure you don't want a beer?"

"No. I don't drink."

"Okay." He opens the beer that he was offering to me and starts drinking it himself. "So, what was my point?"

That Josh is a god and we should worship him. That I'll never be Josh. That you're too stupid to know how to operate a flush toilet or park your car or close the freezer door or cook sausages or put out a simple grease fire or remember your own point.

"Right," he says, seeming to remember. "Here's the deal: Josh knows lots about ass kicking. But he doesn't know anything about getting his ass kicked. You follow?"

I shrug. "I guess."

"He's got nothing to teach you there. He doesn't understand it."

He chugs some more and wipes his mouth with the back of his forearm—the forearm attached to the hand holding the can of beer, meaning he also manages to pour some of his beverage on himself at the same time.

"Whoa," he says, looking down at his shirt.

"You know, I think I might just go back in," I say, starting to stand up. There's only so much moron I can handle right now.

"Now me," Patrick says, "*I* know about getting my ass kicked."

I pause.

"Yeah?" I say.

"Oh, yeah."

We look at each other for a moment. Then he tilts his head to the side, indicating the spot next to him where I'd been sitting. I sit.

"Yeah," he says, noting my renewed interest, "*now* we can talk. Man, I've had my ass kicked so many times . . ." He shakes his head, smiling. "Don't get me wrong—I've dealt it, too, but damn, I know what it's like to just get *pounded*."

He illustrates by smacking a fist into the now-empty beer can, crushing it. He tosses it aside, reaches for another, makes a gesture of offering it to me. "No? Okay." *Shhpritz.* He starts to drink it himself, looking like he might have entirely forgotten that he had been talking.

"You're big, though," I say, not sure if he's done and wanting to prompt him.

"What? Oh. Yeah. I'm big now, but I wasn't always. And, you know, I've always been that guy who will talk smack to anyone—like, *anyone*. I mean, think about it, I got mouthy with your *brother,* and you know, look at that guy. So yeah, I've talked my way into plenty of scrapes."

He takes another beer break and once again seems to remember something.

"Also, my dad used to friggin' beat the crap out of me, pretty much all the time. Get wasted and just go off on me and my mom. Check this out."

He puts down his beer and reaches for my hand, his skin cold and wet from the condensation on the can. He pries open my fingers like he's opening a multi-tool, and roughly presses my index finger against a lumpy spot on the side of his shaved head. It's intimate and weird and off-putting, but I have to admit I also sort of appreciate it, like he assumes that this is normal, meaning he sees us as friends and equals.

"Feel that?" he says.

"Yes."

"Fireplace poker."

"He hit you?"

"Yeah, man. *BOOOM!*"

He swings his free arm, illustrating the blow.

"Your *dad?*"

"Yeah. Put me out cold. You should have seen the blood."

He releases my hand, then briefly touches the spot himself. "A friggin' fireplace poker," he says quietly, rubbing it, then drops his hand. He's looking off now, privately reliving the event, his features twisted and pained. Looking at him, I feel a surge of surprise and then embarrassment, because I realize that he's about to start crying.

"*Buuuuuuuurrrrp*" is what comes out instead. Then his uncomfortable expression vanishes and he looks fine.

"Anyways," he says, continuing on like nothing happened, "I know pretty much every flavor of beat-down. My dad, freaks like your brother, friggin' biker gangs ganging up on me—that's the worst, can't do anything about it, people kicking you in the ribs and the head and crap when you're on the ground. Oh, yeah—I got stabbed once, also."

"Stabbed."

"Yeah, right in the side. Dude with a butterfly knife."

My particular beat-down is starting to seem less horrific.

"You know," he says, "everyone gets beat up."

"Not my brother."

"Maybe not your brother. Yet. But he will, he keeps going the way he is."

"Yeah . . ." I say, and he detects the doubt in my voice, that I'm agreeing just to indulge him.

"Everyone," he repeats. "And the point is this. Listen to me. Are you listening?"

"Yes."

"No, you're not."

"I am."

"Fine. Here's the point: Getting beat up doesn't make you less of a man."

He was right: I wasn't really listening before. Now I am, because he's answering a question I didn't even know I was asking.

"Yeah, you hear me now," he says, seeing my expression. "See, it ain't ever fair. Never. Either you've got more guys or they've got more guys, or you're bigger or he's bigger, or you're on your game or he is . . . whatever. It's never fair. And so you get your ass kicked. But it's just one of those things. It does not make you less of a man," he repeats. "I would say it's actually part of *being* a man."

He looks at me, dropping his head a bit to align his gaze with mine.

"You get it?" he says, and I don't expect this at all, don't expect Patrick the Ear Chewer to be like this, to out of nowhere seem like he has some intelligence and wisdom in him and to offer me this kindness. I can't help the tears welling up, and I have to drop my gaze.

"Yeah," he says, and gives me a few pats on the back while I hang my head and sniffle. "Sucks, right?"

I nod, my head still down, wanting to say something but not wanting any sobs to come out.

"Yeah, it sucks," he says. I hear another beer being opened.

"Here." He holds the can of beer down low so that it appears in my field of vision. "Here," he repeats, and I take it this time.

"Cheers." He knocks his can against mine and drinks. I look at my beer for a moment, hesitating, and then take a sip. I don't like the flavor any more than I ever have, but it seems like the right thing to do at this moment.

"I'll tell you what I learned over the years," says Patrick. "If you're gonna get the shit kicked out of you, there's not much you can do about it. If you can give a beating before you get one, great. But the most important thing is this: When you get stomped you can't let them know they got to you. Right? You get punched, yeah, that hurts and all that. But it's your pride they're trying to hurt. And they can't take that from you. The next time you see them, you walk

178

around with your head up, like *Fuck you. You kicked my ass? So what. So what. I'm still the man, and you got nothing. Nothing.* Right?"

He looks at me, and I nod.

"My dad, he used to leave me all bloody and torn up, and you know what I'd say? I'd say, 'All right, I'm heading out now, you have a good day.' Just like that. Never let him know I was scared. That's punk rock, yo. Show him, you got nothing. You say it."

"What?"

"Say it. 'You got nothin'.'"

"I don't know . . ."

"Try it. Trust me. 'You got nothing.'"

"Uh . . . you got nothing?"

"No. Jesus. You got *nothing.*" He jabs a finger at me.

"You got nothing."

"Better. Big. Like you got some balls."

"I think that's the problem."

"No, no, it's all about pretending. Put on the show. 'You got nothing.'"

I can see what's going on. Patrick wants this to be a big moment. A breakthrough moment. I'm teary and we're sitting here bonding and he wants to go the next step. I appreciate his advice, but I feel ridiculous.

"Say it," he urges.

"C'mon . . ."

"Shut up. Just say it!"

I sigh, shake my head. *Fine.*

"You got nothing."

"Bigger! You got *nothing!*"

"You got *nothing!*"

"Yeah! Again!"

He shoves me, a pop on the shoulder. I'm a little surprised.

"Say it!"

"You got *nothing!*"

I have to admit it's sort of satisfying.

"One more time!" he says, and jabs me again.

"You got NOTHING!" I say, and jab him right back.

"Yeah, man! You got nothing!" *Slam,* on the side of my shoulder.

"You got NOTHING!" SLAM! Smacking him right back.

Something odd is happening. I feel absurd, but also like I'm getting to whatever lies beyond absurd, the place where it starts to feel good.

"Again!" *Smack!*

"YOU GOT NOTHING!!" I scream at the top of my lungs, and hit him as hard as I can.

"Yeah, mofo! That's the shit!" Patrick says, grinning insanely, and slams his beer can end-first against his forehead, the aluminum crumpling into a wrinkled puck. A tiny rivulet of blood starts to drip over his eyebrow. I blink at him.

"Also, later?" he says, not noticing or caring about the blood. "If you get them alone? Hit them with a frigging baseball bat or something. That's good, too."

I learned a lot of things sitting with Patrick on the lawn. I learned how he got in the fight with Josh.

"Oh, yeah, that. I was going through this weird Nazi phase? I know, totally f'ed up, right? Anyways, I see your brother, and he's got the little Jew hat and everything, and I start, you know, blah blah blah," he said, moving his hand like a talking puppet. "So

180

pretty soon we're mixing it up, and I'm thinking it's going okay, and then real quick it wasn't. So we're in the clinch and I bit him, and then next thing I know I'm waking up in the hospital. Kid can *hit*, yo." He stopped then and felt his jaw, like he was checking to see if it was still broken. "But you know what?" he said. "He actually came and checked on me."

"I'm sorry. What?"

"Yeah, I guess I was out for a really long time, and the word was that I was really messed up. So I was in the hospital, and Josh lies and says he's my brother so they'll let him in, and he came to see me and make sure I was okay."

"Josh?"

"Yeah, man. We shook hands and everything. Been tight since then."

Another item for the Josh Mystery File.

Since he was talking, I figured I should pump him for as much information as possible. Next up: Trish.

"Yeah, she screwed him up good. Strippers, man. Never date them. Believe me—I know."

Gotcha. Noted. Lesley?

"She's awesome, dude. Awesome. She's smart, she's funny, she's got a future . . . That's the girl he should be with."

"Was he ever . . . with her?"

"Not that I know."

"Why is he back from school? What happened?"

"Not sure about that. That's Trish, too, probably. I'm telling you, she messed him up."

Does he have some big secret plan?

Shake of the head.

"Don't know, dude. He's thinking something, though. He's quiet that way."

Other valuable things I learned: what it's like to finally punch your abusive dad in the face and break his nose ("friggin' *awesome*"); what it's like to be in juvenile detention ("friggin' *sucks*"); and that Patrick is not, in fact, a meth dealer.

"Meth? Naw. Weed, sure. And X. But not meth. That stuff is nasty."

"Oh. Good," I said, because I didn't have anything else to say.

"Yeah, I don't deal meth. I mean, not anymore."

Great.

We sat and talked until it was dark. Patrick finished the six-pack and the chips and got up twice to pee in the creek. He went up to the house and returned ten minutes later with a soggy microwaved pizza that we ate right off the cardboard. As we were eating I started to hear the familiar *boom boom boom* of Josh hitting the heavy bag in the basement.

"Man, is he pissed at me," said Patrick.

"Me too," I said.

Patrick chuckled, and held a hand out for a fist bump.

Finally, Patrick said good night, gave me a thump on the back, did a halfhearted job of gathering up the trash, and started his walk back up to the house. He stopped and turned.

"Hey, little man?" he said. "Don't pay your brother no mind, okay? You're a good dude."

Then he saluted and went inside, my new, Mohawked, tattooed, drug-dealing friend. I climbed into the tent and tried to sleep, while from the house I could hear Josh hitting the bag: *boom. Boom. Boooooom.*

CHAPTER THIRTY-TWO

ANOTHER ADDITION TO THE HOUSEHOLD

When I wake up, the sun is above the trees, meaning it's late in the morning. Josh is nowhere in sight. I'm not running around the block or doing pushups or being forced to do something dangerous and foolhardy. I wonder if I'm dreaming.

I walk up the slope of the lawn, yawning and rubbing my eyes. I hear the sound of someone yanking repeatedly on a lawn mower cord and look over to see Mr. Olsen.

"Hi," I say, and wave just as the engine pops and sputters to life. He waves back, mouthing something, his words inaudible over the noise of the motor. He watches me for a moment, and then before he starts pushing the mower he does a little shrug and unilateral shake of the head, the sort of movement that signifies an unvoiced *whatever—not my business.* It could be related to the fact that I'm wearing just my boxer briefs.

I go in through the downstairs back door and shower in my parents' bathroom. When I emerge from the bathroom and reach the base of the stairs I catch a whiff of nail polish remover and briefly think that maybe my mom is somehow home. And while I'm thinking that and wondering more about the dreaming thing, I hear hysterical, high-pitched yapping and claws clattering on tile. A small dog appears at the top of the stairs, its whole body quivering and jerking forward spasmodically with each sharp explosion of noise, like it's trying to power-vomit its barks at me.

YAP YAP YAP, says the dog, then hops to the side and repeats the barking, *YAP YAP YAP,* then more hopping and yapping. I'm standing in the middle of the steps, not sure how to proceed.

"Joey!" I hear Patrick shout, his voice mixed in with a female voice shouting the same thing at the same time. "Joey!" Patrick repeats, solo this time. "Shut the hell up!"

Joey doesn't shut the hell up. There's a pause, and some canine-directed profanity, and then Patrick tromps into view and scoops up the dog in one hand.

"Oh, hey, dude!" he says to me, and tromps off again. The angle isn't so good from where I'm standing, but I catch a glimpse of what I think are tufts of tissue paper sticking out from between his bare toes.

When I get to the top of the stairs I hear the female voice again: "Doesn't that look cute?" *KeeeYOOOT,* like that, coming from the den.

"It's really cute," agrees Lisa. The dog makes a whining noise. Patrick shushes it.

I walk to the den and look in. Patrick is stretched out on the floor on his back, holding the dog on his chest, the dog licking his face. Lisa is sitting in the comfy red chair, leaning forward a bit, her attention focused intently on her feet. Sitting cross-legged in front of her, her back to me, is a dark-haired woman who is in the process of painting Lisa's toes. She's wearing a cutoff T-shirt that reaches about to where her ribs stop, revealing the tattoo on her lower back. TRAMP, it says.

"Hey, dude," says Patrick again. "I think there's still some eggs left, if you want them."

Lisa and the dark-haired woman look up, and I let out an involuntary noise that sounds like *heep*. It's Terri the Mean Stripper.

"Oh, hey!" she says with a huge smile.

"Uh . . . hi?" I say.

"Isaac," says Patrick, "this is my girlfriend, Terri."

"We've met," says Terri. Now Patrick's comment about dating strippers makes sense. Of course no bra. I immediately try to find someplace else to point my eyeballs.

"I'm so sorry about the other night," says Terri. "Josh explained everything to me. I was just in a pissy mood, and I was thinking you were staring at my boobs"—hand pointing at boobs for emphasis—"which is, like, silly, because that's why people are there, and . . ."

She goes on, detailing her pissy mood that night at the strip club and some unpleasant customers and their wandering hands that led to that mood. I'm still trying not to look, my eyes roaming everywhere but Terri. The dog is practically licking the boogers from Patrick's nose. Lisa is alternating between glaring at me in wonderment and shock—you did *what? where?*—and gazing at Terri with an expression of the very essence of pure, worshipful love. I'm standing there in a towel, looking for an opportunity to interrupt Terri so she'll stop talking that way in front of Lisa, and distracted by the dog and by the realization that Patrick does have wads of tissue stuffed between each toe, because he has bright red nail polish on his toenails that is still drying.

"— so anyways, I'm sorry for saying you had a hard-on and everything."

"Oh my *God,*" says Lisa.

"Dude, it's totally okay if you did," says Patrick. "Every time I go in there I do."

"Patrick!" shrieks Terri, swatting at him, and they both start cackling. Lisa is giggling. The dog starts yapping again.

"You know she's nine, right?" I say, but they're still cackling and don't hear me. "Lisa, maybe you should, uh . . ."

"What?"

"I don't know. Go play or something."

"No," she says. "Terri, keep going!"

"Oh, sorry!" says Terri, Lisa's new BFF, and gets back to painting Lisa's nails.

"Isaac, you should put some clothes on," says Lisa disapprovingly.

I go to my room to get dressed. Patrick's clothes are strewn about. There is also some underwear of the very wispy, feminine variety lying on the floor, suggesting that Terri spent the night. I get dressed, averting my eyes from my bed, the scene of the crime.

I pass by the den, Terri saying, "Okay, Lisa, let's do your hair."

When I get to the kitchen, Josh is there, measuring the burnt countertop with a tape measure. He straightens and jots something on a spiral notepad, then types something on his laptop, which is resting on the center island.

He doesn't say anything to me, so I finally say, "'Sup."

He makes a grunting noise without looking at me, still typing, then starts scrolling through a web page. I wonder if he's going to bring up what happened yesterday, or if he even remembers it. He's probably just given up on me is what it is.

The room still smells of smoke. I'm sure it has worked its way into the walls and the curtains, tiny particles binding to all the surfaces, and the room is going to stink for weeks. I don't say this to Josh. Instead I say, "What's going on?"

"What do you mean?" he says, scribbling some more notes.

"I mean, I don't know. It's late." I shrug.

"It's the Sabbath. Rest day."

"Oh."

"There's eggs on the table," he says. He's dialing the cordless phone as he talks. "There's also some lox and bagels."

I sit and eat, listening to him on the phone navigating his way through some voice-activated menu: "Kitchen. No, kitchen. Kitchen. Kitchen. Okay, operator. Operator. OPERATOR. Christ."

He waits, then talks with someone about the types of countertops they have and whether or not he can come and buy something today. Halfway through he abruptly says, "Thanks. Gotta go," punches a button, and puts the phone back to his head. "Hi, Mom.

Yes, everything is great. Isaac is better. Yes, he was in school yesterday. Not much is happening. Pretty standard Saturday. Yup, very boring here in ol' Minnesota, Mom."

From the den comes more cackling and giggling and yapping. I roll my eyes and mutter.

"Here," says Josh, and shoves the phone at me.

"Hi, Izzie!" says my mom. "Are you all better?"

All better. Everything is fine. Nothing unusual to report. No former meth dealers living here, or any strippers giving Lisa a makeover.

"Listen, Izzie, I was talking with Roni Weinberg," my mom says. Roni, Eric's mom. "He's very lonely and upset, and you still haven't called him."

"I will, Mom. I've been sick."

"*Very* lonely. And I think he needs a friend."

"I'll call him."

"So Roni and I made a plan."

"Oh, God, Mom, please tell me you didn't—"

"I think that you should spend some time with him."

"Mom, I will, it's just that—"

"I mean, you're becoming a bar mitzvah, and if we're talking about mitzvahs, good deeds, what better thing than helping a friend?"

"I *will* help him."

"Yes, I *know* you will."

"I will. Wait a second—what do you mean?"

"What time is it there?"

"What? It's . . . eleven."

"It is? Oh, well, he should be there about—"

The doorbell rings.

"Mom, I'm going to kill you."

"I love you too, sweetie."

CHAPTER THIRTY-THREE

THE MITZVAH

MERIT BADGE: KINDNESS TO A FRIEND IN NEED

Eric and I say hey to each other when I open the door, neither of us with particular enthusiasm. Then we stand there in silence, the two losers, until he says, "You know what? I don't want to be here either. My mom made me come."

We're at that impasse when my brother looms behind me and starts pushing me out the door, forcing Eric to step back down the steps.

"C'mon. We're going," says Josh, now marching past me and jumping off the front porch.

"What? What are you talking about?"

He turns and walks backwards on his way toward the garage. "We're buying a new countertop." He points a finger at Eric. "You, too, Weinberg. Let's go."

It's the confident tone of command, I think as we pull out of the driveway. That's how he does it. Like the Voice in *Dune,* or Obi-Wan convincing the stormtroopers they've got the wrong robots.

"These are not the droids you're looking for," I mumble from the back seat.

"What?" says Josh, driving.

"Nothing."

Eric is riding shotgun. Josh told him to. "You," he said, aiming with a finger, "in here. You" — to me — "in back." We obeyed instantly. Of course, Eric's unquestioning compliance could be due to the fact that he saw my brother nearly bat Tim Phillips's head off his shoulders yesterday.

Barely out of the driveway, Josh says to Eric, "You're not going to puke on my car, are you?" Eric sighs. "I'm kidding, dude."

That's it for the talking as we drive. Josh snaps on the radio, loud, and yowls along, loud, grinning and nodding and singing to us, inviting us to join in. We decline. I'm thankful for the noise and distraction. I haven't spoken with Eric since the whole bar mitzvahpocalypse, and I feel guilty and excuseless, my craven behavior completely transparent. As we drive I try to think of how, exactly, we're supposed to start over again, what I'm supposed to say.

When we pull into the parking lot of the Home Depot and park, Eric hops out of the car and walks ahead of me without a word or a backwards glance. Maybe he's pissed at me, or maybe, I think, maybe *he's* ashamed to be seen with *me*. Maybe *I'm* the loser here. My disgrace might be fresher, but I don't think getting beat up and humiliated in front of the whole school ranks higher on the loser index than what happened to Eric, which is a lot more exotic and noteworthy, the sort of thing people will talk about for years. I almost want to remind him of that.

We enter the store in stretched-out single file: Josh in front, then Eric, then me. Inside, Josh finds an employee and stops to ask directions. Eric gravitates to a spot a few yards off to the right of Josh,

I end up equidistant to the left, the both of us sort of shuffling around, shifting our weight, not looking at each other. Magnets both attracted to and repelling each other, not moving too far away but unable to get close. Floating in a cloud of awkward.

Josh gets his directions and strides off toward the depths of the store, and we trail behind, dragged along by the main magnet. He quickly starts to outpace us. About halfway down the endless wallpaper aisle I look up and realize that Eric has stopped. He's not exactly waiting for me, but he's not moving, either—just standing there in profile to me, arms crossed. I slow, unsure of what to do, then resume my normal walking speed, thinking to just pass him and catch up with Josh.

Instead, as I get near him, Eric says, "Hey."

I stop.

He looks at me, then looks away, then does it a few more times, squirming a bit, clearly working on getting something out. I do my own squirming, both internal and external. Neither of us wants this confrontation right now, standing in an aisle at the Home Depot under the fluorescents.

"You know something?" he says, and then points an accusatory finger at me. "I thought you were my friend. But I guess I was wrong."

It looks and sounds rehearsed. I can picture him standing in front of the mirror saying that to me, saying it all different ways, some worse than others. I wonder how many versions there were, and where this one lies on the scale from good to bad.

"Eric . . ." I say.

"I guess I was wrong," he repeats, shaking his head.

I start to protest, excuses tumbling out, piling on top of each other: *I didn't do anything, What are you talking about, I was busy, I haven't been in school*—and then something unexpected happens. Something extraordinary. Profound, even. Right there in aisle seven. Something like the scene in *How the Grinch Stole Christmas!* when he hears the *Whos* of *Who*-ville singing and a light goes on in his brain and his heart suddenly swells and he understands how wrong he's been.

I. Was. Wrong.

I say, "I'm sorry."

I'm sorry.

It tastes unfamiliar and exceptional and righteous. It feels like what a grownup would say. Lesley would be proud of me.

I'm sorry.

Whatever Eric had been rehearsing in the mirror, he hadn't rehearsed for this. He's out of words, almost confounded.

"I'm sorry," I say again, because it feels so good. "I was wrong." The repetition is almost unfair, like hitting a guy when he's down.

"Oh," he finally stutters. "It's okay."

He shakes his head, looking down.

"You don't know what it's been like. No one will even talk to me," he says.

"Yeah."

"Not one person. I had frickin' food poisoning. It's not my fault. I could have died."

I nod. "That sucks."

"I've been thinking of changing schools," he says.

Probably a good idea, I think.

"Don't do that," I say.

"Really?"

"Yeah. Screw 'em."

"Yeah," he says, uncertainly. "Yeah. Screw 'em." He smiles briefly and shakes his head again. "How are you?" he says.

"What do you mean?"

"Come on. I saw it. I saw the whole thing with Tim Phillips."

"Oh, yeah," I say, dismissing that nonsense with an airy wave. "Whatever. They got nothing."

"What?"

"They got nothing."

He nods. I nod. We're nodding, agreeing that they got nothing. Then he says, "What does that even *mean?*"

"It means, they got nothing. You can't let guys like that get to you."

"Huh," he says. I have to admit it sounds better coming from Patrick.

We regard each other some more.

"So . . ." he says, "we friends?"

"Of course."

He smiles, relieved. His eyes are wet. "All right." He sticks out his hand. I shake it.

"Friends," I say.

"Thanks," he says, and I can see him trying to keep it together. This is a mitzvah, I can hear my mother saying, a good deed. It makes me feel good, knowing that I'm doing the right thing. I am the water on the parched landscape of his life. The balm on the wound. I am the sun rising after the endless night. I feel ashamed, again, thinking about what a coward I've been—it doesn't matter how close Eric and I are, he's still a friend. My friend has been suffering, and I abandoned him in a time of need. No more.

That's an actual life lesson, maybe the only one I've learned this week: If there's anything that makes you a man, it's sticking up for a friend, even when that friend is unpopular, and there's nothing more important than—OhmyGodthere'sPatriciaMorrison.

Oh my God. She's just rounded the corner at the other end of the aisle with Tracey Howat. They're walking with a man who must be Patricia's dad. They're about ten yards from us, drawing closer, pointing at and discussing the wallpaper samples on the side racks, seconds from noticing the two of us. *Hey, Tracey! Come help me pick out wallpaper for my bedroom, bestie! OMG, is that Eric Weinberg, the pants pooper? And look who he's with! OMG!! Let's tell* everyone!!

Eric is still grasping my hand. He's not even shaking it anymore, he's just sort of holding it while he wipes at his tears with the back of his other wrist, having a moment. The trio have paused about five yards away, having a wallpaper conference, and they're going to notice us in about three seconds.

"Okay, well, I should . . ." I stammer, trying to disentangle myself from his grip, my face starting to burn.

"What?"

"I need to see if my brother—"

Just then Tracey turns to see me and Eric standing there exposed, caught in the spotlight, holding hands, Eric all teary eyed, and I can see the rapid process as her brain analyzes the data, recognizes us, and spits out the result: *losers.* Now she's leaning over to whisper to Patricia and alert her to our presence, and before Patricia can react and turn toward us I jerk my hand roughly free of Eric's and take off running.

"Hey!" he shouts after me. "Hey, Isaac!" but I keep running, dodging fat people and orange shopping carts and leaping over cans of house paint.

I get clear of the aisle and sprint to the left and put some distance between me and the aisle opening, finding a spot amid a floor display of refrigerators from which to do some spying. A few seconds later Eric emerges and looks left and right. I hesitate, hidden in a forest of brushed-steel refrigerators, then step out and raise a hand to get his attention. He sees me but doesn't approach. He just stands there for a moment and looks at me, and the look says it all: He knows exactly what just happened back there in the aisle.

He glares at me hard, anger and grief and betrayal, an expression I'll never forget. Then he walks away, heading toward the exit.

He's not there when I go outside. Maybe he called his mother and she picked him up, I think, or he started walking home, or some combination of the two. I search for him for a few minutes, then kick one of those outdoor garbage cans that's encased in a pebble-encrusted barrel. However much quantity of good I was feeling about myself during my reformed-Grinch moment, I'm feeling that much bad, plus about ten percent. I wasn't the gentle rain on his arid landscape. I was peeing on it.

I can't find Josh in the store, so I wait by the entranceway, finally just taking a seat against the wall. He comes out about half an hour later, pushing a cart with a big box in it. AIR PURIFIER says the box.

"Where's Weinberg?" he says.

"He left."

Josh shrugs. "Okay." I follow him across the parking lot, the cart rattling on the asphalt.

"What about the counter?" I ask.

"Idiots. First they say they can install it today, and then they say they can't do it for a few days. Why'd he leave? He crap himself?"

"I don't know."

"I feel bad for that kid. Know what he should do? Change schools."

CHAPTER THIRTY-FOUR

THE WEIRD FAMILY AT DINNER

Josh makes a big pot of chili and we all sit down to eat, Terri and Patrick included. The new air purifier hums quietly in the corner, laboring to get rid of the smoky smell. Josh already made me scrub every available surface. Joey the dog is out on the back porch, after having crapped on my mother's favorite Persian rug—twice. Lisa sits next to Terri and spends most of her time staring at her in adoration. Lisa now has several tight braids in her hair, threaded with a line of brightly colored beads.

Patrick tells a very funny story about a terrible trip he once took to Duluth, a trip that included a near-fatal encounter with a bunch of hard-ass Rangers, young men from the Iron Range in northern Minnesota. Josh doesn't pay any attention, just periodically checks his phone and sends texts, until Terri, her mouth full of food, says, "Josh, that is so rude."

Soon after that he gets a call and steps out onto the porch to have an agitated conversation while we all watch him. I see a knowing look pass between Terri and Patrick, Patrick shaking his head. When Josh finishes he comes back in and says, "You guys handle cleanup. I'm heading out for a bit."

It's a cooler night so I build a fire in the pit. Patrick and Terri come and join me for a while and we sit peering into the flames, not talking much, until Terri gets tired of the mosquitoes and they go back in. I climb into the tent and try to sleep but can't, so I get out, fetch more wood, and get the fire going again.

As I sit there I think about the day. Of all the failures this week, what I did to Eric was the worst. Everything else was just my failure, a humiliation for myself. Running away from him was piling on his already massive heap of life-is-hell. And now where am I? Abandoned by my peeps, and not even Eric will be friends with me.

I wonder where Josh is. He seems fine, and yet somehow every day he's a bit more tense, like a watch being wound tighter a few clicks at a time. I shift to thinking about Tim Phillips and what happened, and wonder if there is a shoe dangling, waiting to fall. Josh hit him. Something has to happen.

I'm still sitting next to the fire, gnawing on a big ball of dread and musing my dark musings, when Josh gets back a little after midnight. I hear the car pulling into the driveway, the headlights briefly defining the outlines of the house. The car door slams. A few minutes later and the heavy bag starts up again: *boom boom booooom.* I don't think he had a very pleasant evening out. I hug my knees tighter to my chest against the cold and move a little closer to the fire.

CHAPTER THIRTY-FIVE

GET JOSH

MERIT BADGE: SWEET REVENGE

"And here's to Isaac," says Lesley, standing, plastic cup of white wine held high, her gaze affixed on me, "who has been through the wringer and is still doing a great job, even though his jerk brother is a jerk to him."

"I'll drink to *that!*" says Terri, and knocks her cup against Patrick's, while Josh shakes his head and rolls his eyes.

The backyard, Sunday. Perfect summer evening: warm, slight breeze, birds calling. Paper plates, hot dogs blackened and blistered from the grill, corn, potato salad, something radioactive-looking that Terri made, called Strawberry Mess. And the best ingredient of all: the Magic Impenetrable Lesley Force Field protecting me from Josh.

"You *are* doing a great job," says Lesley to me, and leans across the picnic table to give me a big *mmmmuh!* kiss on the forehead before she sits down again. I look over at Josh, grinning, and he's looking back evenly, chewing slowly on the inside of his cheek.

Josh has been looking at me like this the whole afternoon and evening, his gaze saying, *We both understand this game. You can stand on that side of the Force Field and throw turds at me, and I can't do anything about it, not even act upset.*

Until later, when you'll pay dearly.

And I smile back, saying, *Yes, I'll pay later. But in the meantime I'm going to be standing here right at this line, just out of your reach, chucking as much crap at you as possible. Which is what I've been doing.* It's awesome.

Awesome from the beginning, when Lesley arrived, instantly erasing all the pain and horror of the week.

It had been a very full day: hard morning workout with special attention paid to how to escape the mount position, various chores around the house, marathon study session. Around two o'clock I was finishing washing the car in the driveway, Josh the Overseer indicating molecules of dirt that I had missed. I was polishing the tires when I heard a familiar hum and looked up to see Lesley approaching the house on her Vespa.

"Hey," I said, because the sight was so unexpected, "it's Lesley!"

"Good job, Isaac. Figured that out on the first guess. She's here for dinner."

She pulled into the driveway, hopped off, removed her helmet, ignored Josh completely, and came right over to me to give me a big hug and a kiss on the cheek. "Hey, lover," she said.

Lover, like she read my mind the other day at breakfast and remembered it. *Lover.*

Then she turned to Josh and said, "Hey."

"Hey," he said, and there was a pause and some sort of obscure communication between the two of them, and then he held out his arms and they hugged, but I don't think it was anything like what I got from her.

She pulled a bag of potatoes out of the little storage thingy on the back of her Vespa, tossed the bag to Josh, and we all went into the house together, me tagging along as he gave her the quick tour, gruff as always, Lesley glancing over at me with that conspiratorial smile, both of us grinning and making fun of Josh.

Terri and Patrick were out back on the porch, Terri doing Lisa's nails for what had to be the tenth time. Lesley knew both Terri and Patrick—hugs, kisses, how's this person, what happened with so-and-so. Then, to me, "Well, you saw my place. You going to show me your room?"

Yes.

We went to my room, Patrick and Terri's clothes strewn about on the floor and over the unmade bed.

"This isn't my stuff," I said quickly.

"Really? That's not your thong?"

She stepped into the middle of the room and did a slow, full 360, taking it all in. I tried to time it just right, moving behind her field of vision like I was ducking behind the sweeping spray of a rotating lawn sprinkler, making it to the chair and its embarrassing occupant while she was looking in the other direction, hoping she hadn't spotted the stuffed Snoopy. Then she suddenly reversed course and twisted back toward me, and we had a moment of her regarding me as I stood there posterized, holding Snoopy.

"Um . . ." I say.

"I've got one just like that," she said, and gave it a pat-pat. My love grew even stronger.

"So," she said then, "here we are."

"Right."

I know when she's being flirty she's being ironic, but I'll take what I can get.

"Did you get in trouble for being late to school?" she said.

"No. School was . . ." Horrible. "Fine."

She cocked her head. "Did something happen?"

"No."

She squinted. "Really?"

"Yes. Thanks for letting me stay over," I said, hoping to shift things back in that direction. "I didn't want to come home."

She picked up one of Patrick's combat boots, which was resting on my pillow. He really has it in for my pillow.

"Yes, I can see why."

She chucked the boot onto the carpet, then stood with her hands on her hips, tapping her foot, examining me. Then she walked to the door and leaned out to make sure no one was around before turning to me and saying, "How are you?"

"I'm okay."

"I'm not sure I believe you."

"I'm fine."

"Josh is being all right with you?"

"He's . . ."

"Being Josh."

"Yes."

"I let him have it, you know, about everything."

"Oh. Maybe you shouldn't have done that."

"No, I made him promise to be nicer to you."

I nodded. I had a fair idea of what sort of behavior that particular conversation was going to produce.

"You'll tell me if he's being mean to you again?"

"Yes."

"Promise?"

"Yes."

"I like you, Isaac. You're my bud."

"I know. Thanks. I like you, too."

"Good. Hey, you have my favorite shirt?"

And so I had to reveal to her about the whole thing with the Assholes. It wasn't so bad, though, because we ended up sitting on my bed, Lesley telling me what jerks they are and how great I am, her arm around my shoulder to comfort me, and we were sitting like that when Josh came in to fetch us.

"Hey, lovers, hope I'm not interrupting," he said.

"Josh, you jerk," she said, and that's when the game really got going.

We all gathered in the kitchen, the action centering on two activities: cooking, and Let's Get Josh. There was a strange charge in the air—layers of warmth and celebration and joviality, a happy reunion, and intercut with it all was an unmistakable whiff of bitter aggression. It's like everyone sensed that there was Kryptonite in the room, that Josh was temporarily without his powers, and everyone wanted to get in a few shots while they had a chance.

Everyone, it turned out, had a funny story about Josh, each with the same theme: You know about the time when Josh completely lost his temper because of _____ and did _____?

All the tales were like that. You know about the time he got so angry at that dude on the motorcycle and was chasing him down the middle of the street in his underwear, trying to catch him? Did you know about that time when he dumped that whole massive stock pot of cold gazpacho on the dishwasher? Remember the time _____?

It was like a storm cloud forming, organic, spontaneous. Except it wasn't. The more I observed, the more I could see what was happening, could see Lesley subtly orchestrating everything. Little verbal nudges to people. Didn't you have some story about . . . ? Really? Tell us more! And then gentle hints that she knows something juicy but really *can't* share it, really, she *can't*, no, no, never mind, forget I said anything — oh, all right. There was this time . . .

She's got great stories, stories I'd never imagined. So do Patrick and Terri.

But no one's as good at it as me.

I've known Josh for a lot longer than they have, and I've seen the soft parts they haven't: the portions of Josh's existence that are about having parents, about being a child in a family. You know that embarrassing *something*, whatever it is? That feeling of not wanting anyone to see your parents drop you off at the soccer game, because it shows that you're not a totally independent person, that there are people in your life you answer to and who used to wipe your rear end for you, and not that long ago? I'm the witness of that something for Josh. I've seen it and know all about it. I'm the one who can put gouges in his hardened exterior.

The time Josh got so angry he went to sit on the roof and wouldn't come down for hours. The time Josh body-slammed the lawn mower on the driveway. The time my mom got so angry at Josh that she *sent* him up to the roof and wouldn't let him come down for hours. The time . . .

I feel powerful and reckless, everyone's laughter urging me on.

Lisa listens, wide-eyed, giggling when everyone else laughs, especially Terri. Lesley literally says, "More! More!" The frog is very much on the scene, singing and dancing his heart out.

So now we're out back eating, the game of Let's Get Josh still continuing, if not at the same intensity. The whole time Josh has taken it with barely a word, smiling a grimacey, pained smile, nodding. Each story and joke I tell is another deposit into the bank of I'm Gonna Get My Ass Kicked. But that's going to happen anyways, right?

Whenever I want, I can put my gaze on Lesley. That in and of itself is nice. What's better is that as soon as she notices, as soon as our eyes meet, I get our Look. We're still part of the same secret club. At school I might be a friendless loser, but I have Lesley.

"Hey, I've got another story," says Terri, who I think has had a bit too much wine. "Remember that time that Trish —"

As soon as she says that name, Josh shifts in his seat, taking a sharp breath in through his nose. It's the first time he has betrayed any real annoyance at all.

"Hey," he says quietly, and Terri says, "What?"

"Terri," says Patrick, looking at her.

"What, we can't talk about Trish?"

"Yeah, why can't we talk about Trish?" says Lesley, who I think maybe has also had a bit more wine than she should.

"I'm gonna head in and clean up," says Josh.

There are glances exchanged when Josh goes in, and Terri says, "What? What's the big deal?" Then we all sit and talk for a while until it gets dark, and I say, "Why don't I build a fire?"

We sit around the fire pit, Lesley next to me, sometimes putting her arm around me. We sing campfire songs, or the fractions of campfire songs that everyone remembers. We talk and laugh and tell jokes. The air above the fire shimmers, sparks rising up, and I follow their drifting spirals with my eyes. They're like this magical evening, I think, floating and dancing weightlessly into the sky, taking my cares away with them.

After a while Josh comes back out again and tells Lisa to go to bed, and off she goes. He sits down with no explanation or apology. He puts himself on the other side of Lesley, but she mostly ignores him, keeping her arm around me. The Force Field is still in effect.

After a little while longer Terri says, "Let's go in," and we do. Now we're in the TV room. Patrick is kind of spread over my dad's easy chair, Terri in his lap, taking a break now and then from her fortieth cup of wine to trade sloppy, wet kisses with Patrick. I try not to look.

Josh and Lesley and I are on the sofa, Lesley still between us. I'm slouched down, feeling warm and relaxed and contented, included in the circle of big kids. The conversation has been waxing and waning, topics surfacing, discussed, fading away to periods of silence. I know that when Lesley goes home, the Force Field will go home with her, and I'm planning a very rapid retreat to the tent when that happens.

"Okay, y'all," says Patrick, standing and stretching, Terri with her arms around him for support, "we're gonna hit the hay."

They weave out of the room, a tipsy four-legged creature.

It's silent now. I feel almost hypnotized, slouched so low that my body is parallel with the floor, hands folded over my stomach, looking up at the ceiling. Lesley is next to me, our sides touching.

When was the last time I felt this at peace, this happy? The other night when I was in her bed, I guess. Other than that, never.

"Isaac," says Josh.

"What?"

He doesn't answer, finally forcing me to struggle up into a sitting position and look at him. He gives me a look: head inclined toward me, eyebrows up, then a jerk of the eyes in the direction of the backyard.

"What?"

"Bedtime."

"No."

"Yes," says Josh.

"No, I think I'll hang out," I say, and glance to Lesley so we can share our Look.

But it's not there.

I'm alone.

She smiles at me, an apologetic twitch of the lips, and she looks away. Then I see her hand. It's resting on Josh's hand, their fingers intertwined. Josh's eyes are boring into mine, and suddenly I understand what his gaze has been saying this whole time, understand why he never bothered to react, understand what the game really is and that I'm the one who lost.

I get up without a word, without looking at them, feeling a numbness, the kind that comes right after you've hurt yourself and before the pain really kicks in.

"Good night, Isaac," says Lesley, but I don't answer, just keep going down the hall, out the door, into the night.

CHAPTER THIRTY-SIX

PAIN

MERIT BADGE: BROKEN HEART

They should tell you.

They should sit you down and warn you that it's real, that it really happens and how desperately horrific it is, so that you can be ready, so you can know that when they talk about a broken heart it's not some abstract metaphor, that it's the worst thing you can ever experience. Like molten rock like razorblades like broken glass like a beast clawing into my chest, stealing my breath, suffocating me. Like the end of all hope.

Middle of the night. I'm skip-staggering in circles on the lawn, wringing my hands like I'm trying to tear my fingers off, gasping for air and making little moaning noises, now collapsing down to crouch into a ball, rocking myself, arms and hands piled on my head, now up again for more circles, desperate, desperate to escape this agony, but it won't let me be.

I don't know what time it is or how long I've been doing this. It doesn't matter. Let the night go on forever and the moon crack apart and the stars burn out. She's in there with him. She's with Josh, and I know what they're doing, and there's nothing else that has meaning or can have meaning or will ever have meaning. She's taken everything that she gave me, all that soaring joy, and she's torn it out of me and taken everything else with it.

She's in there with Josh.

Lover, she called me, but what she was doing was mocking me. *Lover.* One letter away from *loser.* She was just using me to get to Josh, and I'm the only one who was stupid enough not to understand that. And the way Josh was looking at me today—he wasn't thinking about how he was going to get back at me. He was thinking, *You poor, stupid child.*

I don't remember lying down, but I'm on my back now, sobbing, hands covering my face, elbows pointing up at the black sky. I will never get up. I will never stop feeling like this. This is my new state of existence, and it will last forever.

Forever.

And then I'm up again. I'm up and I'm at the fire pit, squatting to pick up a softball-size stone in two hands, walking toward the house, the stone hard against my stomach, walking faster, thinking, *What are you doing, what are you doing?* and then I'm jogging and then running, then barely breaking stride to spin in an abrupt circle like an Olympic hammer thrower, arms straight, leaning back against the eager weight of the stone, twice around and then releasing it with a grunt to let it sail in an arc toward Josh's window.

BOOOM. That's the sound it makes as it hits the wood siding instead, a timpani drum reverberating through the dark neighborhood. It's still echoing in my head as I'm running back to the fire pit, finding another rock, running back to the house, twirling, letting it loose, *BOOOOM,* running back, another rock, the spin, the throw, *BOOOOM,* again, run rock spin throw *BOOOM,* a light going on in Josh's window, sprint back, rock, run spin release *SMASH!* Success as the rock finds its mark and I stand there, panting.

Good, then. Good. It's done.

"Good," I say out loud.

I turn my back to the house and sit down on the lawn, knees up, calmer now. Listening to my own breathing, the fingers of my right hand absently twisting and burrowing their way into the intertwined roots of grass and the cool, damp earth. *It's not okay, but it's okay,* I think, as my gaze traces the complicated line where the charcoal silhouette of the trees meets the deeper black of the sky beyond. I'm just empty now. There's nothing left inside me to hurt. I could go out there, cross the creek, into the heart of the trees, deeper and deeper, become another shadow, the me dissolving away until it no longer exists and I'm just a part of the darkness.

I don't say anything when I feel Josh standing next to me, or struggle when he clamps his hand on my arm and yanks me to my feet, don't even glance at him as he marches me down the slope of the yard, past the garden, past the fire pit, past the tent, don't protest as he lifts me up above his head, and I don't cry out when throws me into the frigid creek.

CHAPTER THIRTY-SEVEN

TWO CONFRONTATIONS

MERIT BADGE: SUCKER PUNCH

I stayed in the creek until I was numb, until I couldn't feel the muck and sand beneath me. When I finally dragged myself out onto the lawn I was shivering so violently that I could hardly breathe, my muscles clenching and locking into place so hard I thought my bones would break.

I don't know how I made it to the house. The back door was unlocked and not shut entirely, which was good because I couldn't close my hand around the doorknob. I went to my parents' bathroom and somehow bludgeoned the shower on and collapsed onto the tile and lay in the fetal position, still shivering, the transition back to sensation even more agonizing than the knifelike intensity of the creek. I stayed there, going in and out of consciousness, until the hot water ran out. Then I went into my parents' room and got into their bed, and that's all I remember.

The house was deserted when I finally woke up. Or I think it was. Josh's door was closed, and I didn't knock. It was past ten.

I went to school because I didn't know what else to do. I dressed in my old jeans, my old shoes, an old T-shirt. I didn't put any product in my hair. I rode my bike but felt so weak and winded that I could only pedal for short bursts before I had to rest, the bike slowing to a near stop each time.

I'm zombieing my way along the school halls now, hollow eyed, exhausted. A negative space of me, a silhouette cutout of me. Maybe people are looking at me and whispering. I don't know. I don't care.

Sarah Blumgartner sees me. She's in the hallway, walking toward me. Her eyes widen as she registers my condition. *Go away,* I think. *Go away.*

"Hi, Isaac. Are you—"

"Go *away,*" I say, and keep walking.

Lunch, and I sit alone in the corner diametrically opposite from Eric's solitary table. Danny and Paul and Steve are not in the lunchroom. I passed Eric once in the hall, and he didn't even glance at me. I'm even lower now than I was after getting beat up on Friday, off-the-scale low, beneath whatever is there at the bottom. Not a friend left, and no Lesley.

I have no appetite for my food. I feel hot. I'm holding my hand to my forehead as I'm leaving the lunchroom and pass by door seven, which opens to the grassy area behind the school, just as Tim Phillips comes inside.

It's just the two of us there in the ten-by-ten vestibule.

He sees me at the same time I see him, and his eyes widen and I don't even realize what I'm doing until I'm hurtling toward him and ramming my shoulder low in his gut while I grab both his legs. It's a double-leg takedown, just like Josh has made me practice every day, except Tim weighs less than half what Josh does and I lift him easily as he curls over my shoulder, then slam him down on the hard floor and climb on top of him. It's oddly silent, no shouting or swearing or anything, not a word from either of us. He's not even resisting. I'm sitting on his chest like he did to me, and our eyes meet and I then see his expression: helpless, traumatized, terrorized. Not by me, I know, but by Josh, looming behind and through me. In that instant I'm overwhelmed by a powerful surge of misery and disgust and lethargy.

I stand up and stagger away without looking back. It's not supposed to feel like this. I've just defeated Tim Phillips. I'm supposed to feel some sort of triumph, like I've overcome an impossible obstacle, but all I feel is futility, like I can see an endless series of assaults and counterassaults, stretching off into infinity, no resolution ever. It's never fair, said Patrick, and he's right. It's just meaningless.

I drag myself up the stairs, heading to the second floor, and there is Danny coming toward me. There's nowhere for us to go without passing each other. And, seeing him, part of me forgets everything that has happened, as if we're still best friends, and as we both reach the landing I say, "Hey, dude."

He stops.

"Hey," he says, guarded.

I just want to be friends. Desperately. I just want to be able to hit reset, like on the Xbox, and get a new life and start over right now.

"Danny," I start to say, but he interrupts.

"Where's your fancy clothes?" he says bitterly.

Which is how I end up punching him.

CHAPTER THIRTY-EIGHT

INTO THE WOODS

MERIT BADGE: VISION QUEST

Nystrom's dogs are in a frenzy, insane with rage and ferocity. They snap and snarl and bark, climbing over each other to hurl themselves at the barrier of the fence, the chicken wire creaking and squeaking and bowing under their weight. I'm just inches from the diamond interweaving of its surface, inches from them, their teeth, their thick paws, my face so close to theirs that I can feel the heat and moisture of their breath and smell it.

I barely remember how I got here. It must be way after midnight. There's a storm brewing, the air charged and tight with it, hot as a fever. I feel feverish too.

I left the school after I punched Danny, walking away like Josh did after hitting Tim. No one stopped me. The sound was surprising, I thought, the splat of my fist hitting his face. Then the amount of blood streaming from his nostrils. He staggered back and crumpled into a ball, holding his nose, crying. I stood there, watching him, trying to figure out why I didn't feel anything. Then I turned and walked away. Walked out of the school, kept going, walked dizzy and sweating on sidewalks and across yards, aimless. Walked in squared-off circles around blocks, walked and walked, walked until it was getting dark. Then walked home and walked to the back and picked the tent up and threw it into the creek and walked across the bridge and into the woods and into the night.

Above me the clouds thickened like a clenched fist, blotting out the stars, the wind swirling violently through the branches. I pictured a Chinese dragon flying in sinuous circles, bashing his way through the treetops while I followed some mysterious pathway below. Like it wasn't my mind that was controlling me. A spirit quest, Josh had talked about, a spirit quest, and I wondered if that's what was happening, if the spirits were guiding me through the forest, guiding me here to face the dogs.

The dogs want to kill me. They want to seize me in those terrible jaws and tear me to pieces, rend my flesh from my bones. Their eyes are wide and savage, and I've got my gaze locked on theirs, staring them down, driving them even crazier. It's raining now. The fence is deforming, bulging outward a bit more each time a dog propels himself against it. I'm aware that the only thing holding it to the fence poles are thin twists of wire that could give way at any moment, and if they do, I'm dead. I should be afraid, but I'm not. I should run, but I don't. Instead I start laughing.

I laugh at the dogs, laugh at their impotent fury and the insanity of what I'm doing and the insanity of the Quest and the insanity of everything, and then I start barking back at them—*ARF ARF ARF! ARF ARF ARF ARF!!!!*—kicking at the fence as they catapult themselves at me, desperate to get to me, *ARF ARF ARF!!!* The rain is falling harder, fat drops splattering, and I punch an open palm at a dog, the sensation of his wet nose and fur and the chicken wire imprinted on my hand. *ARF ARF ARF!!! YOU FUCKING DOGS!!!*

I start kicking and punching at the fence, barking, deranged, my fury matching theirs. *ARF ARF ARFF!!! ARF ARF!!!* I slam my hands against the fence, back up, throw my body against it in a flying crosscheck over and over again. Then the back door opens and there's Nystrom, squinting into the darkness: "Hey! Shaddup! Shaddup!" and I laugh harder and turn tail and run back up the slope, weak-kneed with hysterical merriment as the rain starts to pour down.

I run through the trees, still laughing. The rain feels wonderful. I squash and stumble across the marshy area, falling into puddles, tripping over unseen roots, the grass slicing my hands. When I reach the trees I run as fast as I dare, bolts of lightning illuminating the path, and then I trip and fall again and try to get up, but this time something is different. Like someone has pulled a plug, all my energy and feral joy gone in an instant, nothing left but utter exhaustion. I lie there, the rainwater pooling around me.

Push myself to a sitting position, confused. Did I come from there? I'm shivering now, almost as bad as when I came out of the creek.

Up to my feet, reeling, panicked, wanting to run but surrounded by trunks and branches and vines and the whole forest pulling at me, weighing on me, the rain pouring down, lightning, thunder, the dragon writhing through the trees above my head. Stagger forward, moving just to move, bounce off the rough surface of an invisible tree, then another, move ahead, waving hands in front of me, my body hot and cold all at once. I don't remember where I am. Did I walk here? Is this the woods behind our house? It feels like it goes on forever in every direction, endless. I can see Tim's frightened expression, and Danny's face as he folded, bleeding, and see Lesley, and Josh, all of them talking at me at once, and Terri's dog barking and snapping at me. Are the other dogs following me? Is Nystrom? Did I really do that?

Wait. What happened? I'm not walking anymore. I'm not moving forward, because now I'm on the ground again, the world twirling around me, my heart racing. I have to get up and keep going, but I can't. I think, *I'm going to die here like this.* And it doesn't bother me so much. Everyone is still talking to me all at once, now calling my name, not leaving me in peace. *Isaac,* Josh is saying. *Isaac.*

Leave me alone, I think.

Isaac, he says, shouting it at me. *Leave me alone,* I say, and this time I think I say it out loud, but he won't leave me alone. He keeps shouting it, he won't just let me be.

"Leave me alone," I say again. "Leave me alone." Screaming it this time: "Leave me alone! Leave me alone! Leave me alone!"

I keep repeating it with as much force as I can muster, over and over again, until my voice is cracking and hoarse, and it dwindles until all I have to offer is a harsh whisper to fend him off. "Leave me alone," I rasp. "Leave me alone."

Leave me alone.

Why can't you just leave me alone.

Then I'm flying, the wind scooping me up out of the mud and lifting me through the trees and high into the storm-tossed night. I kick and punch and thrash about, fighting against it, but it won't let me free. I'm buffeted between the clouds and the lightning and the dragon, and this is how I'll die, lost forever with no one knowing what happened to me, never finding my body.

Except it's not the wind, I see now, it's Josh, and I lash out at him. But he's immune to my violence, holding me tight as I flail and struggle until I'm too weak to fight anymore. He's carrying me now, carrying me through the rain and the forest and the darkness. Cradling me like a child. Murmuring to me in a quiet voice to calm me, a voice I've never heard before. Saying, *It's okay, Isaac. It's okay. Come on. Come on, little brother. Come with me. Let's go home.*

CHAPTER THIRTY-NINE

MISSING THE WINDOW

"There's another piece over there. No, there, behind the toilet."

I crouch down and spot the shard of glass on the tile floor and gingerly pick it up. Josh is perched on the bathroom counter next to the sink, the unit creaking ominously each time he shifts his weight. He's absently tossing and tumbling a large rock from hand to hand, the rock that I had launched through the window. The wrong window, it turns out: the bathroom, not his bedroom window, which is what I'd been aiming for.

There's a piece of cardboard duct-taped over the window. Josh is there in the room with me, but he's not there. His eyes follow me as I put the glass into the brown paper shopping bag with the rest of the pieces, but I'm not really entering his brain. If he's still upset over what I did, he hasn't shown it.

I guess I slept for a full day, feverish and delirious. I remember heading into the woods, I remember the dogs, I remember something about a dragon, but not much more after that. I have a very, very vague memory of Josh carrying me home, or something like that, but I had so many weird dreams I'm not sure what's real. I woke up this morning in my parents' bed around ten, my fever almost gone. Lisa was at school. I don't know about Patrick and Terri. Maybe still asleep. Josh was in the kitchen when I wandered in there.

"Hungry?" was all he said. I nodded, and he jerked his head toward the table. I sat while he cooked sausages and eggs and toast for both of us, and made coffee for himself. We ate together, Josh reading the paper. Not a word passed between us, our residual shared anger hardened into a taut silence. Or maybe not. Maybe a truce of some sort. Or maybe just exhaustion, like so much had happened that neither of us knew where to begin, like a massive tangled knot in a kite string that you just ignore because it's too complicated to even think about.

He didn't speak until I'd finished eating. Then he said, "Let's go clean up the bathroom."

I don't complain about it as I pick up the glass, my hands in gardening gloves that are stiff from dried mud. It seems fair. I did break the window, after all. It's a wordless task marked and measured by the clinking of the glass shards as I place them into the doubled-up paper bag, and by the dry start-stop of Josh tossing and catching the rock.

I was stealing glances at him during breakfast, and I'm doing it again now, trying to detect any evidence of the two Joshes: the Josh I know, the one who very definitely picked me up and tossed me into the creek, and the other Josh, a Josh who may have headed into the woods, into the teeth of the storm, to search for me, and brought me home cradled in his arms. I don't see traces of either of them.

Am I angry at him about Lesley? I don't know. When I let my mind go in that direction I expect to encounter a huge store of emotion. But there's nothing. I don't know why I cared about her at all. I just know that I don't ever want to see her again.

The silence grows longer still, another presence in the room. I hold out a hand, Josh passes me the broom, and I start to sweep, and that uneven rhythm becomes the sound that indicates the passage of time.

Then, into the stillness, Josh says, "I threw a TV set through the downstairs picture window once."

It's been so long since I've talked that I have to clear my throat before I can start: ahem *ahem.* "I remember."

The first thing I've said to him all morning. The first thing I've said to him in days.

"You remember that? You were pretty young."

I retrieve another jagged triangle from near the toilet and carry it to the bag. "Why'd you do it?" I ask.

Josh thinks about it, shakes his head. "Don't know. I was pissed off about something." He makes a sound somewhere between a snort and a chuckle.

It's quiet again as I sweep. He wants to say more. I can feel it. I want to say more, too, all the questions I have piling up into a disordered, impatient line. It's a rare opportunity, right now, a chance to address everything, and I don't want to lose it. I will start with *How long was I out?* which will take me to *What happened?* and from there I will move to *Why did you have to do that with Lesley?* Or start at the top with *What are you doing with your life?* and work from there. I visualize various strategic pathways, practicing them in my head, knowing that whenever I open a conversation with Josh it will most likely veer off in some chaotic direction.

I open my mouth to speak, and at the same time he says, "Isaac

. . ." and then his phone rings. He looks at it. "I have to take this," he says, hopping down from the countertop. "Hey, hold on," he says into the phone, and pauses at the doorway. "Put the bag of glass in the garage with the recycling," he says to me, "and make sure you mop."

Then he leaves.

CHAPTER FORTY

THE OTHER SHOE DROPS

I fall asleep for most of the rest of the day and wake up around dinnertime, feeling woolly headed and grouchy, but not sick anymore. We all eat together, Josh distracted and withdrawn again. I feel strangely calm, but Josh is worse. Like he's pacing inside, moving restlessly from one end of some dark cage to the other, back, forth, not finding any ease.

When I first come in, Patrick says, "Yo, he's up! Dude, what the hell happened to you? You out there having some sort of vision quest?"

"None of your business," says Josh, and Patrick drops it.

Terri has broken three of my mother's snuff bottles. She was examining them and dropped them and they shattered. Between her and Patrick, and Joey's incontinence, I think they've caused several thousand dollars in property damage over the past few days.

We're clearing the table when I hear a car pulling into the driveway and then the slamming of a car door. Then the doorbell rings. The dog starts yapping.

"Joey, shut up!" say Patrick and Terri in unison. Joey doesn't.

The bell rings again, the interval too short for polite doorbell etiquette. Josh is texting and ignores it. The rest of us exchange glances. Joey yaps more, until Patrick nails him with a meatball.

"Clean that up," says Josh, still texting.

The bell rings a third time. Joey can't decide between yapping and eating the meatball.

"Someone gonna get that?" asks Terri.

"Isaac, get the door," says Josh.

I have to pass by him to exit the kitchen. He's focused on his texting, and I slow just enough to be able to do a flyby read of the screen. He's writing, *If I do it, will you show up?*

Do what, I wonder, *And who is he talking to?*

On the way to the front entrance I can see out the picture windows in the living room. There's a massive Chevrolet Suburban filling up our driveway, parked crooked, the sort of car that makes my parents say, *There ought to be a law.*

When I get to the front door the Suburban makes sense. There's a man standing there who could only drive that sort of car: he's big with a gut, and he's got buzzed hair with a flattop, a scowly, craggy face, and overall he looks about as unpleasant as they make human beings.

"Is this the Kaplan residence?" he says the instant I open the door.

I blink at him. "Yes."

"Your daddy home?"

He's clipped and unsmiling.

"Um . . . can I ask what this is in regards to?"

224

That's what my mom says when people we don't know call or come to the door. It doesn't have the effect I'm hoping for. Instead the man seems annoyed.

"Just get your daddy, please."

We've never used Mommy/Daddy in this house, and the way he says it irks me, like I'm his kid to order around. Then before I do anything his eye line shifts upward and his expression changes slightly, like he's surprised and trying to hide it and recalculating the situation.

"Can I help you?" says Josh from behind me.

"Your daddy home?" says the man again, for some reason trying the same tone with Josh—which, well, mistake.

"Isaac, go away," Josh says, and sort of shovels me behind him with one big hand. I take a few steps back but linger.

"My 'daddy'?" says Josh, flat.

"Yes. Is he home? I'd like to speak with him."

"Who are you?"

"That's not your concern. Can I speak with—"

"It is my concern, seeing as how you're standing at my front door."

"Well, seeing as how you probably don't own the house, it's not your front door—it's your daddy's. Can you get him, please?"

"He's not here. Who are you?"

"Name's Tim Phillips."

Oh. No.

Josh shrugs. "Great. Who are you."

"*Tim Phillips.* Senior. Tim Junior is my son. I take it you're the idiot who hit him?"

225

Of course. Of course. Tim Junior finally spilled the beans, overcame his fear of Josh and told his dad everything, and now he's here and it's all catching up to Josh, and he's in huge trouble.

"Oh," says Josh, nodding. If Josh thinks he's in huge trouble, he's not showing it. "Tim Junior. I get it now. No wonder he's such a shit."

My jaw drops open. Tim Senior's face reddens. It literally turns red. His hands drop off his hips. Josh stares back at him, absolutely calm.

"What did you just say?" manages Tim Senior finally.

"I said," says Josh, exaggerating his enunciation, each word a separate entity, "your son is a *shit*. And now that I see you, I understand why, because you look like a shit too."

I don't know why I didn't expect this. I should have. From Tim Senior's expression I'm guessing that he didn't expect this either.

Long moment of the two of them looking at each other. More recalculating and temper management from Tim Senior, who is somehow nodding and shaking his head at the same time, like he's trying to draw figure eights with his nose. Then he says, "You got a mouth on you, don't you."

Josh doesn't respond, just returns his gaze, arms crossed.

"You're real brave, aren't you, beating up on some little kid," says Tim Senior, trying to regain the high ground.

"Your shit of a kid is real brave, ganging up on my little brother with all his shit friends."

"What are you talking about?"

"You teach him to do that? I bet you did. You know something? I never once ganged up on anybody or got in a fight with anybody who didn't want to fight. Ever. But you, I can tell, you're just a shit bully, like your shit kid."

I can see Senior's jaw muscles. His fists are clenched.

"You're lucky I got a back injury," he says to Josh.

"Wow, I really dodged a bullet there," says Josh, mocking him, and it's worse because you can see that they both somehow know the truth: Even in his prime Tim Senior would have gotten his head handed to him. Josh is smiling evilly now. He's enjoying himself, rubbing Tim Senior's nose in it.

I'm going to be honest: I'm starting to enjoy it too.

At this moment I love Josh. At this moment there is actually justice in the universe. *Here, shit bully, meet my asshole brother, Josh. Have fun.*

Tim Senior isn't backing down, but he's not saying anything else. The two of them are just facing each other in a standoff, Josh still smiling. I'm smiling too.

But then there's a subtle shift, Josh's expression darkening as he remembers something.

"You know what?" he says, quieter now. "Your shit kid called my brother a 'stupid Jew.' Who taught him that?"

The instant I hear that tone all the fun drains out of it.

Run, Mr. Phillips, I nearly say out loud. *Go now.*

"I don't know what you're talking about," says Senior.

Don't talk. Go. Now.

"Really," says Josh, in that same quiet tone. He's uncrossing his arms. All that pacing back and forth in the cage, and now someone has wandered too close to the bars. *I'm going to kill your dad,* he said to Tim Junior, and I honestly think it's about to happen.

"Josh," I say. "Josh . . ."

"Is that how you talk at home?" says Josh. "You got a problem with Jews? 'Cause here's your chance." He's now stepping toward Senior, who is backing up, feeling with his feet behind him to find the stairs off the front porch.

"Hey, I got no problem with anyone," says Senior, his hands coming up, palms out. He *really* didn't expect this.

"Yeah? Well, I got a problem with you," says Josh, and I can already see what's going to happen the instant before it does, the jarring shove that sends Tim Senior backwards to trip over the low evergreens that border the front path and land on the lawn on his ass. He has barely stopped skidding when I'm turning and sprinting back to the kitchen.

"Patrick. Patrick!"

He's at the table, reading one of Josh's gun magazines. Terri and Lisa have moved to the back porch, Terri braiding Lisa's hair.

"What?"

"Get out here, quick!"

I have to pull him out of his chair and then push him along the hallway to the front door and out onto the front porch.

"Oh, damn," says Patrick when he takes in the scene, "he's gonna kick that guy's ass."

They're in the middle of the lawn, Tim Senior alternately back-pedaling and trying to get around Josh, who keeps moving to cut off access to the driveway. Tim Senior has a grass stain smeared on the back of his pants and on his shirt. He has stopped talking, everything happening too fast for him. He looks frightened, finally understanding exactly what sort of creature he's dealing with.

"Josh, stop it," I say, "stop it!"

Josh is not stopping it.

"I think you got Jew issues," Josh is saying. Shove. "I think you're a shit bigot." Shove. They're big grown men, but it's just like on the schoolyard, the shoving thing, one kid the aggressor, the other moving backwards and trying to look brave, bringing his own arms up and sort of pushing back at the same time he's shoved.

"Josh, stop it!" I say again.

Whap. A taunting, glancing whap on the side of the head.

"Damn," says Patrick.

"You have to stop him!"

"What?"

"Stop him!"

"I'm supposed to stop Josh?"

"Yes!"

WHAP! Josh smacks Tim Senior again. He's toying with him, humiliating him, and it's a tossup whether he's going to be satisfied with these relatively harmless blows or if he's going to unload on him for real.

"Patrick, do something," I plead.

Patrick scratches his head. "Yo, Josh," he says, not very loud.

I get behind Patrick and shove him in Josh's direction. "Get in there. Stop him!"

Patrick sighs and walks cautiously over to the two of them, slowing even more as he gets close. Then he does the hockey ref thing, waiting for an opening and then stepping between them and hugging Josh and walking him backwards and doing his best to create space between the two.

"C'mon, dude, leave it. Leave it," he says while Josh continues to jaw at Tim Senior, tossing out more schoolyard prefight epithets and making a few efforts to get past Patrick. He's still between Senior and his car, though, and each time Senior tries to go around him Josh moves to block him.

Tim Senior, meanwhile, is pointing at Josh with one finger while fishing in his back pocket with the other hand.

"You think you're tough?" Senior is saying. "You're gonna be real sorry about this, tough guy. I got lots of friends on the police force," says Senior.

"I bet you do," says Josh. He then tells Senior exactly what sort of friendship he thinks it is, a particularly intimate and unsavory type.

"Oh, that's clever. That's real clever," says Senior, and now he's pulling out his cell phone and trying to dial while still keeping an eye on Josh.

"Yeah, the big guy thinks he's tough," says Senior, punching numbers—three numbers, to be exact. "You can show how tough you are when the cops come and Taser you." The phone is at his ear. "I'll be standing here, laughing."

He's right, of course. Now the tide has reversed and is flowing in the other direction.

"They deal with assholes like you every day of the week, big guy. Every day of the week," says Senior, and Josh is hesitating. "Yeah, that's right," says Senior, nodding in satisfaction, "you're gonna see just how tough you are."

He's back in control. Josh *is* in huge trouble, because this is how grownups deal with situations like this: They don't have fistfights, they call the cops and the lawyers. "I thought I could settle this with an adult conversation with your folks," says Senior, now looking at his phone like he's not getting a signal, "but I guess"—he redials—"we'll just . . . do this the hard way."

Then someone roughly pushes past me.

"Hey," says Terri. "HEY!" she says again, and she's got that voice that could penetrate a reinforced nuclear bunker and kill everyone inside. Senior turns.

"I *know* you!" says Terri.

The look of horror on Senior's face indicates he really, *really* didn't expect this.

"I see you in the club all the time, you pervert!" says Terri.

"I don't know what you're talking about," he says, but anyone who says that line the way he says it knows *exactly* what the other person is talking about.

"Oh, yeah? How'd you like me to tell your wife what you do in the club?"

"Now, listen," he says, but she's already in his face, crowding him.

"You know what we think of bastards like you, guys who are always groping the girls?"

"Look—"

"You know what you are?" she says. "You're a . . ."

It's astonishing. I don't think I've ever produced a sentence that long and complex in my entire life, and it's pure obscenities, a nonstop chain-gun explosion of abuse at full volume. I look around, fearful/hopeful that the neighbors are watching, and yes, of course, there is Mr. Olsen, standing in his front yard, not even trying to disguise his fascination. Tim Senior is trying to interrupt Terri, trying to get a word in edgewise. "Now just hold on a minute—"

Fire-hose power stream of insults.

Now he's switching to holding up two hands to placate her: "I can see you're upset."

Increased intensity of insults.

Attempted counterattack: "You listen to me!"

Insults reach white-hot fever pitch.

And then he's just turning tail and fleeing toward his car as she dogs him at every step, still going, determined to drown him in her ire.

It's all a farce now, an episode of *Cops* playing out right there on our front yard. It's going to be okay! Terri saved Josh! There's no way Senior got that 911 call off. He's going to drive away, and we'll go back in and it's all going to be fine! Patrick is laughing. I'm laughing. I think even Mr. Olsen is laughing. It's all fine.

But then Senior kind of pushes Terri away, and Josh escapes from Patrick and strides across the lawn and grabs Mr. Phillips by the shoulder and spins him around and gives him a lightning punch in the stomach.

"OOOoohh!" says Tim Phillips Senior, or something like that, but I can't hear it, because it's blotted out by a harsh staticky squawk coming from the police car that is pulling up to the curb.

CHAPTER FORTY-ONE

TERRI PROVES HER WORTH

MERIT BADGE: LEGAL KNOWLEDGE

Important lesson, learned just this very instant: When the cops show up to your house, do *not* run toward them waving your hands as they're climbing out of their squad car and say, "Please, you don't need to Taser my brother!"

It's immediately apparent that my request has had the exact opposite effect from what I was hoping. They exchange a look, and one of them reaches to undo the snap on his Taser holster.

"Go back inside, please," says one of them.

There's no way they got here this quickly from Tim Senior's call. It had to be a neighbor. It's the two officers from the day of the fire: generic Minnesota faces, almost identical in their blandness, except one has a white patch in his cropped blond hair.

"Inside, please," repeats White Patch.

Instead I run back across the front yard to Josh and say, "Josh, do *not* resist arrest," because he's got that look.

Patrick has a different look, a completely blank expression, the sort you must learn to produce after years of being stopped by the police. Terri is still shrieking at Tim Phillips Senior, who is bent double, one hand on his gut, the other resting on the side of his SUV for support. I'm praying that Lisa is still on the back porch.

"What's going on, Josh?" says the other cop, the wrestling fan from the other day. White Patch is talking into his radio.

"What the hell do you think is going on, you dumb bastard!" bellows Tim Senior, who I don't think is making any friends today. "This sonofabitch assaulted me!"

"Josh, can you come over here for a moment?" says Wrestling Fan. It's not really a request. Both of them have their batons out. Josh hasn't budged.

"That bastard *hit* me!" screams Senior again, his voice breaking on "hit."

"The EMTs are on their way," says the tall one.

"I don't need any goddamn EMTs, I need you to arrest him!"

"Josh," says Wrestling Fan, "I need you to put your hands on your head and turn around. Josh, hands on your head and turn around. There's an easy way and a hard way."

"Josh," I hiss. "Don't. I can see what you're thinking."

There are other neighbors out, watching. A car has slowed.

"He hit my kid, too!" says Senior, who is now standing mostly straight up.

"We'll talk to you in a moment, sir," says White Patch. They're walking slowly toward Josh. Wrestling Fan has put away the baton and drawn the Taser.

"Josh!" says Wrestling Fan, Taser trained on Josh. "Hands on your head and turn around! Now! NOW!"

Strategy. *Think! Chessboard! Consequence mind! What would Josh respond to?*

"Josh, if you resist, they'll Taser you. They'll beat you up with their batons!"

Nothing. He's still keyed up, not hearing me.

"Josh, if you get arrested, Mom and Dad will kill you!"

Of course that's not going to work. *Think!*

"Who's going to take care of us?"

A glance at me, then he refocuses on the cops. He does a little neck roll, a move I've seen him do right before a wrestling match, except this time he's warming up to a felony.

"Josh! If you get arrested, I'll tell Lisa that you're a drug dealer and that you've been dealing drugs to little kids."

This gets him to actually look at me.

"I swear to God, I will," I say.

He lets them cuff him and put him in the back of the patrol car. They call things in on the radio, and an ambulance shows up, only to have Tim Senior shout the EMTs away. He's furious, screaming at the cops, saying, "A fifth-degree misdemeanor? A citation? What the hell does that mean! He assaulted me!"

"Looks to me like he punched you in the stomach," says Officer Thomke, the wrestling fan. "Once." Both he and Federson, the one with the white patch, have been using their professionally polite tones, disconnecting their mouths from their emotions.

"He resisted arrest!"

"You know what?" says Federson, writing something in his note-pad. "I actually know what resisting arrest is. And you can be sure we would have handled this pretty differently if he'd resisted arrest, 'kay?"

"Now, you said something about him hitting your kid?" asks Thomke.

Blink and you'd miss it—Tim Senior glances over at Terri, who is watching from about ten feet away. She raises an eyebrow.

"He hit your kid?" repeats Thomke.

"No . . . forget it," says Senior.

Another lesson learned: If you punch someone in front of a cop in Hennepin County, they don't arrest you and take you to jail unless they think you're planning to commit another crime. Instead they give you a citation for a fifth-degree misdemeanor, just like Tim Senior was complaining about. You have to go to court, though.

We watch from the porch as the cops talk to Josh. Terri comforts Lisa, who finally came outside to see what was going on and is now crying and clinging to her adopted older sister. Tim Senior has left, screeching off down the road, the cops looking at each other and shaking their heads. Now they've taken Josh out of the squad car and uncuffed him, and Federson is writing out a ticket. The mood seems very different: I can't hear them, but from their movements, Thomke seems to be querying Josh about wrestling techniques. At one point Josh even demonstrates on an eager Thomke, grabbing one of his legs to illustrate the finer points of a takedown, both Federson and Thomke nodding—*Ah, now we get it.*

"See that?" says Patrick. "That's the thing about your boy. He knows how to make friends with people."

"When he's not punching them," I mutter.

There are handshakes all around, and then Josh walks toward us across the lawn. Thomke calls after him: "You're gonna make that court date, right, Josh? And stay out of trouble?" Josh twists and gives him a little half salute/half wave in confirmation.

"Josh, I'm dead serious about this," says Thomke. "You get into trouble again before the arraignment, even something small, and I guarantee you're gonna end up in jail."

"Got it."

"Gonna behave?"

"Scout's honor."

"Okay, then."

As we watch the cops drive off, Josh's phone pings. He digs it out in a hurry and reads it. Whatever it says, it transforms him, fills him with joy. It's a type of smile I don't remember seeing from him before, a moment of pure, unguarded happiness and excitement, like a kid who was expecting coal but instead got a pony.

"What?" says Patrick.

"Remember that party you were talking about?" Josh says to me.

"The one we're not supposed to have?" I say. "That party?"

"Yep. We're going to have it."

CHAPTER FORTY-TWO

PARTY PREP

"Josh, you heard those cops. You can't get in trouble again."

"What trouble? What's going to happen?"

It's about an hour after the cops left our house. We're in the parking lot of a liquor store. He's placing the second large keg into the trunk, the car sinking visibly under the weight.

"Uh, you're buying forty-five gallons of beer?"

"So?"

"You're underage?"

"Not according to my ID I'm not."

Patrick is grunting, trying to lift the third keg. Josh grabs one of the handles and they put it in the trunk. Josh starts to tie the trunk lid closed.

"Is this part of the Quest, Josh?" I ask.

"Sure, yeah. You're learning how much beer to get for a house party."

"Josh, Mom and Dad—"

"Aren't home."

"You signed the contract."

"The situation has evolved."

I know how it evolved. I did a little more electronic espionage, snooping on Josh's phone. There was a string of text messages between him and Trish.

TRISH: *You could have a party.*

JOSH: *Not like youd come.*

TRISH: *I might.*

JOSH: *You wont get a drink w/me but youd come to a house party.*

TRISH: *Maybe.*

And so on, back and forth, until the sentence that I saw him composing earlier: *If I do it, will you show up?*

And the magic, golden-smile-inducing reply:

TRISH: *Yes.*

So we're at the liquor store. I don't know why, but I try again: "Josh, you can't have a party."

"Why not?"

"Things could happen. Things could go wrong."

"Like what? It will just be a few people. It will be fine."

CHAPTER FORTY-THREE

AN INVITATION

I still wasn't feeling great, so I spent the next day at home too, mostly napping. When I woke up this morning Josh was still asleep. I'm not sure why, but I went for a short run and did some pushups and sit-ups. Also, I actually studied my haphtarah by myself after last night's beer run, because Josh seemed pretty distracted. I'm not sure if the Quest is still on or not.

I decide on an old pair of jeans and a T-shirt from the summer soccer league. I'm not employing any product. Other than my haircut, there is no trace of the Lesley-influenced New Isaac. All right, I am wearing boxer briefs, but no one is going to know about that unless things get really weird.

The scratches on my face have scabbed over into three semi-parallel lines running down my cheek. Like Ged from *A Wizard of Earthsea,* with the scars on his face from the nameless black beast that he summoned from the lonely outer darkness.

I ride my bike to school, timing it so that I arrive just before homeroom starts, meaning there will be fewer kids outside or walking through the halls, and those who aren't in classrooms will be concentrating on getting to them as quickly as possible. Before I step through the doors I take a moment for a deep breath. *You got nothin',* says Patrick. *Right. You got nothin'.*

The school is a foreign country. It feels like a century since I've been here. I walk through the halls, past the lunchroom, the gym, the trophy case, and I wonder if it will ever seem normal again. It's like one of those optical illusions, where once you see it one way you can't go back to seeing it the other. But it's not the school that has changed, it's me.

The first test: homeroom. But Paul isn't there. Maybe he's out sick. I sigh in relief. I sit and bury my head in a book. If people are looking at me, I don't know it. When the bell rings and I'm walking out, Mr. Leopold pulls me aside.

"You all right? Not like you to be absent."

I give him the note that Josh signed for me. Mr. Leopold reads it.

"You feeling better?"

"Yes."

"What happened here?" he says, wiggling his finger at his own face, asking about the condition of mine. A nameless black beast from the outer darkness is what happened.

"Nothing. Just wrestling with my brother."

I make it through the next two periods without incident. No one pays any attention to me. I don't spot the Assholes. I don't have any classes with Paul or Steve or Danny today, and I don't intend to seek them out at lunch.

It's right before third period that I spot Danny. I'm just turning away from my locker, and there he is, walking straight toward me. He looks determined.

"Hi, Danny," I say when he gets close.

He punches me in the face.

In the forehead, really. It makes a bonking noise, sort of a mini-version of what it sounded like when Josh elbowed me. I reach my hand up and touch the impact point, surprised. Danny has taken a step back and is standing there, his fists clenched, his eyes wide, looking as surprised as me. And scared. And in pain. I think he hurt his hand on my forehead.

We're both nearly motionless, except for me rubbing the spot where he hit me. He is breathing hard, waiting for me to make the next move. So I do.

"My brother is having a party tonight," I say. "Wanna come?"

CHAPTER FORTY-FOUR

THE PARTY

MERIT BADGES: TOO NUMEROUS TO COUNT.

The floor is a living thing under my feet, vibrating, pulsing like a heartbeat under the collective weight of the ten thousand people packed into our home, all those individuals blending into some sort of supercreature bouncing ecstatically to the music.

"This is a fucking awesome party!" bellows Patrick, his words less comprehensible through hearing than through lip reading, the music overwhelming his voice.

I'm used to his enthusiastic speaking style, and I've got my mouth shut and eyes reflexively squinted. Danny and Steve and Paul are just meeting him now, though, so I'm pretty sure they caught some spray, especially with the way that they're goggling at his appearance, mouths agape.

"Patrick!" I bellow up at him. "These are my friends, Danny, Paul, and Steve!"

"What's up, Motherfuc*kahs!!*"—the last syllable in a ghetto falsetto. High-fives that nearly take each of our arms off, a "Yeah, dude!" accompanying each slap, and then he bends and grabs Steve's head like a melon and mashes his forehead against Steve's in a primitive greeting, giving him three gentle-ish head butts. "Yeah!" says Patrick as he's doing it. "Gimme some *pain!*"

Then he straightens and dance-squeezes his way through the throng and is lost to sight, his Mohawk scraping the ceiling.

"What the hell was that?" shouts Danny, wiping punk-rock spittle off his face.

"That's just Patrick," I shout back.

The Four Geekateers, together again.

After Danny punched me and I invited him to the party, we went for a long walk around the school. And we talked. I apologized for hitting him. He apologized for hitting me. We agreed we were even. I told him a little bit about my adventures the past few days, with plenty of lingering on the strip club part of the story.

Mostly we had one of those awkward but hopeful talks you have after a bad argument, where you're both hideously aware of the issue but you're intentionally avoiding it and doggedly talking about other things, giving each other verbal pat-pats, both of you smiling and laughing just a bit too hard because you're so desperate to get things back to Normal.

The three of them showed up around nine o'clock, as the party was starting to pick up speed, dumping their bikes on the front lawn. I hadn't yet talked to Paul or Steve, and there was a good ten seconds where no one said anything when I opened the front door. Then Paul pointed at my Ramones shirt and said, "You are so gay."

"*Sooo* gay," seconded Steve, and I knew everything was going to be all right. Things are right back to Normal.

But in the back of my head there's a little voice telling me that everything has changed, that it will never be quite the same.

A new song starts, louder than the last, everyone cheering. So much for "a few people": there are cars parked in our driveway, cars halfway on our lawn, cars up and down and probably around the block. There are people crammed into every square foot of the upstairs, the downstairs, the backyard. The musics are loud — *musics* plural, because there are at least three competing sources *thumpa thumpa thump*ing against each other in an epic battle for dominance: the stereo in the living room, a portable boom box in the basement, and another one out back where the kegs are. I saw Josh out there earlier in the center of a cheering mob, hoisting one of the 170-pound kegs above his head and drinking directly from the nozzle that someone held in his mouth. Somebody may call the cops because of the noise, but it's not going to be Mr. Olsen. He's in the sardine-packed kitchen, beer in hand, big grin on his face, chatting up one of Terri's stripper friends.

Lisa is already asleep in her room. She can sleep through anything. She slept through a thunderstorm in which lightning hit the tree outside and hailstones shattered her window.

It's so packed, all of our other neighbors might be here, too, as far as I know. It's hard to describe the crowd: imagine some sort of high-energy collision between twelve very different types of nightclubs, resulting in an entirely novel and unstable element. There are hipsters, and young businessfolk, and punk-rock friends of Patrick's who look like they're going to rob the businessfolk, and stripper-girlfriends of Terri who look like they're going to seduce and rob everyone, and small solid men who look like the Mexicans who work behind the scenes in restaurants, and college students, and high school students, and muscly dudes who must have been on my brother's various sports teams, and then just random people that I can't categorize.

And then a handful of scrawny, pimply junior high kids, scurrying around like rodents under the dinosaurs' feet.

"It's not the static weight, it's the shock load," Steve is saying to Paul, the two of them still arguing over the structural integrity of the living room and whether there will be PARTY TRAGEDY headlines in the paper tomorrow. "Look at the amount of displacement of the floor," he adds, indicating the worrying manner in which the floor is flexing under everyone's weight.

My peeps.

"Isaac! Hey! You hear me?" Danny grabbing my arm, pulling my attention back from scanning the crowd. "I said, check out the tits on that girl!" He's indicating one of Terri's friends. Appreciative noises from Steve and Paul.

"What? Yeah, nice," I say. It seems cheap to tell them that I've already checked them out at the club, and without any fabric intervening between my eyeballs and her nipples. I go back to my distracted crowd scanning.

"You waiting for someone?" asks Paul.

"No."

I am. Partially, I'm waiting for the police to show up and drag Josh away.

But I'm also waiting for Lesley. Not because I want to see her. I don't.

Danny grabs my elbow again. "Isaac, check it out!"

Eric Weinberg. He's wandering amid the forest of larger folks, searching for a familiar face.

"What is *he* doing here?" says Steve.

"I invited him," I say.

I did. I sent him an e-mail and then called him and then texted him from Josh's phone. I didn't think he'd actually come, but I'm not unhappy he's here. It seems somehow right that he would be.

He spots us and holds up a hand in greeting, makes his way over to us. When he reaches us I notice that he's got a plastic cup of beer in the other hand.

"Hey," he says, or shouts, when he's close. Heys all around. It's loud enough that we all have an excuse to just sort of stand there without talking, pretending we're observing the party all around us, which is what we do for a stretch. Then there's a pause in the music.

"Is that a beer?" says Danny.

"It's a party, right?" Eric says, and takes a cautious sip. It's his magic item to regain entry to the world, I realize, his way of one-upping us all: *Long have I walked the dark realm of Loserdom,* he's saying, but I return now, beer in hand, cooler than you all.

"Yeah, where's the beer?" says Steve to me. Eric's gambit is working.

"Guys—look!" says Danny.

No.

Sarah Blumgartner.

No.

"Oh, *snap!*"

"Damn!"

"Oooh, your girl is here!"

"I didn't invite her!" I say, to jeers and derision, and then she has spotted us and is heading over.

"Someone's getting laid tonight!" says Danny, elbowing me. More hilarity.

"Hi, guys!" she says.

If Eric was out before, he's in now, the boys instantly bonded into a unit by the arrival of Sarah, the enemy.

"Hey, Isaac," she says.

"Hi."

"Are Theresa and Erica here?" she asks.

No, and you know *they're not, because I didn't invite them, and I didn't invite you, either.*

"Haven't seen them."

"Weird — they said they were coming."

"She's all yours, big guy," Danny whispers in my ear.

"We're gonna go get some beers," says Steve, indicating a group that clearly doesn't include me and Sarah.

"I'm coming," I say.

"I'll come," she says.

"It's okay — we'll get you some," says Paul, and they all vanish, leaving me with her.

So there we are.

"Everyone's been talking about this party," she says, by way of excusing her presence. "It's like the whole school knows about it."

"Huh," I say. I'm wishing the music would start again.

"Are you all right? What happened here?" She reaches out and touches my black eye. I shy away, not hiding my annoyance.

"Nothing."

"Haven't seen you in school."

"Haven't been there much."

She nods. I can see her expression changing. Whatever hopes and dreams she had when she came are meeting the hard wall of reality, which is that I don't like her. I know I'm being insufferable and rude, but I'm angry that she's here, that she decided to invade this celebration.

"Okay," she says. "Well . . ."

Then I see Lesley.

She's just across the room, watching us. When our eyes meet she smiles and waves to me.

I reach out and grab Sarah's hand.

"C'mon," I say.

"What?"

"Let's go. Let's go get a beer."

I pull her away and we dodge our way through the bodies just as the music is starting up again.

We swim our way through the various strata of the party until we're out back, and wait our turn at the keg. She goes right at the beer, drinking it like she's done it a hundred times before, and looks at me expectantly, so I drink, too. She's talking to me, and I'm nodding and responding, but my brain isn't really engaged. I'm on full alert for Lesley, hoping to see her again. Hoping she'll see me with Sarah. The backyard is far less populated than inside, the crowd densest near the house. I'm nodding, yessing, noing, looking for Lesley, sipping my beer from its soft plastic cup.

"Want another?" asks Sarah, her cup empty. I realize mine is, too. I feel a bit dizzy, but warm and almost happy.

"Sure," I say.

We stand and sip our beers and talk about bar mitzvahs and math class and the blood red Jell-O mold her mother makes at Passover dinner and what classes we'll be taking next year. I've known her forever. She's not a bad person, really, and not so annoying outside the context of school. My mother says she thinks Sarah is beautiful, which, uh, no, but then again she doesn't seem that hideous at this moment.

She's standing very close to me, which makes sense, because it's loud out here, too, and hard to hear each other. Every once in a while she reaches out and puts a hand on my lower back when she leans in to listen to me, and I don't mind it. At one point she says, "Wanna go inside?" Lesley's in there, I think, so I say yes. On the way in I catch a glimpse of Josh in the midst of everyone. Someone is talking to him, but Josh isn't hearing, his attention focused on texting something, brow furrowed.

Sarah and I end up in the packed basement, gravitating toward a dark corner. People are talking around us, but I feel hidden in our spot. I don't see Danny or Paul or the rest of them. Sarah's standing even closer now, and her hand is on me more often. Once or twice I mirror her gesture, my hand on her back, both our heads inclined toward each other, nearly touching.

Lesley. She's nearby, watching me. Watching us. I'm midsentence when I see her, my eyes flicking over briefly, then returning to Sarah. She's leaning in close to listen to me, her eyes luminous and full and never leaving my face. Aware of Lesley watching, I lean just a little bit closer and Sarah responds and I put my chin up just a bit and she responds and her hand reaches out to rest on my forearm and we're closer and we're kissing.

CHAPTER FORTY-FIVE

BACKFIRE

MERIT BADGE: FIRST KISS

One of those moments when everything changes. One of those moments when you realize you've crossed a border. Forever.

I'm kissing Sarah Blumgartner. We're kissing. It's happening. Ten seconds ago I was the Isaac who had never really kissed anyone. I am now a different Isaac, an Isaac who has kissed someone. *Is* kissing someone.

Her lips are soft. She opens her mouth and her tongue is in my mouth and it's the most amazing thing I've ever experienced. Her hands are caressing my face. Her breath smells good. I pull her in close, but not too close, because I have a sudden hard-on and don't want her to feel it, so our chests are touching but not our lower bodies, her breasts pressed against me.

We kiss. We kiss more. We kiss and kiss and kiss, tilting our heads back and forth like they do in the movies, noses first on one side, then on the other, mashing our faces together. Part of me is saying, *This is incredible.* Why did it take me so long to do this with Sarah? Sarah is smart and funny and cute, and we could have been doing this for a long time. Another part is saying, *I really hope Lesley is watching*.

I disengage to check. Lesley's still there. She *is* watching. It's almost like she was waiting for me to look again. I'm hoping to see jealousy, a frown, anger. But what she does is *smile* at me. It's a maternal, I'm-happy-for-you smile, a condescending pat on the head of a smile. A farewell of a smile. Then she turns to go.

I realize that Sarah is talking to me, saying my name.

"Isaac? Isaac."

"What?"

"You okay?"

"I'm fine."

But I'm not. I'm furious.

"What happened? Do you want to stop? Isaac?"

"What?"

"Do you want to—"

"I want," I say, "to pierce my ear."

"Pierce your—"

"Yes. I want to pierce my ear. I want *you* to."

"Me? Now?"

"Yes. Will you do it?"

She starts to laugh. "Okay."

I pull her into the crowded kitchen and spot Josh standing against the wall near the center island where the stove is. And yes, there she is, Lesley, talking to him, her hand resting on his arm. He's upset about something, but isn't he always?

I steer Sarah so that we walk near them, making sure that I don't glance over at Lesley as we pass, then park us just a few feet away.

"Which ear should I pierce?" I say, loud. "Which ear should I pierce?"

"The left one," says Sarah, but I'm worried that Josh and Lesley might not have heard me, so I say it again, louder. "Which ear should I pierce?"

"Left! The left one!!"

I position her by the stove, just a few yards from Lesley and Josh. I tell her to wait, then shoulder through the crowd to the corkboard on the wall and remove the pushpin that's holding up the NO PARTIES sign. Back to Sarah, handing her the pin, turning on the gas flame.

"Here, sterilize it," I say.

"You sure you want to do this?"

"Yes!" I leave her again, going to the pantry to get a potato. When I return, Sarah is holding the needle over the flame, the tip glowing red. I know Lesley has noticed me now, know that she's watching me and Sarah, her eyes leaving Josh now and then to glance over distractedly.

"Here? Like this?" I say, holding the potato up behind my ear. "And then you just jab it through?" I motion with my other hand, pantomiming it, aware that I'm overdoing it for Lesley and Josh's benefit.

"Don't you want to ice it?" says Sarah. "Make it numb?"

"No, just do it," I say.

"Are you sure?"

"Do it! Just do it!"

She's grimacing, wrinkling her nose, suddenly girly and squeamish. Out of the corner of my eye I can tell that Josh has turned to see what Lesley is looking at. They're both watching. Now is the time. Now. Sarah is hesitating, lining up the needle, pausing, aiming, pausing, saying, "Ewww! Ewwww!"

"Do it! Go!"

Sarah makes one more *ewwww* sound and jabs the pin into my ear.

There. Done. Good.

Then: "Ow, *shit!*"

"Oh my God!" says Sarah, "I totally messed that up!"

The line at the bathroom is long, several songs' worth of waiting. My hand is cupped over the side of my head so that other people can't see the pin still hanging out of my ear.

When I finally get in I lock the door and go directly to the mirror. The pin is sticking straight out of my ear, about a half-inch north of where it should be. It's in the cartilage, the tip barely protruding through the other side. I grit my teeth and yank it out — *"Ow, shit!"* again — then squeeze out a few drops of blood and wash it with soap and water and finally dump rubbing alcohol over the whole area, someone pounding on the door the whole time.

When I go out again, I can't find Sarah. I can't find her, I can't find my peeps, I can't find Josh, I can't find Lesley. The party seems to have intensified and grown more wild, more dangerous. Like people have taken the part of them that makes them obey all the Thou Shalts and Thou Shalt Nots and drowned that part in alcohol and put it away in a box for later. I wasn't scared of it before, but I'm scared of it now, my buzz totally gone.

I see Sarah. She's there across the room. I start walking toward her. *Wait.* She's not alone. She's with Eric. Eric Weinberg. They're close. They're — *no. No.* They're kissing. She's *kissing* him. She was kissing *me* ten minutes ago, and now she's kissing *Eric.* Eric! I had Lesley, and then I lost her, and then I had Sarah, and now I've lost her, too, and now I'm nothing.

While I'm trying to take that in and figure out what I'm going to feel when the shock wears off I see Josh coming toward me, looking even more upset than before, and Lesley is right behind him, harrying him. He passes right by me like I'm not there, and she does too and she's saying, "What's wrong? Trish busy?"

I take all those awful emotions, the ones that were about to slam into me and crush me, and put them on pause.

Josh stops in his tracks, close enough to me that I could almost reach out and touch him.

"Why?" he says. "Why do you have to start with me?"

"Oh, no, did she stand you up?" She's still smiling as she says it, but it's brittle and mean, and she sounds drunk and slurry. I don't move, not wanting to call attention to myself. "This big party's all for her, isn't it, and she didn't even show up?" says Lesley. "What a surprise!"

"You know what I don't need right now? I don't need you giving me crap."

He pushes past her and starts to walk back the way he came, and she follows.

"Do you know how many guys she's with?" she says loudly as she walks after him. "Do you? Listen to me!"

She grabs his elbow and he shakes her off, tries to keep walking.

"She doesn't love you! She never loved you!"

He reverses direction again, coming back toward me, attempting to lose her.

"You know it's true!"

He stalks past me and goes down the hallway toward his room, Lesley still in pursuit, and I fall in line behind them. He goes back into his room and slams the door shut to escape, but Lesley pushes it back open and goes in. I can hear her saying something, crying now. I follow and stand just outside the door, unable to resist. It's the key to everything, the mystery, all to be revealed now, and I can't miss it. Through the half-open door I can see Josh pacing back and forth, hands pressed against his head like he's trying to hold his skull together. Lesley is sloppy crying, screaming at him: "I love you! *I* love you! And you screw me and pretend it doesn't matter! She *never* loved you!"

He's seated on his bed now, hunched over, still holding his head.

"And now you're just running away, running away and doing this stupid thing . . ."

"They were all assholes anyway."

"Who? Everyone at college? Why, because they didn't buy your act and didn't give a shit about you being such a tough guy? Who cares? That's not why I love you!"

He's shaking his head now, trying to shake her words away from his ears.

"I love you, Josh! I *love* you! Why do you have to be so stupid?"

She looks so drunk and small and needy. I'm ashamed for her, embarrassed to be watching, but I can't stop.

"Why can't you answer me!" she says to him, and he suddenly

springs up from the bed and I have to step aside as he storms out of the room.

"Great! Great! Go get yourself blown up in Afghanistan!" she screams after him. I'm not sure which direction to go in, to follow him back into the party or go to Lesley, who's lying on the floor, bawling. I go to her and kneel down, touching her tentatively on the shoulder.

"Are you okay?" I say, even though it's pretty clear she's not.

"Why'see goddabeli'thah!!" she says, or something like that, impossible to tell through the alcohol and the tears. "Why!!?"

"Lesley, what did you mean about Afghanistan?"

"She doesn't fuggin' love him!"

"What did you mean about Afghanistan?!"

"He's not going bag to shchool, he's joining the fuggin' Marines!"

While I'm frozen there in shock, thinking, *Oh, shit,* and also, *Of course he is,* Patrick leans into the room, his nose bleeding, and says, "Yo, Isaac, you gotta go talk some sense into your brother."

CHAPTER FORTY-SIX

FLAMEOUT

MERIT BADGE: HONEST-TO-GOD BAR BRAWL

"Move your fucking car!" Josh is bellowing as I run out the front door. The blond-haired guy he's talking to looks terrified, but he's saying, "Josh, I don't think you should be driving."

"He said he's going to the bar," says Patrick as we racewalk toward the driveway. Josh's car is parked in front of the garage, the blond-haired guy's car right behind it.

"Move. Your. Car," says Josh again.

"Josh!" I say, coming up to them.

"Go back inside," he says.

"Josh, everyone's still here. There's still a party going on."

"Go back inside, Isaac."

Other people have filed out of the house to see the show.

"Josh, if you drive, the cops will arrest you, and they're going to put you in jail."

"Josh, dude," says Patrick. "Seriously, let's just go back inside, get a beer . . ."

Josh makes a flicking motion with his hands like he's flinging us away in disgust, and climbs into the car and starts it up. I start pounding on the window.

"Josh. Josh!"

He puts it in gear and lurches forward, smashing into the garage door, turns the wheel violently and reverses, crunching against the bumper of the car behind him. He does it again, trying to back-and-forth his way out of the tight spot.

The blond-haired guy says, "Stop! You're ruining my car!" Patrick is behind me, saying, "Josh, Josh, cut this shit out . . ."

Boom! The car plows into the garage door again, the whole thing shaking. *Bamcrunch* into the car behind. I'm still pounding on the window uselessly. Then I see that the passenger window is open, and I jump across the hood of the moving car, like something out of a cop movie.

"Josh," I say through the passenger window, "you can't go!"

I don't know if I'm talking about going now or about the Marines, or both. He ignores me, reversing the car again. I try to open the door, but it's locked, and I try to unlock it as I'm stumbling backwards with the movement of the car. In another second he'll have cleared enough space to drive across the front lawn to the street, which is what he seems to be aiming to do. As he's spinning the wheel to reposition the car and make his escape I dive headfirst through the open window, my legs hanging out as we fishtail across the front lawn and hit the pavement with a huge bump and screech. I wriggle and scrabble myself in as Josh hits the accelerator, my feet on the ceiling, my face mushed against the rubber mat in the passenger foot well. About five seconds later Josh stomps on the brakes and the car screeches to a halt again.

"Get the hell out of the car!" says Josh.

"No," I say from under the dashboard.

"Get the hell out!"

"No!"

He reaches over and opens the door and starts shoving me out, but I get my left leg wedged between the seats and brace my right foot against the top of the door frame.

"Get out!"

"No! I'm going with you!"

"Ah, screw it!" says Josh, and stomps on the gas again, the door slamming by itself as the car rockets forward.

It takes me several minutes of uncomfortable contortions to get my head and my feet in the correct orientation, all while Josh is driving way too fast and cutting in and out of lanes. When I finally get myself upright and buckle myself in, we're on the freeway.

Would you say anything to Josh, sitting next to him in the car, feeling the dreadful anger pouring out of him? His hands are clenched tight on the steering wheel, and I can see that tension in his arms, his jaw, his neck, his whole body. I can barely fit in the car with all the baleful energy vibrating off of him.

We park at the curb and Josh leaps out of the car, me following. "Josh," I say, "Josh," even though I know he won't listen and there's no reason to waste my breath. I don't even know why I'm following him, other than the need to observe what happens next.

There's a line at the door of the club, but he walks right to the front, barely slowing as he enters to give the doorman a curt nod. I speed up, hoping that if I arrive within the right number of seconds the bouncer will still recognize the invisible bond that connects me and Josh and let me in.

"Whoa," he says, a big arm thrust in front of me like a turnstile. "I'm with Josh."

The bouncer is distracted, trying to decide while checking IDs and letting other people in.

"Please, I have to go in. I'm with Josh," I say. "Josh," I repeat, his name a talisman. The bouncer, irritated, makes some sort of gesture that could be dismissing me or waving me in. I decide to take it as the latter and shoot inside the club.

It's as crowded and loud as the last time, with recorded music instead of a band. It doesn't take me long to find him: he's at the bar, talking to Trish. I watch from a dark corner of the room, standing on a chair so I can see over everyone.

They're discussing something. Or he's trying to tell her something, trying to get a reaction from her, and she's not giving it to him. He's got a beer in one hand, and he drains it during a pause in the conversation as she serves someone else. *She's hot,* I think, but nothing like Lesley. Lesley is right — how could he choose Trish over her?

Things are deteriorating fast. Now they're straight-up arguing, all pointed fingers and shouting and Josh slamming his hands on the bar for emphasis. People are starting to notice, awareness spreading out in a growing ripple.

There's a group of three guys to Josh's right, big football player types. The biggest moves to Josh's side and places a hand on his shoulder, and I can see him mouthing, *C'mon, buddy,* but Josh shrugs and bats the hand away without even looking at the guy.

I'm starting to walk toward Josh, picking up speed, as the guy tries the hand on the shoulder again, and Josh suddenly pivots and gives him an impossibly explosive shove that sends the guy tripping back on his heels to plow into his friends, the three of them going down in a tangled mess of arms and legs and barstools.

Now everyone in a thirty-foot radius has stopped whatever they were doing and turned toward the altercation. I'm speeding up, trying to get to Josh, and the three guys are trying to sort themselves out and get to their feet, and then I see the bouncer rocketing across the room toward Josh. As he slams into Josh, Josh turns and does some sort of move and the bouncer goes sprawling, but now the three guys are back on their feet and coming at Josh, everyone throwing punches and clawing at him, and now the bouncer is up again and grabbing Josh from behind as Josh twists and turns and lashes out in chaotic fury.

"Josh!" I scream, but he can't hear me. "Josh!"

He connects solidly on one of the football players and the guy goes down, clutching his face, and then Josh nails another and drops him. Josh shakes off the bouncer and turns to deal with the third football player, and even in the midst of my fear I can't help but think, *Jesus, that guy can fight.*

And another part of my brain is saying, *Jesus, he looks like an idiot.*

Now the other bouncer has joined in, and more guys pile on Josh like a rugby scrum, the whole mass staggering unpredictably back and forth as they try to force Josh to the floor. I reach the outer layer of the scrum and pull uselessly at thick arms and legs, screaming for Josh, no one noticing me in the least. The whole group, by design or chance, is lurching toward the exit, Josh somewhere in the middle, somehow still on his feet. I trip and get up again just as a sort of shuddering outburst of energy shimmers through the pack, and suddenly Josh is free again, throwing punches, and I dive through an opening to grab at his arm, but he shakes me off with one violent movement without realizing who I am. I'm literally airborne a moment, and then my feet hit the ground and my head hits something else and everything goes stars.

I'm on the floor, stunned. When I woozily get up, the two bouncers have somehow gotten hold of Josh and are marching him unsteadily toward the exit. He's bleeding. They're bleeding. There are bleeding frat boys and barstools and tables strewn on the floor.

I catch up to Josh and the bouncers in the entranceway, the three of them barely able to fit through the space together.

"I love you, man, but you got to chill the fuck out, Josh!" one of the bouncers says.

One of them kicks the front door open and they struggle to squeeze through the door to the outside, then they hurl Josh out to do a face plant on the sidewalk. I see him framed by the bouncers and the doorway as he struggles to his feet and turns back toward the bar, taking a moment to get his balance. He's got blood streaming from his nose and from a gash on his eyebrow, but he looks ready to fight again, his hands coming up as he steps forward.

"Josh!" The bouncer is pointing a finger at him. "Josh!" he repeats. "Go the fuck home, Josh. Don't make me call the cops. Just go home and we'll forget all this."

Josh is still moving toward us. I pinball my way past the bouncers, ricocheting off their bodies as I push through while they get ready to fight Josh again.

"Josh!" I shout, and run to him, grabbing him around the waist.

"Get away from me," he snarls, and effortlessly peels me off and pushes me aside. But as he pushes I get two-on-one wrist control, just like he taught me: I fasten both my hands around one of his wrists and drop my hips and yank at him, and he's so unsteady and off balance that he crashes to the pavement again. I've taken him down.

He lies there, not moving, blinking slowly, like he has given up and is content to stay on the sidewalk forever. His cell phone is on the pavement next to him. I pick it up and shove it in my back pocket.

"Josh," I say, pulling at him. "Get up. We gotta go."

He takes a deep breath and lets it out.

"Josh, c'mon, let's just go."

A few people are passing on the sidewalk and glance at us curiously.

"Josh."

He hoists himself up into a sitting position.

"We have to go, Josh! Now!"

"I'm going back in there."

"No, you're not!"

He's climbing to his feet, ignoring me as I try to pull him along the sidewalk.

"Josh. Josh! We have to go! The cops are coming!"

He shakes me off and starts walking back to the bar. The bouncers are watching, shaking their heads and trading glances, disgusted. Something bursts inside me, an explosion of anger and frustration. I run around Josh and plant myself in front of him, wind up, and punch him as hard as I can in the stomach.

He stops in his tracks, startled, and looks down at me stupidly.

"Josh!" I scream. "We're going *home—now!*"

"What happened to your face?" he says.

"What?" I say, baffled.

"Your face."

He reaches out a hand and touches the side of my head. When he pulls it back it's covered in blood. I feel a surge of vertigo and then notice the pain. I gingerly put a few fingers up and feel the wetness along my cheek and my jaw line.

"Here," says Josh, and rips the remnants of his tattered shirt off and holds it out to me. It's filthy, covered with blood and beer and whatever mixture of grime coats the floor of the bar. I wave it off impatiently.

"Hey, kid."

It's one of the bouncers walking toward me, holding a clean bar towel. "Here," he says, and tosses it to me. I catch it and press it against my temple.

"Thanks," I mumble. A small crowd has gathered. Josh is still standing there, dull eyed, like he's watching all this on TV, and I feel overwhelmed by shame and embarrassment.

"You want an ambulance or something?" says the bouncer.

"No," I say without looking. I grab Josh by the arm and pull. "Come on."

He's like a horse, immovable for a moment, and then he lets himself be led away from the bar. With his other hand he starts digging in his pocket and pulls out the car key.

"Josh, you're not driving," I say.

"I'm fine," he says, and proves it by dropping the key. I snatch it up before he has time to even register what happened.

"Give me the key," he says. "Give me the key, Isaac."

"No."

He reaches for it. I jump backwards and start walking away, still facing him, one hand holding the towel against my head, the other holding the key while I simultaneously try to pull out his cell phone. Josh starts walking after me.

"Josh, no. We're taking a cab."

"Give me the keys, Isaac."

"No."

"Give me the fucking keys!"

"No."

"Isaac, fuck you. Give me the fucking keys."

I stop.

"No," I say, "fuck *you*." Then I let the keys drop, and they rattle through the parallel bars of a sewer grate. I don't hear them hit bottom, however far down that might be.

"Oh, goddamn it, Isaac."

He sits down on the curb and puts his head in his hands.

I realize I don't know how to get a taxi. In the movies people always just wave their arms or whistle, but that's always in New York. I don't think it works that way here. I pull out his cell phone, thinking that I'll call information, and freeze. There's a voice message from our home phone. It has to be Lisa.

CHAPTER FORTY-SEVEN

THE EMERGENCY

MERIT BADGE: JUNIOR DOCTOR

In the cab I try calling the house again, but no one answers. Lisa was scared in her message, crying, asking where we were, saying she was sick and her head hurt. I picture her alone and unconscious and dying while a party rages around her and we're in some stupid bar downtown. I redial. Nothing.

"Shit!" I jab the end call button.

The cab driver took one look at us and didn't want to take us. I offered him a hundred dollars from Josh's wallet. He took us.

It's a long, tense ride, and I drum on my legs and jiggle my feet. Josh is slumped down, leaning against the door and staring up and out the window like he's lost in thought.

"She said she was going to move to New York with me," says Josh out of nowhere, still looking out the window.

"Trish?"

He doesn't answer. Instead, after a long pause he says, "I hated it there. Hated school. Couldn't hack it. Total fail. I failed, Isaac. Didn't even like wrestling anymore."

"But you're going back," I say. "You're going back, right?"

Again he doesn't answer. After more looking out the window he says, "You know what you should do? You should get a tattoo of a dragon."

"What?"

"A dragon. Get one here," he says, pointing to the inside of his forearm.

"What are you talking about?"

"I think it's your spirit animal. You kept talking about dragons that night I found you in the woods during the storm."

"Josh, are you joining the Marines?"

Nothing.

"Are you joining the Marines?"

"Yep."

"Do Mom and Dad know?"

"Nope."

"But you can't! When?"

"The day after your bar mitzvah."

"Josh, no! They'll send you to Afghanistan!"

"Hope so," he says.

Now I'm the one who's quiet, thinking.

Then, "There's no such thing as spirit animals, Josh. It's bullshit. *You're* bullshit. You and all your crap. Your tattoo and your frigging yarmulke. It's just like Patrick with his stupid Mohawk and leather jacket, just something to put on so you can be different and show off. All bullshit. This whole two weeks has been bullshit."

He watches me talk, expressionless, maybe not even hearing me. Then he turns back to the window.

• • •

When we arrive at the house the cars are gone from our driveway and from the block. I'm out of the cab a lot faster than Josh, not caring if he's coming or not. I can see the extent of the damage to the front lawn: an S curve of tire tracks slashing diagonally across from the driveway to the curb. Before I go in the front entrance I take a quick moment to note the splintered wound in the garage door.

The house seems empty, all the partiers gone. It's a wreck, plastic cups and bottles everywhere, a large spill in the entrance hallway that countless people have tracked through. I go right to Lisa's room, the hallway light enough to illuminate her in her bed. She's asleep, flushed, tossing about. Her forehead is hot as hell. I get the thermometer from the bathroom across the hall. Josh is there when I get back, hunched over her. He straightens when I come in.

"She's really sick!" he says. He looks freaked out. "Look at her face!"

"Josh, she's got Terri's frigging makeup smeared all over her face."

"She's burning up! You have to get the thermometer."

"I've got it."

"Give it here."

"I'll do it."

"Give me it!"

I hand it to him. Of course he can't get it to work. He keeps pressing the button too many times and resetting it before he puts it in Lisa's ear, and then he swears each time he reads the error message on the display.

"Here," I say, then just take it from him. "Move over," I say, and he does, and I take her temperature.

"One hundred and three point four," I say.

"Oh, man, that's really high. That's really high." He's looking even more freaked out and helpless. Helpless and overwhelmed, like a child, a way I've never seen him before. "She could be in a coma!"

"She's not in a coma. She's asleep."

"Lisa!" He starts shaking her.

"Josh, let her sleep. She's just sick. She probably has strep. The fever, all of it, these are exactly her symptoms when she has strep."

"Lisa!" He shakes her more. She opens her eyes and starts bawling.

He holds on to her as she cries and says her head hurts, her throat hurts.

"She has strep," I say. "Remember the diagnosis game I play with Dad?" He ignores me, trying to get her to quiet down.

"We gotta go to the hospital or something," he says. "I'm gonna call an ambulance."

"What?"

"We have to get her to the hospital! She could have—I don't know! She could have anything!"

I'm not sure why, but somehow that statement doesn't help calm Lisa down. She starts bawling harder.

"I don't wanna go to the ho-ho-hospital!" she sobs.

"I'm calling an ambulance," says Josh, clumsily trying to dial his phone. I can already envision being stuck in the emergency room for the rest of the night while they deal with actual emergencies. Plus, someone probably reported what happened at the bar, and there Josh would be, showing up at the hospital, all bruised and matching the description of the idiot who started the fight.

"Wait!" I say. "Just hold on!"

"Where are you going?" says Josh.

"I'll be right back."

I sprint across the hall to the bathroom, open the medicine cabinet, find one of my dad's pen flashlights, the kind with an advertisement on it for some sort of medication. Back across the hall.

"Lisa, let me see your throat."

She does. I shine the light in. Her throat is covered with white spots.

"See? It's strep. We'll get her penicillin tomorrow and she'll be fine. Let's go to bed."

"What are you talking about? I'm calling an ambulance!"

"You're driving me insane! Look, stay here, don't call an ambulance!"

Now I run down the hall, down the stairs, to my parents' bathroom. On the way there I spot more party wreckage, including Mr. Olsen and two random people passed out on the L-shaped sofa. I don't stop to check on them. In a drawer in my parents' bathroom I find a rapid strep test, which my dad keeps on hand because Lisa gets it so often.

When I straighten up I spy myself in the mirror and pause for an instant, fascinated. I have a deep cut that splits my right eyebrow, which looks like it's going to heal into a scar like the one Josh has. The area under that eye is starting to purple into a black eye to match the one on the other side. Each nostril is decorated with that dark red crust you get when you have a bloody nose, so I guess I must have had one. I don't have time to wash the cut, but it's starting to bleed again, and as I leave the bathroom I snag a washcloth to press against it.

I run back to the stairs, get halfway up, pause, go back down to the sofa to give Mr. Olsen and the other two a hard shake. Only Mr. Olsen responds with anything resembling consciousness.

"Whuh?" he says, opening his eyes and sort of focusing on me.

"Mr. Olsen, it's time to go home."

"Whah?"

"Time to go. Isn't your wife waiting for you?"

"She's outta town." He closes his eyes again. I shake him again.

"Mr. Olsen, you *have* to *leave.*"

"Leave?"

"GET THE HELL OUT OF OUR HOUSE!"

"Jeez, kid."

"And wake these two other idiots up and get them out, too. Now. NOW!! GET UP!!" I yell, kicking at his shins for good measure.

I can hear him mumbling and muttering behind me as I sprint up the stairs to Lisa's room.

Josh is sitting next to her on the bed, stroking her forehead. He still looks panicked. I doubt he was this scared when *I* was sick.

"I'm calling an ambulance," he says again.

"Hold on. Lisa, open your mouth."

I've watched my dad do this half a dozen times, and try to imitate his deft motion with the throat swab. Then I put it in the test tube and wait and dab it on the little strip and maybe ten seconds go by before the two parallel lines appear.

"There. Positive. It's strep. Good night."

"She's never had that before."

"Josh, Lisa gets strep, like, every two goddamn weeks, but you just don't pay enough attention to know it. She's a carrier of group A streptococcus."

"You don't know what you're talking about."

How is it that after every absolutely bizarre thing that has happened this week, that one statement makes me angrier than anything?

"I might be a total pussy, Josh, but I *do* know what I'm talking about," I say to him, very quietly. "And you know it."

I can hear Mr. Olsen and the people from downstairs talking drunkenly as they make their way to the front door. One of them is speaking stridently now, arguing with the others. I can't tell what he's saying, but he sounds remarkably like my —

Holy shit.

"Who are you, and what are you doing here?" I can hear him clearly now, very clearly.

Josh looks up.

"Oh my God," says a very familiar female voice. "Oh my *God.* Herb, look at this place! I am going to kill Josh!"

"Oh, shit," say Josh and I together.

CHAPTER FORTY-EIGHT

JOSH GETS BEAT UP

My mom punches Josh, the final punch of two weeks of punches. Right in his already-bruised and bloody face.

A girl punch, I guess he'd say, the wind-up all awkward and the fist in the wrong position, but I swear that punch hurts him more than anything that happened at the bar. It's like a magic wand, the contact instantly converting him back to being a child. He puts his hand up to the spot and his eyes go teary, the first time I've ever seen him close to crying.

My mom is certainly crying. Scary crying. Hysterical furious shrieking out-of-control incoherent sentences crying. I've never seen her like this. After she hits him, she screams, "I can't stand you! I want you out of this house, and I never want to see you again!"

It's worse than the punch. I can see it. At first I think Josh will just shrug it off like he has shrugged off everything my parents have ever said, but this destroys him.

Everyone gets beat up, Patrick said. This is Josh getting beat up.

CHAPTER FORTY-NINE

THE RETURN

The house is trashed. The lawn is ruined. There are drunken strangers in the foyer. Your clothes are shredded and your face is bruised and bleeding. Your little sister, whom you were supposed to be taking care of, has French braids, is wearing fingernail polish, lipstick, and eye shadow, and has strep throat. Your little brother, whom you were also supposed to be taking care of, has two black eyes, a screwed-up ear piercing, and a claw mark on his face, and is bleeding steadily from a split eyebrow. What do you do? If you're Josh, you stride out to the entranceway and demand, "Mom, Dad, what the *hell* are you guys doing here?"

I heard it all from Lisa's room, where I was hiding.

"What's going on?" said Lisa.

"Mom and Dad are back," I said. "Shhh."

I could hear my mom and dad yelling at Josh and could track their progress through the house, marked by an exclamation of outrage at each new discovery: the charred countertop; the trashed condition of the living room; the shelf of snuff bottles Terri had destroyed ("My *snuff bottles!*" I heard my mom wail).

While my mom was screaming at Josh, I heard the heavier sound of my dad passing in the hallway outside Lisa's room, on his way to my room. *Oh, God,* I thought, *I hope Patrick and Terri aren't—*

"Who the hell are you?" my dad roared. "What the hell is this?"

A few seconds later Lisa's door opened. I shot out into the hallway past my dad before he could grab me.

"Hey, Dad," I said as I receded down the hallway, washcloth against my face. "That's Patrick and Terri in my room. They're okay people. Also, I just administered a rapid strep test to Lisa and it came back positive."

This was all prepunch. I ended up colliding into my mom as she rounded the corner to the hallway. "And what happened to you?" she said, and roughly pulled the cloth away. She was white-hot raging at that point, but when she saw my face is when she really lost it.

"What did you *do* to him?!" she shrieked at Josh, and the scary crying started. "Nothing," I kept saying, "he didn't do anything," but I would have needed a bullhorn for her to hear me, and that's when she hauled off and let him have it.

Now she's shrieking: "Herb. Herb! Have you seen Izzie?!!"

"Mom, I'm okay," I keep repeating. Josh is now sitting on the floor, head in hands, crying. Josh is *crying,* his body racked with sobs. Our dad is talking at the same time as our mom, saying that there are strange people in Izzie's room, Lisa has a fever, and Christ, look at Izzie's face, Jesus, what happened to you, and what the hell is this goddamn dog doing here?! He kicks at Joey, who is yapping at everyone.

Which is when Eric Weinberg makes his grand entrance: shirtless, red faced, teetering out of the TV room to join our merry group. One by one we fall silent, gaping at the new arrival. Even Joey the dog stops yapping.

"Hi," Eric says to us, wobbling on his feet, "what's going on?"

Then he throws up everywhere.

We all take a moment to grasp the impressive volume of material that he just deposited on the walls and floor.

"Jesus," says my dad, "can't this kid keep anything down?"

CHAPTER FIFTY

AFTERMATH

It's remarkable how loud the world is when you're sitting in a room with your father, neither of you speaking for a long time. I can hear the air molecules themselves, knocking around against each other.

We're in his den. It's Saturday afternoon, the day after all the fun. Why are they home a day early with no warning?

"I was concerned about a patient."

Of course.

Patrick and Terri departed midmorning in his beater Camry. Josh, whose face is all lumpy and purple, has been cleaning the house all day under the unsympathetic supervision of my mother. Lisa is resting, already on the penicillin that my dad picked up from the pharmacy. He briefly switched duties with my mom at midday so she could deliver a very hung-over Eric back to his house. As far as his parents knew, he was just sleeping over.

"Please don't tell my mom," Eric begged as they were leaving.

"Eric," said my mom, "do you think I'm a goddamned retard?"

When my mom got back, my dad took me into his den and asked me to sit down. He was very quiet and formal when he did it, and I imagined it's how he talks to his patients. "Isaac, can you come in here for a moment? I'd like to speak with you."

"Isaac," he said after we'd both settled, "I'd like you to tell me what happened over these past two weeks."

I thought for a while, then said, "Actually, I'd prefer not to talk about it."

Right after Eric threw up, my dad went into triage mode. I could see it happen: He flipped a switch, sent whatever personal feelings he had on a minivacation, and became Dr. Kaplan in the trauma ward. It was completely cool, actually. *Boom:* "Judy, take Eric to the bathroom and clean him up." *Boom:* "Josh, get off your ass, get paper towels and the mop, and take care of the vomit." Josh, still crying, complied. Incredible. *Boom:* "You, come here." He got down on a knee and examined my face, turning my head from side to side.

"The window!" wailed my mom from the bathroom. My dad looked accusingly at Josh, who had just returned with a roll of paper towels.

"No, that one's on me," I said. "I broke the window."

"We are going to need to talk," said my dad.

He sent Josh and me downstairs to their bathroom while he checked on Lisa.

"Strep?" I said when he came in.

"Yes."

I raised an eyebrow at Josh.

"You were right," said Josh. "Isaac was right, Dad."

Because Lisa is his daughter, my dad keeps strep tests on hand. Because Josh is his son, he also has a supply of stitches and anesthetic. My dad ended up giving me three stitches in my eyebrow. He gave Josh six—two on his forehead and four over his right cheekbone. He wasn't particularly gentle with Josh as he scrubbed his face and cleaned out the wounds.

My dad was silent as he worked, expressionless, still in doctor mode. He'd been shaking with anger before, and looked exhausted and jet-lagged, and must have been overwhelmed by all the chaos that greeted him on arrival. But I couldn't see any of that. All I could see was pure focus. And I thought, my dad can't ride a motorcycle or throw a punch or shoot a gun, but he could take the bullet out of you, and he could do it while the house was on fire around him. I liked him a lot right then.

Afterward there was some contention as our mom and dad huddled and discussed what should happen next, what to do with Lisa, what to do with Eric, and whether to boot out Patrick and Terri.

This conversation was interrupted by a brief visit from our friends Officers Thomke and Federson, responding an hour late to a noise complaint (Thomke to my dad: "Boy, I feel like we've been here a lot this week! Well, good night!" leaving my dad with an expression somewhere between stunned and resigned).

When the fuzz left, my parents restarted their discussion/argument, even more heatedly. This time I interjected.

"Listen: Here's what's going to happen. Leave Terri and Patrick in my room, because I told them they could use it. I'll sleep on the sofa. Eric sleeps on the downstairs sofa. We can deal with everything and clean up in the morning."

And you know what? They actually listened to me.

So now here we are in his den, my dad trying to make sense of the past two weeks.

"What do you mean, you prefer not to talk about it?" he asks.

"I'd just rather not talk about it."

"Isaac, I'm sorry, but that's unacceptable. I'd like to know what happened, and what happened between you and Josh."

I don't answer.

"Isaac, did he threaten you?"

I snort. I can't help it. It just slips out. Josh has threatened me so many times it's like background noise.

"What? What does that mean? Has he told you not to talk? Are you afraid of him?"

I think about that. Am I afraid of him? Not anymore. I'm not sure what else he could really do to me.

"Isaac?" says my dad.

"No. I just don't feel like talking about it."

"I guess we can just wait until you do," says my dad.

It takes some effort not to smile. It's what he used to say when I was a child and didn't want to cooperate: We'll just wait until you do. No yelling, no grabbing me and forcing me to do something. He would just out-patience me until I caved. But I'm not a child anymore. It makes me feel proud and sad all at once, and like I want to give my father a consolation hug, because he doesn't know that era is gone. Instead we both lapse back into our current silence. We've been sitting like this for several minutes now.

He sighs. "Isaac . . ." he says. He's given up, the first time that has ever happened. "Will you at least explain to me why you won't tell me?"

"Because," I say, "it's between me and Josh. It's between me and my brother."

He doesn't say anything, but he nods. He doesn't like the explanation, but he doesn't press me any further.

"Okay," he says, and gets up, the process labored, like he's exhausted. He rubs his face. "I'm really sorry, Isaac. This is my fault. I shouldn't have left you at home with Josh. You were right."

"It's okay."

"Sounds like it was quite a time."

My hand goes up to the stitches on my eyebrow. I reconsider what I said in the car to Josh last night, about it all being bullshit.

"Worst two weeks of my life," I say. "And the best."

CHAPTER FIFTY-ONE

THE LAST NAUGHTINESS

MERIT BADGE: SLAYING THE MINOTAUR

Friday morning. One day left until my bar mitzvah. I'm on my bike, but I'm not heading to school. I'm skipping again, a fugitive for the final time.

I've spent the week making up homework and tests. I've also been studying my haphtarah on my own and going for solitary runs in the morning. I rescued the tent from the creek and dried it out, and I've been sleeping in it, even though Patrick and Terri have moved on and my room is available. My mom wrinkled her nose but didn't say much about it.

I've barely seen Josh. He met with a judge this week, an accelerated hearing so that he could hurry up and join the Marines. He pled guilty to a fifth-degree misdemeanor assault and received a stay of adjudication and was placed on administrative probation, which basically meant he had to stay out of trouble or they'd toss him in the can. There was also a one-thousand-dollar fine that the judge waived, in light of the fact that Josh was heading off to serve his country.

During one of my morning runs I got an idea and went to Nystrom's house and rang the doorbell. When he finally answered, glaring at me suspiciously from behind the screen door, I could barely hear him over the racket the dogs were making, bunched up on the side of the house where the fenced-in area extended almost to the front.

"Is this the Brown residence?" I asked.

"Who?" he said.

"I'm sorry, I guess I made a mistake."

The dogs were still there on the side of the house when I jogged away.

I lock my bike to a street sign in front of the apartment building. No one answers the buzzer after the first few stabs, so I lean on it until Lesley's voice finally crackles from the speaker, her tone irritated: "Hello? Who is this?"

"It's me. Isaac."

She buzzes me in without another word. She opens her apartment door before I even raise my hand to knock, and she stands just inside the foot-wide gap and regards me, her eyes sleepy.

"I need your help," I say.

An hour later. I'm hiding in the brush that overlooks Nystrom's backyard. All four dogs are there, lazing about in the morning sunlight.

"Can you still hear me?" says Lesley quietly. She's speaking to me through the wireless earpiece of her cell phone to the wireless earpiece of mine, the new one my parents bought me to replace the one Josh chucked into the creek.

"I can hear you."

When I got to her apartment in the morning, I told her my plan. She stood silently for a few moments, then said, "Okay."

We left my bike there and rode on her Vespa. We barely spoke, just going over the details a few times. We didn't talk about the party, about her and Josh, nothing. She let me off early so I could cut through the woods, while she continued on to Nystrom's.

"You ready?" she says.

"I'm ready."

"You sure you want to do this?" she says. "It's pretty stupid."

"I'm sure."

"All right, then," she says. "I can't believe I agreed to this. Okay. I'm going to ring the doorbell now."

She rings it, and I watch the dogs do exactly what I was hoping they would—they sprint around the side of the building toward the front and start barking insanely at Lesley.

I'm up instantly, running down the short hill toward the fence.

"Hi there," Lesley is saying in my ear, except she's talking to Mr. Nystrom, who must have answered the door. "I'm with a film crew, and I'm scouting locations for a shoot," she says. I reach the fence and start climbing as quietly as I can. "No, a film crew. Right. Like a movie."

I drop down from the fence into enemy territory, pulse pounding, managing to score a direct hit with my right foot on a fresh pile of rottweiler crap. That's the least of my worries, though. The dogs are still out of sight, barking at her, but they're just around the corner, and if they lose interest in her and return to the backyard I'll soon be in several of their stomachs.

"Wait, please wait. Could I just show you the shot we'd like to get? No? Please? Pretty please? Your house is perfect. We'd pay you, also."

I'm sure Patrick would have agreed to help me out, but I think most people would call the police if Patrick showed up at their door. Terri would have probably volunteered, too, but God knows what sort of chaos would have resulted. I really don't know any other adultlike people I could have asked. It had to be Lesley. Because, well, Lesley is Lesley. She's beautiful and engaging, and I figured even Nystrom wouldn't be able to resist her charms. Plus she has those official-looking laminated film-crew badges.

"Well, there really *is* no better spot," she's saying. I can hear the smile in her voice. "It's just here along the side of the building, where your . . . *lovely* dogs are. Can I just show you?"

It's working. The dogs are getting louder in the earpiece, meaning she's moving closer to them, closer to the fence, meaning hopefully they'll keep paying attention to her while I slay the minotaur.

The minotaur stares back at me cherubically. It turns out to be heavier than I expected. I won't be able to just throw the statue over the fence. But I'm prepared for that: I have my backpack. I lay the bag on the ground, roll the statue into it, zip it up as much as I can, hoist it on my back, struggle not to fall over.

"These really are lovely dogs," Lesley is saying now. "Although I feel like *someone* told me they were poodles."

In a harsh whisper she says, "Isaac, you are so gonna get it . . ."

Okay, I wasn't entirely honest with Lesley when I described the mission, figuring she might balk if she knew the dogs might actually kill me if things went bad.

"Oh, nothing," she says to Nystrom. "Just talking to myself. So, what are their names?" Pause. "How wonderful! Which one is Adolf?"

It's a lot harder climbing back up the fence with the backpack pulling me down, the straps cutting into my neck and shoulders, the chicken wire painful on my fingers. I'm running out of time. My heart is pumping hard, and I'm trying to hide the sound of my breathing. Nearly there. Then it happens. My foot slips, scraping down the fence, making a huge rattle. I freeze.

"Wait, where's that one going?" Lesley says, loud, warning me. "Where's he going?"

I twist around just as the dog clears the corner.

There's a moment when monster dog and statue thief regard each other.

Then it's game on. The dog doesn't even bother to bark—he just charges, hurtling at me. I feel a burst of adrenaline such as I've never felt in my life. I don't so much climb as launch myself over the fence, somehow landing unhurt on the other side just as the rottweiler slams into the barrier, and I'm up the slope and into the brush, pausing just long enough to give Adolf the finger.

Lesley and I sit on a fallen tree in the forest behind Nystrom's house and look at the statue.

"That's it, huh?" she says. "That's what you nearly died for?"

"Yep."

She shakes her head. "Boys are weird," she says.

"So are girls," I say.

The forest is quiet except for the distant sound of an airplane. Lesley looks at her watch.

"I need to go to work," she says. "And you need to go to school."

I nod.

"Thanks for helping out," I say.

"Sure."

Neither of us moves.

"Isaac," she says after a pause, "I'm sorry. I didn't mean to hurt you. I really like you, you know. I think you're a special guy. I hope that you don't hate me."

I'm still for a bit, not answering. There's a bird chirping somewhere. Another plane is in the air, invisible. At school, third period is just about over. My dad is at the hospital seeing to his patients. Josh is doing whatever he is doing, and Patrick is out there somewhere, and Terri with her yappy dog, and the world and the universe continue on their way. When I answer, it's quiet, because I'm afraid that the world might hear me, and even that she might hear me.

"I *love* you, Lesley," I say.

There. All done. Nothing left to hide.

Next to me, she's silent. I'm content to sit there. When I chance a look at her, she's looking back at me, smiling in a strange way, and her eyes are brimming.

"Aw," she says. "Aww," she repeats, and holds her arms out to me, and we hug, a tight hug, twisted awkwardly toward each other on the log. She rocks back and forth a little and I rock with her, and I hear her sniffle and feel her remove her hand from around me so that she can wipe her nose or her eyes. Before she releases me she puts her right hand on my cheek and brings me closer to her so that she can kiss me on the temple: once, twice, a third time.

"Isaac," she says, "you're the first guy who's ever said that to me." She pulls me in for another hug, and it's a long one, even longer than the first. I'd felt distant from her before. I did hate her. But now my mind is full of the impossible, the fantastic, of realities less probable than my fantasy books. I know that the chasm between us is too broad and deep, that by the time I'll truly be a man and be ready for her we'll both be different people and she could be married and have kids and live in Los Angeles likes she wants to. It will never work. It's like losing her again. It's like a death, a whole future eliminated and vanishing, and now we're both sniffling and teary eyed.

We separate and she fishes around in her jean jacket for a packet of tissues.

"I've taken to carrying these things," she says, offering me one. "I've been crying a lot more lately."

"Yeah, me too," I say, and she laughs, and we sit there dabbing at our tears.

"Hey," I say, "want to come to a bar mitzvah?"

CHAPTER FIFTY-TWO

THE QUARRY IS PRESENTED

"Josh."

"Mmm?"

"Josh, wake up."

"Mmmm."

1:39 a.m., less than ten hours left until my bar mitzvah. I'm standing next to Josh's bed, watching him sleep.

"Josh," I say again, and cautiously reach out like I'm trying to snatch a jewel guarded by a cobra and give Josh a few fingertip shoves on the shoulder. I'm ready to duck if he's the lash-out-in-his-sleep type, which I'm assuming he is. Instead he makes another *Mmmm* sound, and then takes a big breath in through his nose and brings a hand up to wipe his face.

"What's going on?" he says. "Ow. Turn that off," he adds when I put the flashlight beam on him. See how *he* likes it.

"Let's go," I say.

"What are you talking about? What time is it?"

"About two a.m."

"Christ."

"Let's go."

"Where?"

"You'll see."

I have to hand it to him—he didn't ask anything else. He just looked at me for a moment, shook his head to wake himself up, then got up out of bed and got dressed without another word.

He follows me outside into the night, asking no questions as we walk. The last time we made this journey together I wanted the answers to the Mystery of Josh: Who is the girl at the bar? What are his plans? What happened at school? Now I know the answers, and they're small and simple and maybe a little bit sad, and there's no romance or intrigue to them. But I guess they're just human.

Josh doesn't open his mouth until we're huddled in the brush near Nystrom's backyard and I hand the statuette to him. I hid it here after swiping it, figuring it was too heavy to carry home. Josh twists it around in the moonlight, examining it.

"How'd you do it?" he says.

I shake my head. He nods, letting the question go. Josh holds a hand out to me. "Well done," he says. "You killed the minotaur."

CHAPTER FIFTY-THREE

MANHOOD IS ACHIEVED, AT LEAST ACCORDING TO THE TENETS OF REFORM JUDAISM

MERIT BADGE: BAR MITZVAH

"Today, I am a man."

I'm the one at the podium now, everyone staring up at me. My voice is even. My hands are steady.

I finally admitted to my dad that I was afraid of getting shaky and passing out. He gave me ten milligrams of atenolol to take. It's a beta blocker. Apparently it prevents your body from responding to adrenaline. All the big musicians in major orchestras use it because it keeps their hands from trembling.

"Take it," he said. "You'll be fine."

I hack my way doggedly through the sections that are in Hebrew. I'm not going to lie—there are a few bumpy moments, lots of starting and stopping and glances at the rabbi for guidance. At one particularly sticky point I pause and say, "I'm really sorry, everyone. I've had a pretty eventful few weeks." This is greeted with an appreciative chuckle from certain quarters of the assembled and a raised eyebrow from my mother. From the back comes a voice: "You can do it, little dude!"

More laughter.

"Thank you, Patrick," I reply, and slog on. I'll admit to being somewhat touched that he's attending, and that he went so far as to make a special alteration to his Mohawk for the occasion: shaving a five-inch strip out of it at the crown of his head so the yarmulke has a place to sit.

Terri is here too, and a few of her friends who I assume were curious about what a bar mitzvah looks like. I'm guessing that my event has a higher stripper turnout than is generally the case. I'll say this: My grandfather seems pretty pleased with that part of the guest list.

I kludge my way through the Hebrew jungle and emerge on the other side with what I'd call a C+, or maybe a B- with credit for sheer effort. Not Talmudic scholar material, but not Shabbat short bus, either.

Then it's time for my speech. You have to give a speech to demonstrate how mature and thoughtful you are. With the Hebrew part all I wanted to do was survive. But I really, really wanted to say something in my speech, something with weight and substance, something that might actually make people think that I'm, well, mature and thoughtful.

You'd think I'd have something to talk about, considering the past weeks' fun. But the more I tried, the less I could make sense of my own thoughts. So I end up delivering the speech I had prepared a long time ago, a generic blah about how the environment is precious and everyone should get along and there should be no more war. Rabbi Abramovitz stands next to me, smiling, eyes closed, nodding sagely. Probably thinking, *Oh, for fuck's sake, why can't these kids ever say anything interesting?*

I glance up now from the podium. I'm nearly done. Josh is

watching me solemnly. Lisa is fidgeting. My mom has her smile. My dad looks bemused. There are some cousins and my aunt and uncle from Connecticut and my grandfather from Florida, and assorted family friends.

Danny is here. Paul is here. Steve is here. Sarah and Eric are here, sitting together, holding hands.

Lesley isn't.

Before the ceremony got started I asked Josh if she'd called or texted or anything. Then I asked him again. And then again a few minutes later, at which point he promised me that if she did, I'd be the first to know, and if I asked him again . . .

"What?" I said, waiting for the threat.

"Nothing. Just go get bar mitzvahed."

Maybe she'll show up late, I told myself. But inside I knew that she wouldn't. And somehow I know she's gone from my life forever.

I finish. There is applause. I step off the podium to hugs and congratulations, a bar mitzvah at last. My dad says, "You were steady as a rock! That beta blocker really worked, huh?"

"Sure did," I say, and thank him. It seems ungrateful to tell him that the pill is still wrapped in tin foil in my pocket, untouched.

CHAPTER FIFTY-FOUR

GOODBYE

"You want any of this crap?" says Josh.

"I definitely want the Navy SEALs poster."

"Yeah?"

"No."

We're in his room. In a few minutes Patrick is going to show up in his beat-up Camry and take Josh to the airport so that he can fly to South Carolina for the beginning of boot camp. My dad offered to take him, but Josh said he had it covered.

"Really, anything in here, you want it, it's yours," says Josh. "They don't let you take anything along with you."

"I'll poke around."

"The porn is all in that bottom drawer."

"Yeah, I figured that out about three years ago."

He nods. "You always were smart. You can probably just dump the rest of the shit that's in here."

No, we'll keep it for when you get back, I want to say, but it gets stuck somewhere, so I don't say anything.

This whole week I kept expecting the moment when Josh would take me aside and say, *Let's talk. Let's talk about everything that's hap-*

pened and everything that's going to happen. But no. I don't know if I passed the course or not. It's like we're back at the beginning, nothing changed, not knowing if we're friends or what he thinks of me or *if* he thinks of me.

"Josh . . ."

"Yeah?"

"Nothing."

"Okay."

Outside, someone honks. Josh looks out the window.

"Patrick's here."

I nod. Josh stands up.

"Well," he says.

"Yeah," I say. *This is the last conversation you're going to have with him, ever,* part of me is saying, and another is trying to build a wall and block that thought out.

He extends his hand. I shake it.

"Good luck," I say.

"Thanks."

I follow him down the hall to the foyer. I watch as he has a brief conversation with my mom and dad—my dad puts a hand on his shoulder, patting it, then a hug; my mom strokes Josh's face, looking at him sorrowfully, an embrace that lasts longer than Josh wants.

"Lisa," says my dad, "come say goodbye to Josh."

Lisa emerges from the TV room. Josh picks her up and hugs her, kissing her face. She starts to cry. He whispers something to her, Lisa nodding as she listens, sniffling. He puts her down and pats her on the head. A last handshake with me.

"All right, guys, see you later."

Lisa and I go out on the front porch to watch him climb into Patrick's car. Patrick waves to us, a little salute, and I wave back. *Remember this. Remember this moment, just in case it's the last time you'll see Josh.*

The car pulls away from the curb, the crap muffler making the engine sound phlegmy. Lisa, weeping, stays outside to wave at it as it disappears down the block, but I go back in.

And that's it.

I go to my room because I don't want to be around my parents and their grief. I sit down on my bed, then lie down. The wall cracks and gives way and I'm flooded with the certainty that I didn't want to face, the knowledge that Josh is gone forever, gone to boot camp and then to some valley in Afghanistan, his pride forcing him to always race to be the first to meet the bullets in each firefight, to walk point on paths lethal with IEDs. He won't come back, because he doesn't want to come back.

Then I hear the farty sound of the Camry again, growing louder, and then honking. I get up and look out the window. The car is back out there at the curb. Lisa comes into my field of vision, running across the front yard, Josh scooping her up and hugging her more. *He's staying! He's not going!*

I run out the front door and across the damaged lawn to him. He's still holding Lisa, talking in her ear. When I get there he says, "All right, go back inside. I have to talk to Isaac for a second." He puts her down and she wipes her tears and hesitates, and he says, "Go on, go on, I'll see you soon. Go on, Lisa," and she goes to the front porch and stands watching.

"Did you change your mind?" I say.

He shakes his head. He looks around, as if he's making sure no one is watching or listening. The block is empty, except for Patrick waiting in the car and Lisa on the porch.

"Gonna miss your flight, Josh," says Patrick, leaning to talk out of the open passenger window.

"I'll be right there," says Josh. He looks pained and uncomfortable, unable to form his thoughts into words.

"Josh," says Patrick again.

"Yeah," says Josh. Again the struggle. I hold my breath, waiting for something, anything, from him, some acknowledgment of me. The final merit badge, the thumbs-up from Josh. Instead: "Look . . . just . . . take care of Lisa, okay?"

"Okay."

"Good. And, you know . . . take care of yourself, okay?"

"Okay."

He nods. "Okay. Okay, good." He reaches out a hand again, the soul handshake, and we do the jock bump thing, a few pats on each other's back.

"All right, then," he says, and climbs back in the car, and they drive away for good, all of it ending like every conversation I've ever had with Josh: unfinished, incomplete, the most important parts left unsaid.

EPILOGUE

The person who comes to your door is called a Casualty Notification Officer. He is accompanied by an Appropriate Member of the Clergy, which in this case was a rabbi in military dress uniform.

It was dinnertime. It was Lisa who answered the door. She came back into the dining room, carrying with her a swirl of frigid air from outside, the January cold sticking to her like an arctic forewarning of the news that was about to be delivered. She told my parents that there were two army men who wanted to talk to them. My mother and father looked at each other across the table for a very long moment. Then my father put his fork down and stared at his plate as if gathering himself, stood, and left the room. And I knew.

"Stay here," my mother said, and followed him.

"What's going on?" whispered Lisa after they were gone. "Isaac! What's going on?" she said again.

I put my elbows on the table and buried my face in my hands and just sat there, because I couldn't talk.

As far as I know, Josh sent exactly three e-mails after leaving home. The first was that he was in basic training and it was fine. Then it was that he was being sent to Afghanistan, and it was fine. Then, he's in Afghanistan, and it's fine. Except I knew it wasn't fine, because I knew which Marine unit he was with and I read an article about them, about how they were in combat almost every day. He got a Purple Heart from some earlier combat mission, but he never mentioned it. We found out about that after he died, killed by an IED that also killed two other Marines. I try very hard not to think of his indestructible superhero body being torn apart by an explosion.

Lesley didn't come to the funeral. I didn't expect her to. Patrick came, though. I didn't cry at all during the ceremony. Patrick cried like a baby. My mom comforted him. Then they both went outside and smoked cigarettes in the subzero temperature.

Two weeks after the service I was gathering the mail and froze in place, a chill up my spine. There was a letter addressed to me in Josh's handwriting.

I had a moment of thinking, *He's alive. Josh is alive. They were wrong. It was someone else.*

But then I thought, *No. They don't make mistakes like that.*

I don't know why, but I took the envelope back to my room. I didn't tell anyone about it. I held it for a long time, looking at the envelope, the stamp, the address in his handwriting from a base in Helmand province. But I didn't open it for weeks. I couldn't. I finally opened it on March twenty-third, Josh's birthday.

It was handwritten on thin paper in his bad script.

Isaac,

    I asked a buddy of mine to send this if I was KIA. So if you're reading this, I'm dead. Which sucks, but whatever. I knew that was part of the deal when I signed up.

Good luck with everything. Take care of Lisa.

I want you to know that I love it here and love what I'm doing. Mom and Dad will never understand this, but this is what I was born to do.

I also want to explain why I put you through what I did.

The world is full of assholes (people like me). People like you are rare. You're smart and you're hard working. You think about things and care about them, and you can make the world a better place.

I just don't want you to get eaten up by the bad people. I wanted to show you that you're tough enough to stand up to them. Because the world needs you.

You know I have a hard time saying things. I wasn't able to say this before I left, and I guess I won't be able to tell you this in person. But I want you to know: I'm proud of you. You're already a better man than I ever was.

Josh

I read the letter, and then I read it again, and then I read it ten more times. Then I read the last two lines over and over again, trying to experience them anew with each and every repetition. I didn't cry during the funeral, but I read that letter and sobbed for an hour. Then I folded it up and carefully put it back in the envelope and put it in my dresser. And then took it out and read it again.

Summer is coming. I'm going to be fourteen. It's nearly a year since my bar mitzvah. Eric and Sarah are still going out, and suddenly he's cool, because there are rumors that they've done it. I still hang out with Danny and Steve and Paul, but I was right, things are somehow different. I thought they'd be my peeps forever, but I wonder—ask me in a year, and maybe we'll all have moved on.

A few times now Patrick has stopped by unannounced. Just showed up, knocked on the door, and hung around. Once my parents even let me go play pool with him. I saw Durwin there. He came over and said he'd heard about Josh and he was sorry. I said it was okay. I told him I was sorry I thought he was a drug dealer. He said that was okay too.

I haven't seen or heard from Lesley since the day I invited her to my bar mitzvah.

No one bothers me at school anymore. Now I'm The Kid Whose Brother Was Killed in Afghanistan. A genuine war hero. There's a plaque with his picture on it in the trophy case, next to all the awards he won for the school over the years.

Sometimes I use product in my hair. When I'm old enough, I think I'll get that tattoo Josh described, the dragon on my forearm. Maybe I'll put his name on it.

I've started to spend time in Josh's room, going through his things. I found a book on his shelf, a collection of Zen stories. He had dog-eared one. It was about a demon who cuts off his horns, like Hellboy, and files down his fangs and joins a monastery and tries to lead a virtuous life. Except of course after a while he can't bear it any longer and ends up devouring everyone. Because that's his essential nature. It's who he is. I didn't need any explanation as to why Josh had bookmarked that particular tale.

"So foolish," my mom said about Josh. "So foolish." My dad said, "Isaac, I pray to God you never have to go to war." I told my mom, "It wasn't foolish, it was who he was." And to my dad I said,

"I hope so, too. But if I do, I pray to God I have a guy like Josh next to me."

My dad thought about that a long time in silence, and then just got up and left the room. I thought he was angry with me. Instead he came back a few minutes later and his eyes were red. He said, "You're right, Isaac. You're right." And he said, "Thank you for that. That makes me feel a bit better." Then he squeezed my shoulder and left again.

I take Josh's letter out and read it almost every morning before I go to school, a little ritual that connects me to my brother, and to the two weeks we spent together. Two weeks that changed me in ways that I'm still trying to figure out.

I started those two weeks as a boy. When I emerged on the other side I wasn't exactly a man, but I certainly wasn't a child anymore. I was transformed. Maybe not in the way that Josh intended or hoped, but transformed nonetheless.

Don't get me wrong: I'm still me. I don't think it works like that, that you have one big experience and suddenly you're brand-new and totally different. I still get nervous and anxious and think too much about everything and see consequences and worry. I guess those thoughts and feelings are part of who I am. They might be pains in the ass, but I went on a very intense journey with them as very close traveling companions, and along the way I got to know them better and maybe even appreciate them a bit.

Josh once told me that his heart rate would actually drop before he got in a fight. I'll never be that guy. I'll never be the guy who thinks it's fun to run and jump off a cliff. But I know that I can, because I did. I also know what it's like to be in a pool hall and a topless club. I spent the night in bed with a woman. I made friends with a stripper and a semiharmless drug dealer. I've shot a gun and crashed a motorcycle and gotten beat up and beat someone up, and I've been in a real live, honest-to-God bar brawl.

I'm not saying I recommend those things as healthy pursuits, exactly. But they did whack me around and open my eyes, and I guess I have Josh to thank for that. Also for pushing me too hard and making me do more than I thought I could. And for setting the scene so I could fall in love, and yes, get my heart stomped on, which is probably one of those horrific lessons everyone just has to experience. At least I got the first one out of the way early on.

If I'm honest with myself, I'd have to say that it wasn't just him making me do everything. If I'd really wanted to, I could have put a stop to the Quest at any time. Despite all my complaining, I was a willing participant.

That last time I saw Lesley, she said, "Josh knows how to be a man. But he doesn't know how to be a *Man*. You know what I mean? A grownup? I wonder if he's scared to be."

I've rolled that around in my head a lot. I always thought it would be hard for *me* to be a man. But maybe Lesley was right. Maybe it was even harder for Josh. I mean, think about it: What would Conan the Barbarian do these days?

It made me start thinking about my bar mitzvah speech. I wish I could give it again. Because now I think I have something worthwhile to say. Not that I'm any sort of expert, but I'd talk about becoming a man.

I'd say that I think there are different ways to be a man, that sometimes it means being brave and strong and aggressive, and sometimes it means thinking and caring and being responsible and seeing consequences. And everything in between all that. Knowing how to play chess *and* do a double-leg takedown. You don't just say, *I'm* this *sort of guy, so I can't be* that *sort of guy.* Maybe you can't be all those things, but you should at least know about them and respect them and try to experience them and have as many bits and pieces of them as possible be part of you. Because I think a real man is all those things.

I would also say this—and again, I'm no expert. But I bet that you probably never quite get there, that becoming a man is something that never, ever stops, and all you can do is just keep trying. Maybe that should be number 614.

POSTEPILOGUE

THE FINAL MERIT BADGE

I almost forgot: I finally spoke to Patricia Morrison. One sentence. Done. Check it off the list.

It was the Monday after the party, the bar fight, everything. There I was, walking by the trophy case, and there she was, walking toward me. There was a moment when her eyes flickered randomly over to look at me and lingered, no doubt needing a moment to let her brain assimilate my novel appearance: exhausted, two black eyes, bruises, scrapes, stitches. In other words, totally cool.

"Hey," I said, and her eyes widened more realizing I was addressing her, "you missed an *awesome* party."